THE ONE THAT GOT AWAY

A.J. PINE

Entangled Publishing, LLC
2614 South Timberline Road
Suite 109
Fort Collins, CO 80525
Visit our website at www.entangledpublishing.com.

Select Contemporary is an imprint of Entangled Publishing, LLC.

Edited by Karen Grove
Cover design by Louisa Maggio
Cover art from Shutterstock

Manufactured in the United States of America

First Edition April 2016

Fill with mingled cream and amber,
I will drain that glass again.
Such hilarious visions clamber
Through the chamber of my brain—
Quaintest thoughts—queerest fancies
Come to life and fade away;
What care I how time advances?
I am drinking ale today.

"Lines on Ale"
Edgar Allan Poe

Prologue

A turtleneck would hide it. It didn't matter that it was Memorial Day weekend and the warmest day of the year so far. Brynn was going to the party. Sure it hurt to swallow, and *maybe* she was running a fever, but this was it. Her last chance. All year she'd promised herself she would kiss Spencer Matthews before she graduated, and graduation for the class of 2005 was in one week. Time was running out. This was it, their last hurrah before he left for school in California. There was no way she was going to miss it.

"Oh…my God. What's wrong with your neck? Ew, Brynn. What are those bumps?"

Leave it to her sister, Holly, to notice…and with a flair of drama only Holly was capable of. She stood in Brynn's bedroom doorway but already looked poised to make a run for it.

"Nothing's *wrong*," Brynn insisted, but even her voice

was a dead giveaway. She could barely get that second word out. It sounded more like a gurgle than a word. It didn't matter. She would power through. Spencer was going to be at the party, and he expected her to be there, too. It would have been enough if he'd just stopped by her locker to say hi, but she played his words over and over again now.

"You're going to be at Becket's tomorrow night, right? Promise me I'll see you there." It was a simple request, and Brynn was determined to comply.

Jason Becket was her class's notorious party thrower, and tonight's festivities were guaranteed to be epic. So, of course, she promised Spencer she was going. He was single for the first time this year, and so was she. *Still.* The stars had finally aligned, and nothing was going to stop her from turning fantasy into reality. Mind over matter, right? If she didn't admit she was sick, she wouldn't *be* sick.

"And your *voice*!" Holly continued. "You sound like the worst Kermit the Frog impersonator I've ever heard."

Holly was two years younger and a typical drama student. She performed whether she was on stage or not. Tonight was no exception. And anyway, who was she to say Brynn's voice was the *worst* Kermit she'd ever heard? Cut a sick girl some slack. If she was going to sound like a frog, she was going to sound like a *good* frog.

But she *wasn't* sick. So it didn't matter. She needed to focus, keep her eye on the prize.

"Do you know what's supposed to happen tonight?" she asked her sister, and Holly recoiled. Did she *sound* contagious? It was possible her ears were clogged. Hell, everything was clogged, and everything hurt. But this was *her* night, and she was *not* contagious because she was a healthy, seventeen-year-old girl who just couldn't swallow without the threat of tears.

Holly took a step back toward her own room. "Ugh,

Brynn. It's so cliché to like a guy like Spencer Matthews. He's, like, *too* perfect. Any girl would get an inferiority complex around someone like that. Better yet, I bet he's *so* good his girlfriends don't even get mad. They get bored. I think the best guy is the one who pisses you off every now and then. Like…like Patrick and Kat in *10 Things I Hate About You!*"

Life was not some romantic comedy. Holly was full of shit. Of course Spencer was perfect. That's why she'd crushed on him the whole year, biding her time until he was single and would maybe, hopefully, look at her the way she looked at him. Today she was sure he did—or *would* once they found a moment alone tonight. If being a hot, smart, football-playing-marching-band drummer was a crime, Brynn wanted to be his willing accomplice. Seriously, a guy who started pregame on the field with the band—in his formfitting football uniform—and spent the rest of the game as running back…how hot was that?

Brynn attempted a groan, which really freaking hurt, but she wouldn't give whatever plague she was carrying the satisfaction. If anything, a twenty-four-hour bug had taken up residence in her throat, which meant she was at least a quarter of the way through it at this point. She was probably already on the mend.

"Have you ever felt fireworks?" she asked.

Holly answered her sister with a roll of her eyes and slid down the wall until she sat on the floor in the hallway, still keeping clear of Brynn's room.

"Okay," Holly said, waving her on. "I'm comfortable. And this feels like a safe distance from patient zero."

Brynn wanted to groan, but she thought better of what that would feel like on her throat and instead plopped down on the foot of her bed, sweat beading at her hairline.

"Fireworks," Brynn said again. "Falling in love—*knowing* you're in love because when you kiss the guy who's the right guy…" She closed her eyes and smiled dreamily, despite how miserable she felt.

Holly took the liberty of finishing her sentence. "Fireworks?"

Brynn nodded, then opened her eyes. "That and 'I'm a Believer' will start playing in my head."

"Love doesn't come with fireworks and soundtracks filled with songs by the Monkees, not that I'll *ever* understand how Mom got you obsessed with a forty-plus-year-old boy band. I think you might be delirious with fever or something." Holly laughed. "Hey, maybe that explains your taste in music, too!"

Brynn huffed. "Whatever. You're only fifteen. You've never been in love."

Before Holly could offer a rebuttal, the front door opened, and Brynn let out a tiny whimper of relief because if there was one thing Holly *could* call her on, it was Brynn never having been in love, either. God, if she could just make it to the party and kiss Spencer, she *knew* there'd be fireworks… plus Mickey Dolenz and Davy Jones harmonizing in her head, no delirium necessary.

But with the sounds of footsteps bounding up the stairs, Brynn's dream slipped further away. It was for sure Jamie because he never knocked. He was practically a resident in the Chandler house. Jamie would take one look at her in a turtleneck and yoga pants and put the kibosh on the whole operation.

Time to rally.

Brynn pulled her hair out of the bun sitting atop her head and finger-combed the curls. Then she swiped on some lip gloss and affixed her best smile—until she tried to swallow, and her eye betrayed her with a rogue tear.

Jamie appeared at the top of the stairs and stopped in the doorway, his too-straight, sandy hair slicked back like Leo DiCaprio in the *Titanic* ballroom scene. Brynn sighed. She loved *Titanic*. Why couldn't Rose just move over on that piece of driftwood? There was definitely room for two.

Brynn blinked a couple of times. The fever must be rising, because she could swear Jamie looked super cute tonight, and she did *not* have thoughts like that about Jamie Kingston.

He ran a hand through the product in his hair, and a shock flopped down over his eyes before he pushed it back again. She did *not* find this adorable, either. Because that would be the weirdest, looking at her best friend like that. Besides—Spencer. *Spencer* was the issue at hand.

"Holy shit, B. What happened to you?"

. . .

Jamie wasn't sure whether to take a step into the room or back down the stairs. He always thought Brynn was beautiful, but she looked bad. Like, really bad. Her eyes were bloodshot and her cheeks flushed. And her swollen neck? Whoa.

She stared at him through the thick lenses of her glasses perched mildly askew atop her nose. Her wild brown curls were matted to her face, dampened with sweat. But this was just at the hairline. The rest was a tangled sort of nest-like display, which could only mean she'd just taken it down from a bun. Jamie was the only one Brynn let see her immediately post-bun, and he took a certain pride in this—even if he was here to take her to a party where she planned to kiss another guy.

"Sleepy Jean, I say this with love, but you look like shit."

She flopped back on her bed and groaned. This was how he knew something was really wrong. He didn't call her Sleepy Jean solely for her inexplicable love for the sixties TV band, the Monkees. Brynn really was a "Daydream Believer." She saw opportunity in every situation and never took *no* for a final answer until she'd exhausted all other possibilities.

Jamie took a chance and moved toward the edge of the bed. Screw it. He sat down next to her, resting a hand on her leg.

"What's with the turtleneck, Dieter?" He raised his brows.

Brynn laughed. At least he thought it was a laugh, but she also could have been trying to blow bubbles in mud. *Sprockets* was her favorite *Saturday Night Live* skit, another one of Brynn's retro faves, this time from the nineties, and although Mike Myers wasn't on the show anymore, Jamie had a stockpile of his parents' VHS recordings for them to watch whenever the mood struck. He smiled to himself. Brynn was clearly sick, but he made her laugh, and that was something.

She sat up, tears pooled in her eyes. When she pulled the turtleneck down to her collarbone, Jamie sucked in a breath.

"Duuuuude. You've got mono." The glands in her neck swelled on each side like she was a cartoon character who had swallowed a small branch that got stuck in her throat just below her head.

The tears came fast now, tears that tugged at his heart because he knew what they were for. He knew *whom* they were for: Spencer Matthews.

"My throat hurts so much, Jamie. I can't even swallow."

Okay, so maybe he was a selfish asshole. It's quite possible the river of tears was for the extreme pain she was in. He knew what it felt like because he had had mono sophomore year, and it sucked.

He brushed a damp curl off her forehead and tried to tuck it behind her ear. But Brynn's hair had a mind of its own and had no intention of obeying. Kind of like the girl herself.

Jamie bit back a smile.

"Mono?" Brynn croaked.

Holly was still in the hall, standing up now and, at the utterance of the word "mono," she ran to her own room and slammed the door.

"Let me know when you're on some antibiotics or something, and then I'll come out!" she called from the other side.

He chuckled. Typical Holly.

"Where are your parents?" he asked, and Brynn flopped back down on the bed.

"Out," she whined. "My dad has some work dinner thingy in the city, so they're staying the night in a hotel."

He looked at the pout on her lips, letting his mind wander for a few seconds. What would it be like to kiss those lips? What if *he* was the guy Brynn was willing to risk her health—and others'—to see?

She whimpered, and he drifted back to reality.

"Holly!" Jamie kept his eyes on Brynn while he called for her sister.

"What?"

His eyes grew wide. Holly sounded much closer than she should have, considering she was barricaded next door.

"The vent," Brynn said, and Jamie couldn't help but laugh.

"You guys still do that?" he asked, heading toward the wall Brynn's room shared with Holly's. He dropped to a squat and directed his request toward the metal slats of the vent in the floor.

"Holly?" he called, using his indoor voice this time.

"James?" she responded, and he had flashbacks to when he and Brynn were in middle school, sitting in her room doing homework while Holly and her friends giggled and squealed next door, some of them professing their love to him—through the vent, of course. Brynn had always laughed and rolled her eyes.

"Don't they know you're practically our brother?" she'd once said. Jamie hated that she still saw him like that now.

"Call your parents and ask if I can take Brynn to urgent care," he told Holly.

"Okay, James." He could hear her smile.

"And Holly?"

"Yes, James?"

"Stop calling me James."

He smiled, too. Then he heard Holly speaking to her mom.

"Are you sure it's mono?" she asked him.

"Pretty sure," Jamie said. "I had all the same symptoms."

He glanced back at Brynn, who had turned to her side to watch the back and forth between Jamie and Holly. He wondered if she had any clue what she did to him, if she knew how much he wanted to scoop her up in his arms and hold her until she felt better. And maybe after that, hold her a little more.

He lay down next to her and tilted her glasses up so he could swipe a thumb across her tear-streaked cheek.

"You're burning up, B." He let the frames fall softly back against the bridge of her nose.

"I know," she whispered. "I took my temperature. But I thought if I didn't admit how bad I felt that I could ignore it."

He pressed a kiss to her forehead, her skin like fire against his lips. But he didn't care, not if he could give her the smallest bit of comfort.

"You know I'd give my left arm to make you feel better, right?"

She pressed her lips together and nodded. "It's not *that* big of a sacrifice, considering you're a righty. If you really cared—" She cut her own joke short to attempt a swallow, and it only made her cry more.

"For you, Sleepy Jean, I'd give them both."

Fuck. He was a goner. How he made it through this year without blurting out his feelings was a mystery, because when she looked at him like that, like he was the only one who could fix the mess that was her night, the words repeated over and over again in his head: *I'm in love with you, B.* But she'd made no secret of how she felt about Spencer Matthews since the school year started, which meant Jamie was well practiced in the fine art of holding it all in.

"Mom wants to know how high her fever is."

Brynn tried to clear her throat, then moaned in pain before she said, "One hundred and two."

Jamie repeated the response to Holly, then sighed as he looked at his miserable friend.

"Does she want them to come home?" Holly asked, and Brynn shook her head, her eyes still on Jamie.

"Are you sure?" she asked. "Because this is it. Our last high school party. I don't want you to miss it, too."

Shit. If she only knew how many other parties he would have skipped if it meant a night alone with her instead… But all he said was, "I'm sure."

Brynn tilted her head back in the direction of the vent.

"My night and, let's face it, my goal for the year are out the window," Brynn said. "Tell them Jamie will take me to the doctor, and then I'll go to sleep. They don't need to ruin their night."

After Mrs. Chandler insisted she speak to Brynn, Holly chucked her phone into the room and ordered Jamie to sanitize it when Brynn was done.

And that was that. Instead of taking Brynn to the final bash of their senior year, he'd take her for a blood test, maybe top off the night with a throat culture. Man did he know how to impress the ladies.

"This was supposed to be my night, Jamie," she said after getting off the phone. "*My* night. And now all I want to do is chop off my own head to end the pain."

He laughed. He couldn't help it. She was cute when she was a mess.

"First of all," he said. "I think the whole beheading thing might be a little more painful and a lot less practical than, I don't know, going to urgent care? And second, this can still be your night. Just a different kind. We'll see a doctor, get you a nice prescription for some codeine, a pint of Cherry Garcia, and a stack of Dieter tapes — as long as you still have the VCR hooked up."

She sniffled and sat up. "Aren't you afraid you'll get sick?"

He shook his head. "I'd chance it to take care of you. Plus" — he gave her a knowing smile — "you're not supposed to be able to get mono twice. I'm probably immune to your plague." To prove it, he kissed her on the forehead, happy to show her she didn't have to be alone tonight. But even in her state, all the kiss did was prove to him how hard it was to just be her friend.

"Okay, maybe we'll get you a quick shower, too." The least he could do was lighten the mood, for both of them.

She sniffled again. "Can we listen to the Monkees in the car?"

He put his arm around her, pulling her head to his shoulder.

"Anything for you, Sleepy Jean."

And he would do anything for her, even step aside for someone else. He'd made it all the way to junior year *not* falling for her. It had taken him dating Stephanie Delaney to realize no other girl made him feel the way Brynn did. Though who's to say it wasn't always there, this thing between them? Correction — this thing between them only Jamie seemed to feel. And who was he to stand in the way of her dream? He wouldn't be that guy, letting his feelings interfere with her happiness. They had too much history for that kind of selfishness. Brynn made her choice, and it wasn't Jamie. But tonight the universe seemed to be on his side, postponing the torture of watching her fall for someone else. Tonight was not for Spencer Matthews. It was for Jamie and Brynn. Even if they were only friends.

Chapter One

If there was one fashion accessory that made Brynn Chandler deliriously happy, it was boots—the taller the better—and the ones she had on now were devastating in the most gorgeous way. They made other boots cower in shame and other women green with envy. Rich black suede hugged her calves and folded over just above her knees. The three-inch heels that gave some stature to her five-foot-four-inch frame, making her legs look long and lean and—dare she say—*hot*, topped off the look. And, amazingly, they were crazy comfortable to walk around in. She nodded at her reflection, twisting her foot side to side so she could admire the view. She didn't often think it of herself, but tonight Brynn knew it. She was lookin' *good*.

Some of her former classmates complained the committee hadn't planned a summer reunion, but not Brynn. Nothing topped the perfect dress like the perfect pair of boots, and *these* boots were made for a girl to wear to her high school reunion. She couldn't believe it had been ten years already. Maybe she hadn't done big things with her career or met the love of her life, but she had the boots, and tonight that would be enough.

"Holy shit, Brynn. If you fuck up my babies, we are through."

Okay, so maybe the devastating boots weren't *hers* per se, but they still looked exquisite with the dress, and Holly did say she could wear them. Brynn just tried not to think about the price tag of Holly's *babies*.

"I should remind you," Brynn started, "that you're my sister. So the whole *we're through* threat doesn't really work on me. Plus, you need me for the other half of the rent, so…"

Holly huffed. She was good with that—the drama. A theater girl all throughout high school and college, Holly Chandler was always *on*. Sometimes Brynn couldn't tell if her sister was adding a little flair or if her emotional reactions were genuine. This seemed a little bit of both.

"Please remember they retail for four hundred dollars, okay? To me that means they're irreplaceable—unless you are sitting on a wad of cash I don't know about, in which case I'd love your portion of the rent on time this month."

Brynn sighed. She didn't have to think about things when Holly was always there to remind her. Eight years out of high school, and Holly was already working her way up in Chicago's fashion scene.

"Of course I'll be careful." Brynn groaned. She could play the drama card, too. "It's not like you *paid* four hundred for them."

Holly shrugged. "That's why they can't be replaced. A perk of working in the fashion industry is the samples, but they don't give me replacements if my sister ruins them."

Brynn crinkled her nose. So what if her baby sister was already pulling in more bank than she was *and* scoring extras like the boots? Brynn could make more money as a CPA for a larger company, but she liked doing the books for her favorite independent bookstore, Two Stories. The aptly named two-story bookshop might not be a cash cow, but her close friend Annie owned it, and there was no place Brynn enjoyed more.

Holly gave her sister the once-over. "You do look fucking hot. I'll give you that."

Brynn smoothed her hands over her dress and shook out her hair. Thanks to the wonderful developments in anti-frizz curl cream, she no longer sported the nest she had trouble taming in high school. Brynn's hair hung in soft spirals from crown to just below her shoulders, and the natural gold highlights shone especially bright in her soft brown hue. She wondered if hair could reflect her mood, because tonight she felt all sparkly. Not *vampire* sparkly. More like a firecracker.

On any other Saturday night, Brynn might be on a blind date. Some of her married friends and her mom felt an obligation to the poor, single twenty-seven-year-old doomed to a life surrounded by a litter of cats. Was that the name for a group of cats? She'd have to look it up to be sure. Not that it mattered. Didn't everyone know she was allergic…to cats *and* bad dates? It's not like she had never had a serious boyfriend. She just hadn't had one in a year. And she couldn't keep taking her best friend, Jamie, to all her family functions now that he was officially off the market. That had worked extremely well when she needed a plus-one and didn't want to deal with questions about her love life. But now that she was the single one and Jamie wasn't, Brynn had no choice but to say yes to the many, *many* setups foisted upon her by well-meaning individuals who, judging by the men they set her up with, really didn't know her at all.

Her last date turned out to live with his parents, who *funded* their date because the guy was in a "job transition" phase that had already lasted two years.

What was wrong with being twenty-seven and single anyway? It's not like it was nineteenth-century England, and if she didn't marry her obnoxious cousin, her family would lose the estate upon her father's death. On the contrary, Brynn and Holly's parents pushed them out of the nest as soon as each of them graduated college and just as quickly turned each of their rooms into a scrapbooking studio for their mom and a reading room for their dad.

It was the grandkids—or the lack thereof—that prompted her mother's interest in her love life. Holly was always dating *someone*, even if it never lasted longer than six months. Plus, she was twenty-five, still far enough from thirty and the approach of "advanced maternal age," as their mom liked to say. Brynn, on the other hand, was one preschooler's lifespan away from that next decade. According to those in the know, something had to be done, even if it meant a life with Tom who lived with his parents. He could probably still reproduce, right?

It didn't matter. Tonight would be different—what it should have been ten years ago.

"I do look pretty good, right?" she asked Holly.

Her sister crossed her arms and nodded. "In a sexy librarian kind of way, yeah."

She groaned, then took off her glasses. "I'm not a librarian." She marched out of her room and into the bathroom to retrieve her contact lenses. Holly followed, giggling.

"I meant accountant. You're a sexy accountant. Come on, Brynn. Look at you. You're gorgeous. And I bet you're the only accountant who not only knows that sixty-nine is a number but also how to do it!"

"Not helping," Brynn said.

She's just trying to push my buttons. We can't all be twenty-five and perky, with the straightest hair known to man, and 20/20 vision.

She straightened in front of the mirror, but her contacts weren't in yet, so she couldn't really check herself out. Thanks to her extreme farsightedness, the image staring back at her was nothing but a blur. It was true she put a lot of thought and work into how she looked tonight. The past month saw her making extra trips to the path along Lake Michigan for a run, and she cut back on the imbibing, which was always difficult with a best friend who owns a brewery. Four weeks ago, the belted black knit dress fit all her curves just a little too snugly. Tonight, she felt she had room to breathe, and Brynn enjoyed easy access to oxygen.

As she raised a contact lens balanced on her fingertip, someone pounded on the door, startling her and sending the contact flying into the sink.

"Shit!" she yelled and waved her sister toward the door. "Let him in. Then tell him I'm going to kill him if I don't find this lens. I don't want everyone to see me as a sexy accountant."

Holly giggled some more as she headed for the door, and Brynn muttered to herself as she shoved her face into the sink to find the contact.

It was no use. Brynn couldn't see what was right in front of her face if she didn't have her glasses on, and she'd left them in the bedroom on her nightstand.

She braced her hands on the counter and blew out a breath. "Sexy accountant," she mumbled again. Brynn pouted, thinking about how people saw her ten years ago—the smart girl with too much optimism and too much hair. In their senior superlatives she was voted "Best Smile" and "Most Likely to Be Concealing a Carrier Pigeon." Yeah, they made that second one up just for her. As an assistant editor for the school paper, she'd even approved it going to print. Because that was Brynn—go with the flow and smile at everything— but tonight she wanted to be something else.

"Can't I just be sexy?" she murmured to herself.

"Sure thing, Sleepy Jean."

The familiar voice came from behind her, and she smiled

despite her irritation. Jamie brought that out in her. But right now, she was annoyed with him, and he had some damage control to do.

She turned toward her friend and blinked at his blurry outline.

"Where is it?" he asked, and she could hear the smile in his voice even if she couldn't see it. She rolled her unfocused eyes.

"In the sink…I hope. If it went down the drain and I have to go to our ten-year reunion looking like I'm balancing my checkbook, you're in for a world of hurt."

He brushed past her, and she hummed a small, "Mmmm." He smelled good. Different, but good. Something fluttered in her belly, and Brynn groaned softly. She could pass it off as annoyance if he questioned her. Which it *was*. Her belly wasn't supposed to get all fluttery for him.

"Is that the new cologne Elizabeth bought for your birthday?" She grimaced a little. It's not that she didn't like Jamie's girlfriend. It's just that she and Jamie loved going through the fragrance section at Bloomingdale's together, making fun of the latest celebrity perfumes and colognes. The one that made them laugh the most was always the one she bought him for Christmas that year and vice versa. This year it was going to be Adam Levine's aptly titled scent, Adam Levine, but if he was into whatever Kenneth Cole or Hugo Boss his girlfriend bought him, the fun would be lost.

Jamie backed away from the sink so he stood in front of her again. He pulled out her hand and gingerly dropped the lost lens into her palm.

"Even cleaned it off with your solution," he said, and she quickly inserted the contact into her right eye and proceeded to do the same with the left. "And to answer your question, no. It's not the stuff Liz got me. I ducked into Sephora on my way here and sprayed on some Michael Jordan 23. I'm going old-school Chicago tonight."

Brynn couldn't help the satisfied smile, even if the edges of it were dulled by him having a nickname for his girlfriend after only three months. When she had first met *Elizabeth*, Jamie introduced her as Liz.

"Elizabeth," she'd corrected and winked as she shook Brynn's hand. "James seems to like Liz, and I kind of like when he says it. But everyone else calls me Elizabeth."

She'd never begrudge Jamie his happiness, even if it was with a girl who winked. She just didn't like the idea of their sharing private jokes or nicknames. But *Liz* still called him James, and *Liz* had no clue about their celebrity cologne obsession. Some things were sacred.

When she turned around, Jamie crystalized into focus, and damn did he look good. Not that he didn't always, but his work attire was overly casual, usually just a Kingston Ale House T-shirt and jeans. And even though tonight's affair was being held at that very same establishment, Jamie cleaned up for the occasion.

"Looking pretty sharp, Mr. Kingston," Brynn said as she took him in. His hair was cropped short on the sides but left slightly longer on top, enough to require a little pomade to give it some lift. It looked darker when he wore it shorter, and Brynn liked it like this. The outfit was typical Jamie: white oxford with the sleeves rolled up, charcoal and black striped tie, a fitted black vest, and, of course, always jeans. Tonight's pair was dark-washed denim, a fitted straight-leg that stopped atop a pair of red suede Pumas.

He bowed humbly. "And what scent are you wearing this evening, Ms. Chandler?"

Brynn bit her lip and grinned. "Meow by Katy Perry."

Jamie threw back his head and laughed. "Is this your way of outsmarting your future as the crazy cat lady...by becoming the cat?"

Despite her allergies, Brynn couldn't help being sucked in to the worry factory sometimes. What if she didn't meet someone by thirty? Would she be required to get a cat at that point? Is it something you sign when you turn thirty, the *if-I-don't-marry-at-least-I-have-my-cats* contract?

He kissed her on the cheek and whispered in her ear, "Ya look sexy no matter what, Sleepy Jean."

Brynn sighed. At least she had a *real* nickname even if she didn't have a guy.

"That's what I told her!" Holly materialized behind Jamie. "She doesn't think she's sexy with her specs, but they're hot when she wears them, right, *James*?"

Holly had always called him James to annoy him, and now she took great pleasure in pointing out how Liz called him that every day. Brynn wouldn't admit it, but she enjoyed Holly's teasing, too. Tormenting Jamie about his girlfriends was nothing new. There was always something to mock, though never with malicious intent. Only to push Jamie's buttons and maybe, in the back of Brynn's mind, to alleviate that tiny stab of jealousy, something else she'd never admit, not after the debacle that was Jamie and her ten years ago.

Sometimes fault was hard to find, and they had to admit, Elizabeth—or *Liz*—was a pretty tough nut to crack. She was pretty, always had great shoes, and she was an ER doctor. Hard to find anything wrong with that, so they had to look for little things, and for them it was the formality of his name. *James*. Even though more and more in his adult life he'd been leaving Jamie behind, introducing himself as James to new people he met, Brynn and Holly couldn't get over Liz calling him that.

Jamie rolled his eyes. "It's my *name*, you two." His look may have spelled irritation, but his smooth baritone hinted at a smile, one that told Brynn he knew the teasing came from a place of affection. He pulled out his phone. "That reminds me.

I need to call Liz before her shift starts or we might not get a chance to connect tonight. She's working straight through till morning."

He strolled into their small kitchen to make his call, and Holly nudged her sister on the shoulder.

"You really missed the boat with that one," Holly said.

Brynn leaned back against the sink. "What do you mean?" As if she didn't already know.

"Look at him, Brynn. Jamie's always been cute, but damn. The boy grew up *nice*. Haven't you ever thought about…you know? Or can I call dibs if *Liz* ever leaves the picture?"

Brynn pushed past Holly and into the living room. She needed to move, to shake off the horror at the thought of Holly and Jamie. It wasn't like she wanted him for herself. Not anymore, at least.

Dammit, Jamie. You are not sidetracking me from the plan.

Brynn missed her chance with Spencer in high school, and for a blip on the radar, she thought getting mono was actually some sort of gift because it made her see Jamie differently—made her *feel* differently about him. And kissing him? Well, she thought that would have changed everything. But two words from him—*I can't*—had broken her heart… and had nearly broken their friendship for good. Tonight the plan would go down the way it was supposed to years ago, the way that would have ended happily instead of putting her friendship with Jamie in an uncomfortable limbo for four years.

The way she saw things now, the only reason their friendship survived was because of the distance and perspective of being at different universities and because they'd never crossed that line again. They'd barely spoken their freshmen year apart, and though she'd never tell him, it was the hardest year of her life. In the long run she'd gotten what mattered most—Jamie in her life, always.

"Relax," Holly said, which told Brynn her sister saw right through her. "I'm not going to date Jamie. He's like my brother. *Ew.* I just don't get you guys. The only difference between you two and a real couple is the whole sex thing." Holly's brows drew together. "You're *not* sleeping with him, are you? Because then I'd have to break it to you both—you *are* dating."

She narrowed her eyes at her sister. The night of that high school kiss, Holly had slept at a friend's house to avoid Brynn's *plague.* She knew nothing about what had happened between Brynn and Jamie. No one did. So why the third degree now? True, Jamie was a good-looking guy. And that smile and laid-back air, like nothing ever fazed him, made him easy to be around. It's why Jamie was friends with everyone—the guy who avoided a label in high school and just kind of fit in everywhere. Holly suspecting anything now was just Holly being Holly, which meant button-pressing little sister.

"No," she said, her voice firm. "We're not sleeping together. He's my friend. I wouldn't mess with that."

She had enough failed relationships to know she didn't want to add Jamie to that list. She was glad he met Liz, especially since he seemed happier these past few months than she'd seen him in a long time. It might be weird to watch him fall head over heels for someone, but she'd be happy for him if it happened—*when* it happened.

Just not with her sister.

"Anyway," Brynn continued, "you're only bringing that up to mess with me about tonight."

Jamie had found Liz, and tonight Brynn would get a second chance at her own fireworks.

Holly threw her hands up in the air. "I'm just asking you a question. I'm not trying to foil your ten-year plan."

"What ten-year plan?"

Jamie walked in, and instinct told her to change the subject.

She had by no means been pining for Spencer Matthews for a decade. But if the stars were aligned again, who was she not to see where they led her? A second chance at a guy she *could* have fallen for when she was a teen ranked much higher than another setup from her poor, grandchildless mother.

"What do you think? Is everything working the way it's supposed to, you know, work?" she asked, doing a quick twirl and shaking out her hair. Then she smoothed her hands over the fabric, making sure the A-line skirt was straight and that the back of the dress wasn't somehow caught in her underwear. They'd take a taxi to the ale house, so she wasn't wearing tights. Though the dress stopped above the knee, her fabulous four-hundred-dollar boots that weren't really hers protected enough skin to make braving Chicago's unexpected late-September chill doable.

Holly and Jamie nodded.

"You're sure, both of you? It's a thumbs-up?"

"Yes," Holly said. "You're hot, B. Own it, honey."

Brynn laughed.

"Can I ask you something?" This from Jamie. "Did you pick a turtleneck dress on purpose?" He raised a brow.

Brynn's cheeks went hot, and Holly's brow creased. She ignored the twist in her gut at Jamie bringing up that night now. But, if she had to admit it, yes. On some level the turtleneck seemed fitting. Jamie stood there, a knowing smirk on his face.

Busted.

• • •

Jamie didn't know what bugged him more, remembering that Brynn wore a turtleneck that night ten-plus years ago, or that she was wearing something to remind her of the night she wished she'd had back then instead of the one she spent with him.

He laughed, a little too loud to be casual and a little too forced to be genuine. Still, he hoped he'd saved face.

"You're wearing something to remind you of your attempt to pass on a potentially life-threatening illness to another human? That's twisted, Brynn."

She winced, and he knew he'd gone too far. It just slipped. *Brynn*. Sleepy Jean, Dieter, B, even SJ on occasion, but Brynn? That only seemed to come out when he was angry. He'd nicknamed her the day they were paired up for a think/pair/share in eighth-grade language arts class. She'd introduced herself as Brynn, and he found her later in the library pretending to read her history book. Her head bobbed to whatever was playing in the earbuds hidden in her wild, curly hair, and he sat down at her table, pulling one free so he could listen.

"The Monkees?" he had asked, eyes wide with incredulity and maybe a little embarrassment at recognizing the band so quickly.

She'd snatched back the bud and paused the music.

"Not like I should have to explain everything to you, James, but everyone knows the Monkees are my favorite band. My mom grew up loving Davy Jones, and she was good enough to pass that love on to me. No one seems to have a problem with it."

He crossed his arms and pushed his skater bangs out of his eyes.

"Not *everyone* knows if I didn't know, and you can call me Jamie. My friends do."

She sighed. "Who said we were friends?"

He had smiled at her then. "Come on, Sleepy Jean. After all we've been through since third hour?" Right then something cracked in her veneer, a twitch of her lip that let him know he'd won her over.

"Fine, *Jamie*." She'd sighed. "We're friends."

And that had been it. Since then they were Jamie and Sleepy Jean to each other, and when formal names were verbally lobbed, the other knew something was up.

"Mono is not a life-threatening illness," Brynn scoffed. "You should know. And what do you have against Spencer, anyway, *James*?"

Touché. He deserved that.

He had nothing against Spencer Matthews, not anymore. But the mere mention of his name brought back feelings of that night when Brynn had been more than a best friend to him. Jamie liked to tell himself he was over it, but the memory still stung. Just the idea of Spencer had won Brynn over. She'd barely even spoken to him senior year yet was sure he was *the* guy...until an ill-timed sickness gave Jamie his opening. One kiss. That's as far as they got. Then, when everything in his family went to shit, he let it drag the possibility of Brynn and him down, too.

Tonight he'd let the plan play out the way it was supposed to. If Spencer got the girl ten years ago, Jamie would have been crushed. True. But he never would have known what he was missing. Now he did. At least the teenage version of him did. But that was the thing about tonight. It made him feel only a blink away from seventeen, which meant his actions and reactions were not necessarily those of a twenty-seven-year-old man.

"I've got nothing against self-important author types," he said, digging the hole deeper with his petty dick-headedness. "And you shouldn't take your spleen for granted. Mono is *not* something to fuck around with."

He laughed at his own joke, even though a ruptured spleen was no laughing matter.

Brynn rolled her eyes, and Jamie knew he was in for it. He'd heard nothing but Spencer Matthews's name this past week, from more than just Brynn. As owner of Kingston Ale House, he'd been in charge of maintaining tonight's guest list, and Spencer's name was definitely on it. Then there was the fact that the guy was Jamie's age and releasing his first novel in a couple of weeks. It seemed like everyone who knew Spencer wouldn't shut up about what the guy had accomplished at such a young age.

What about Jamie? Maybe he didn't create a literary masterpiece, but it was *his* name on the brewery's sign, and he also made a great pale ale and was working on a chocolate stout. Everyone loved a chocolate stout, right?

"You're sure he responded without a plus-one?" Brynn asked, and she seemed to let go of the tension pooling between them.

"Positive," he said. "And don't worry. I'll be busy enough with the party end of things that no one will think we're there together, so no accidental cock-blocking."

This got a smile out of Brynn, and he told himself the sting it gave him was just a result of those residual high school feelings, the ones he'd put aside and buried deep when he finally got his friend back. So what, he fell for his best friend when they were teens. So they'd kissed, and Brynn had actually told him she wanted more. But Jamie had told her it was shit timing, that he needed a friend instead of a relationship. That didn't mean he couldn't be supportive if she found happiness now. He just kind of, sort of, maybe wished it could be with another guy—preferably one who shared no part of their history.

"It's actually good Liz is working tonight," he added. "Things will probably be too crazy for me to be a good date."

Brynn poked him in the ribs, in that spot only she knew was his most ticklish, and he fought hard not to laugh. Instead he grabbed her finger, and they stood there in silence for several seconds. Then Brynn cleared her throat.

"You sure you're not just worried about taking such a big step?" she teased. "I mean, introducing her to the high school crowd? That's probably bigger than meeting the parents, huh? Has she met your parents yet?"

He let go of her finger, and her hand fell to her side.

"We should go," he said, ignoring her questions.

Liz wasn't the issue tonight. All that mattered was he'd be busy enough that when Brynn aimed her arrow at her target, he'd have plenty on his plate so he wouldn't have to watch.

He put his arm around Holly and gave her a brotherly squeeze.

"Good night, Miss Holly. Don't wait up."

Brynn came at her sister from the other side, planting a kiss on her cheek, and said, "But don't forget I'm coming home and accidentally chain lock the door."

Brynn had to crash at Jamie's place on more than one occasion due to this oversight before.

Holly pushed them both away playfully.

"I'll leave myself a note on the door," she groaned, and Jamie and Brynn both watched as she followed through with the statement as soon as she uttered it. They trailed her to the door where Jamie helped Brynn on with her coat before grabbing his, too.

"Have fun storming the castle, you two," Holly said. "I expect to hear everything at brunch. And take care of my boots!"

Brynn blew her sister one last good-bye kiss, and Jamie ushered her out the door and into the small hallway that led outside.

A snap of wind startled them, and Brynn lost her footing in the boots only to have Jamie catch her in his arms before she hit the ground. He chalked up the shiver that ran down his spine to a breeze off the lake.

"My hero," she said, giving him a patronizing pat on the

cheek.

Jamie righted her and hailed a taxi, and they were surrounded in warmth within seconds.

"Kingston Ale House on Southport," he said to the driver, then turned to Brynn.

"You know I'll always catch you, right?" He meant it. No matter what happened tonight or another ten years from now, he always wanted Brynn Chandler in his life.

She responded by smiling and nudging his shoulder with hers.

Jamie sat back and smiled to himself.

Maybe he was over what he felt for his best friend in high school, and maybe she would finally get her kiss tonight, the one she hadn't forgotten about for ten years. But Jamie hadn't forgotten, either—what it felt like to love her from afar and lose her, even if it was his fault. That's what kept him at a distance now. That's what the memories did—reminded him the only way he'd always have Brynn was like this. Funny what the mind did, though, on a short cab ride to revisit his decade-old life. It brought all the memories crashing down, and he could do nothing to stop it.

Jamie had been the one to play caretaker the night Brynn *didn't* kiss Spencer Matthews. He'd sat with her at urgent care and later waited outside her bathroom door to make sure she had the strength to shower and brush her teeth before settling in on the couch for the night. The pharmacy had been closed, so she would have to wait until the next morning for the codeine.

"Looks like it's just us, Cherry Garcia, and Sprockets," he'd said, getting her situated on the couch. She'd lain with her head in his lap, and even now in the back seat of a cab,

Jamie's heartbeat sped up at the memory, just as it had done in real time.

"Talk about worst night ever," she'd said. "And I'm ruining yours, too."

He'd brushed his fingers across her forehead and along her hairline.

"Not possible, B. A night with you—healthy or not—beats a stupid party every single time."

He remembered her smiling at him and then dozing off. The truth was there was nowhere in the entire freaking world he'd wanted to be than with Brynn that night, no matter how she saw him.

At midnight, she'd woken, her head in Jamie's lap. Her fever had broken, and she'd put on her glasses and stared at him with eyes so clear Jamie didn't know what to make of it until she'd asked him the question that catapulted them from just friends to something more.

"Jamie?"

"Yeah?"

"Can you really not get mono again?"

He'd shrugged. "I remember my doctor saying you weren't supposed to, but it's not a guarantee." He held his breath, too afraid to hope where the conversation might be headed.

"But you stayed with me anyway?" she'd asked, her eyes wide with recognition.

And he'd nodded. He couldn't imagine being anywhere else.

She'd sat up then, still holding his gaze. "I was supposed to get kissed tonight."

At that point, Jamie couldn't even nod. He couldn't move. And he certainly couldn't speak. So he'd waited.

"Kiss me?" she'd asked. "I know it's stupid. I've never… we've never… I just… Jamie, you *stayed.*" She'd tugged the hair tie off her wrist and pulled her curls back into a bun. "I don't have a fever anymore, but I get it if you're scared of getting sick again…"

She didn't have to finish. He'd pulled her to him so quickly, there wasn't time to think. In that moment, Brynn had wanted him, and it didn't matter if it meant putting his health at risk. *That* he could do. And for a few sweet minutes, his lips had been on hers. There were smiles and sighs and the taste of a *Hall's* throat lozenge, yet he hadn't cared. Because a weight had lifted from his chest, one that had been pressing down for an entire year. But always in the back of his mind there was that voice, and it told him again and again, with every brush of her lips, that this couldn't last. It was only a brief interlude, but in that time he'd let down the walls, let self-preservation fly out the window.

"Jamie," she'd said when they finally parted, his name a breathy sigh. God, he could hear it again, could conjure it at will. Why wouldn't his brain forget?

"Yeah?" he'd asked, his voice hoarse, his heart hammering with anticipation.

"We just kissed," she'd said, and he'd nodded. "We should do it again. When I'm better. We should…"

Her eyes had been wide with realization, and he'd threaded his fingers with hers.

"Yeah," he'd told her, beaming that what he never thought was possible was actually happening. "We should."

The next morning brought the fever back, and Brynn's mom had filled her prescription as soon as she got home. For a week she was in a codeine haze, and Jamie barely saw her. When she was finally well again, Jamie's family had fallen apart. His parents had ridden the wave of a miserable marriage until he'd graduated high school—the last of the Kingston boys to leave home. Brynn had spent the week miserable and in bed while Jamie spent his hiding out to avoid the vicious verbal lobs his parents threw at each other. Funny, they'd never fought that he could remember. But once his dad said he was leaving, everything they'd held back came pouring out.

"I can't do this, B," he'd told her when she was finally well again. "I need my friend. Because if it goes any further…I just can't watch us turn into them." That had been the only explanation he'd had—the only thing he thought would make sense to her. Because the truth of it was, everything he'd thought he knew about love had detonated in an instant. How could he let himself fall further for her when all his life he'd been taught a lie? So he'd caged his heart—enough to keep it safe and enough to keep Brynn in his life, even if it meant hurting her to do it.

She'd cried, but she hadn't argued. Why would she fight a losing battle? Because that's what Jamie was. For a year he'd played it safe, never fought for what he wanted. Then when he finally got it, he pushed it away after one amazing kiss.

Jamie turned his head toward Brynn in the cab now, sliding his arm around her.

"We're good, right?" he asked, and something wistful rose to the surface in her eyes. He wondered if she knew where his mind had wandered, wondered if hers ever wandered there, too.

"Always," she said, and leaned her head to his shoulder.

Friends, he thought. *We're good as friends.* That's what he kept telling himself, and he was sure by now he believed it.

Chapter Two

One of the perks of knowing the owner of the establishment was making sure her stuff was safe when it was time to get her drink on, and Brynn did not take this for granted. Jamie led her to his office at Kingston Ale House, her secret hideout where she would leave her purse and coat for the remainder of the evening.

"Has *Liz* been here yet?" she teased him, and Jamie gave her that look, the one that asked, *Are we done with this yet?* But the only way she knew how to deal with him dating was to act like the annoying little sister. It wasn't like he was going to marry the girl.

Wait. Could he marry this girl? Brynn laughed quietly to herself. She and Jamie never got that far in relationships. They wouldn't have to think about marriage—to other people, of course—and how that would affect their relationship for years, right?

"Not yet," he said, oblivious to the convoluted places her mind seemed to be taking her. "She works mostly night shifts, and well, so do I, so there hasn't really been the occasion for her to visit while I'm here."

"Hmmm," she said, then hooked her arm in his. "Guess I'm still your work spouse for now."

Brynn took a selfish satisfaction in this. Sure it made her feel a bit petty, but she liked that there was a part of Jamie that wasn't Liz's yet. He had always been Brynn's fallback when they were single together, and he'd been a big help during this most recent dry spell. It seemed like every other weekend, someone they knew was getting married and, thank the stars, Jamie was there when she needed a date. Well, until three months ago. And really, it was her own fault she lost her backup date in the first place.

He chuckled. "Yeah. I don't think that's how it works. Regardless of how much time you spend loitering here, you don't actually take home a paycheck."

He winked at her and stepped through the door.

Jamie checked his voicemails on the office phone when Brynn stepped in front of him and rubbed her finger over the fading scar on his chin.

"She does do good work," she said.

He closed his eyes for a brief couple of seconds, and Brynn held her breath. Then he jerked his head back, a totally acceptable reflex now since she'd stabbed him in the face with a letter opener.

"Thanks," he said, his voice unusually strained.

"You're still mad at me," she said. "It was three months ago, and it was an accident. *Plus* you got a girlfriend out of the whole deal, so you really should be thanking me. I did you a favor."

He laughed. "Can we take a poll tonight to see how many people would like the favor of you impaling them in the face with a sharp object?"

She threw up her arms, her right hand knocking a shelf above Jamie's desk where his coffee mug, the one that read

SHHH…THERE'S BEER IN HERE, held all his multicolored dry-erase markers. Brynn caught the mug as it toppled from the shelf, but the markers scattered across the desk and the floor.

Jamie raised his eyebrows, and she groaned. At least she wasn't gesticulating with anything other than her hands. No danger of drawing blood. And it's not like she was some bull in a china shop, either. That day in *her* office, Jamie had sneaked up on her while she was opening bills. When someone pokes you in the ribs and yells, "Boo," you react. And Brynn reacted much like right now, her arms flailing. Only that time, Jamie's face got in the way instead of a shelf.

"First of all, you weren't *impaled*," she said. "It was little more than a scratch."

She stepped away from the desk, then stopped short before she erased his calendar with her back. How Jamie worked in such a cramped space was beyond her. He must knock stuff off shelves on a daily basis.

Brynn sighed. Wild gestures weren't Jamie's thing. He was too even-tempered, too controlled for something like that.

"It required stitches," he argued.

She laughed at his use of the plural.

"Two," she reminded him. "Two stitches and a girlfriend. You're welcome."

She did feel bad about him having to take a taxi to the ER, but Annie, her friend and owner of Two Stories, had just run to the bank to make a deposit. Brynn couldn't leave the store unattended. Now she wondered what would have happened if she *had* gone, if she'd been with Jamie when he met Liz. Would it have been anything more than an ER visit? This line of thinking wasn't going to get her anywhere.

She set the mug on his desk and helped him collect the markers.

"Sorry," she said. "About almost killing your mug."

They alternated dropping markers back into their

makeshift container. For as long as they'd been friends, Brynn had only ever been reckless around Jamie, and it was never intentional. He just had a way of pushing her buttons...or scaring the shit out of her. Sometimes there were casualties, but she'd never, before her office incident, drawn blood.

"What's this one for?" she asked, holding up a brown marker. "A new brew?"

Jamie smiled, the kind that was full of pride when he got to talk about his work. She'd always known he was brilliant at math and science. When, in college, he started experimenting with brewing, he quickly changed his major to business while simultaneously enrolling in online brewing classes and apprenticing with a local brewmaster. It was funny. She used to be the one who took all the chances, saw the cup as half full. But her outlook changed after high school, and now she was happy to play it safe—steady job, reliable yet moderate income, and surrounded by people she knew would always be there, like Holly and Annie and Jamie.

"That," he said, pointing to the whiteboard calendar behind her, "is for my chocolate stout. We're going to launch it in the new year."

Brynn licked her lips. "I get an early preview, right? Before the general public."

Jamie kissed her on the forehead, and she sighed with relief. He wasn't *really* still mad about the whole stabbing thing. The warmth that spread through her, that gave her a little tingle, *that* was the security of having Jamie as a friend. An accidental stabbing was nothing. They'd weathered worse.

"Of course. How else will I know if it's ready for the masses?"

"And when do I get my Blue Moon?"

Jamie groaned, but she knew it was an act. He'd always promised he'd top her favorite beer, a Belgian-style white ale from a brewer in Colorado. That's what having Jamie in her life did. It made her a beer aficionado whether she wanted to be one or not. Forget the watered-down crap they'd drank for two bucks a cup in college. Now she could tell the difference between a lager, ale, stout, porter, IPA, you name it, and Brynn's favorite was a beer Jamie still didn't brew.

"I'm not going to do it until I get it right," he said. "You know too much now. Too sensitive of a palate. If I fuck it up, I could lose you as a customer."

She smiled at his appreciation of her beer knowledge. It was going to be a good night. She could feel it. In fact, she was already believing tonight's glass would be half full.

"Hey. What's this?" she asked, pointing to the words "Road Trip" followed by a question mark on the calendar. "You going on a trip without telling me?"

He shrugged. "It's just this beer thing in California that's happening in a couple weeks. I was maybe going to drive cross-country. I don't know. It could be good for business, but I'm not sure I should take that much time off. I'll probably skip it."

She narrowed her eyes at him. "Jamie. You *never* take time off. You might actually enjoy relaxing for once." She bit her lip as she contemplated her next question and then mustered up the breeziest voice she could find. "Would…Liz go with you?"

Her stomach clenched as soon as she asked the question. But she reassured herself that any friend would be curious about this type of progress in a relationship. Jamie road-tripping with Liz? That would be huge, right? The forced intimacy of being in a confined space with someone for a prolonged period of time—that could make or break a couple.

He shook his head. "She definitely can't take off that much time. I don't think residents actually get any time off, come to think of it. Nah. It'd just be me and my truck."

He put his hand on the door knob, and Brynn took a deep

breath and smiled.

"Good," she said. "I mean, some *you* time would be good."

He nodded.

"Are we ready to reunite?" he asked, and she knew he was referring to Spencer Matthews. Because *yes*. She was ready. After a decade of relationship disappointment, she was going to get her kiss—and then some—hopefully, because hello? She was twenty-seven, and it had been *a while* since *then some*.

"Lead the way, Mr. Kingston." And he did, straight out of his office and up the stairs to the indoor party deck that overlooked the rest of the brewery.

It was time to find out if things would have been different had the events of that late spring night ten years ago gone differently. If anything, she'd get the chance to answer a newly resurfaced *what-if*.

Finally, she thought. *Everything changes tonight.*

• • •

Jamie couldn't wait to get upstairs. Parties were never his thing, but he had ultimate home-court advantage here. So if reliving high school got to be too much, he could always pour himself a pint and claim he had work to take care of in the office.

"Mr. Kingston and Ms. Chandler. I take it you're here for the Arlington High School reunion?"

Brynn bounced with excitement, then leaned across the upstairs bar and gave their greeter a kiss on the cheek.

"Is your sister here yet?" she asked. Jeremy was Annie's younger brother. He'd worked here as a server during his last year of grad school, but he just kind of stayed, and Jamie was glad for it. He was more of an assistant manager now, practically running the restaurant side of the brewery, and tonight he was overseeing the reunion.

"Yeah. She's back there talking to that asshole she dated senior year. What's his name?"

Jamie and Brynn craned their necks to search for Annie on the other side of the room. There she was, talking to Ryan Freeman who was, as Jeremy put it, the asshole Annie dated for an entire year. Of course no one thought he was an asshole until the students took a cruise around Lake Michigan on the *Spirit of Chicago* for their post-prom activity. That's where Jamie, Brynn, and Annie found him on the lower deck of the boat making out with a junior whose date had fallen asleep after spending an hour in the bathroom trying—and failing—to keep his dinner down.

"How does she do it?" Brynn asked.

"What?" Jamie asked.

"Stay friends with all her ex-boyfriends, even guys that do stuff like kiss other girls while we're all trapped together on a boat. Kinda hard to avoid your cheating boyfriend when you have two choices of locale—upper deck or lower deck."

Jamie laughed, but there was a bitter edge to the sound. This was what it was going to be like—every little memory, no matter how insignificant, bringing him back. He and Brynn had gone to prom together, as friends. The mono incident had been only a week after that, the best night of his life. And then he'd pushed her away and buried those feelings because at the time he thought the only other alternative was he and Brynn breaking each other's hearts. He had to remind himself that he was a grown man, and that heartache was a decade behind them. He prided himself on being a level-headed guy who never let his emotions get the best of him, and he wasn't about to start tonight.

"Not everyone holds on to ten-year grudges, B." Then again, he thought, it seemed like Brynn held ten-year crushes, so she'd probably disagree.

"There's no statute of limitations on passionate emotion," she argued, her arms crossed as her brown eyes blazed into his.

He swallowed and looked away. It was either that or try to read something in her eyes that he knew wasn't there.

Jeremy shrugged. "I'm with Brynn. I still passionately think he's an asshole after ten years."

"You're a good baby brother," Brynn said, then ruffled Jeremy's auburn waves. He slapped her hand away, and the two laughed.

Some things never changed.

The party had barely started, and Jamie had already had enough. "Just get us our name tags, Denning," he growled. He was outnumbered, and Brynn was enough of a match one-on-one. Besides, a crowd was heading up the stairs, and Jamie wanted a pint in his hand before he had to do the whole socializing thing. He snuck behind the bar to grab something that wasn't on the menu for the rest of the guests.

Brynn caught his eye with a knowing look. "You aren't," she said, but the corners of her mouth were already turning up.

"I am," he told her. "The only question is whether or not you're going to join me." His pulse quickened. Regardless of what happened tonight, at least they'd start it together, something that was just for them.

Brynn looked from him to Jeremy.

"I'll cover for you two," Jeremy said, so Brynn followed Jamie behind the bar.

He didn't even serve hard alcohol here, though he did have the license for it. Hell, the wine was brought in special just for the party. A brew house was meant to serve beer. If patrons came looking for anything other, Jamie was fine if they didn't come back. But every now and then, an opportunity presented itself that required a little something extra, and tonight was one of those nights.

They both dropped to a crouch, and Jamie reached a hand to the back of a small shelf, producing a 750 ml bottle of Jack and two shot glasses.

"Just like high school," Brynn said, leaning an elbow against the shelf for balance. Jack Daniels was Jamie's dad's go-to drink. There was always a bottle in the house, which meant there was always enough for them to sneak a shot on certain occasions.

"Just like high school," Jamie echoed, and he let himself remember, for a moment, what it felt like to look at Brynn with possibility. Like they had everything ahead of them and that maybe, someday—just for a moment... Then he let it pass.

He filled each glass to the line, and they clinked a messy "Cheers," whiskey dribbling on to the tips of their fingers.

Jamie cleared his throat and steadied his voice. "I hope you find what you're looking for tonight, B."

All he really wanted was for his friend to be happy, and she hadn't been, not like she was when she was a kid. The Sleepy Jean he knew since their teen years had lost her spark of hope. Tonight was the first time, probably in years, that he'd seen that fire lit in her again, and he hoped he had *something* to do with that, even if she'd never admit it.

"Thank you, James," she said as her grin widened. "I hope I do, too."

They threw back the shots, Jamie unprepared for the severity of heat that burned its way down his esophagus. Come to think of it, the infrequency of their Jack Daniels shots in recent years made it so he never got used to it.

And then, in her best—meaning world's worst—German accent, Brynn declared, "Now's zee time on Sprockets ven ve dance!"

He laughed, loving the sight of that glint in her eye, even if it meant she was taking the express lane to buzzville. They stood just in time to see Jeremy checking in a group that had come up the stairs. He wasn't sure who saw who first, but when Brynn grabbed his hand and squeezed, he knew it was the last he'd see of her until it was time to go home. And without warning, something equally strong yet long ignored squeezed inside his chest.

"Brynn? Brynn Chandler? Is that you?"

Jamie was wrong. He could handle everything up until now just fine. But hearing that voice and watching Brynn turn toward it—it was like something out of *It's a Wonderful Life*. He was about to witness what would have happened had the kiss between him and Brynn never occurred. Tonight events would play out like he assumed Brynn wished they had, and he would have to stand by and let them. He had no claim on her. Jesus, every part of this night was a sense memory taking him back, and the night had barely even begun.

Shit. Even Jamie had to admit the guy was freakishly good-looking—blond hair, blue eyes, and a goddamn California tan. That would have been enough, but the dude was wearing a suit that only a guy from L.A. could pull off—trim and tailored—even if said guy wasn't really from there at all. But Spencer had lived in L.A. since he left for college, and there was no doubt that the California sun agreed with him.

I have blue eyes, Jamie thought, then wanted to throat punch himself for his jealousy.

He poured another shot. Okay maybe it was two. He kept telling himself that he was a completely different person than he was a decade ago. He owned his own business. He had just met a great girl. But then, that had never really been the problem. He met girls easily enough and had been in his fair share of committed relationships. What didn't come easily, though, was the whole falling in love part, and he had always assumed it was because he was protecting himself, outsmarting heartbreak by never truly giving his heart to someone else.

Jamie shook his head and laughed quietly. He just had to make it through tonight, just a few hours surrounded by memories and decade-old feelings. He loved Brynn, but he wasn't *in love* with her anymore. Yet as he tried to fast-forward through how the evening would play out between Brynn and Spencer, he found it hard to breathe.

This is what you wanted, asshole, to just be friends. Well, it's what seventeen-year-old Jamie *needed*, to keep her in his life. The only other option was to risk losing her completely, and he wouldn't have survived that.

Everything would go back to normal tomorrow. *He and Brynn* would go back to normal, to their routine, to the friendship whose foundation couldn't be rocked again. But he couldn't shake the thought, the questions that kept gnawing at the back of his mind: *What about twenty-seven-year-old Jamie? What did he need?*

In that moment, Brynn let Jamie's hand go. It fell to his side as he watched her stride away from him with an ease that punched him in the gut, and right into Spencer Matthews's arms.

Chapter Three

"Brynn Chandler."

He said her name like it was a revelation, like it was the answer to a question, and she really wanted to know what the question was.

"Spencer. Uh, hi."

Not the most graceful response, but when he leaned in and brushed his lips against her cheek, she decided it was good enough.

Of course she had been thinking of this moment all day, if not all week. Oh hell, who was she kidding, she'd fantasized about it on and off for ten years. She was convinced so many things in her life would have gone differently if she had made it to that party senior year. For one thing, she would have kissed a beautiful boy, one who had grown into the gorgeous man standing in front of her. Instead she'd kissed Jamie, unexpectedly falling for the boy who put his health at risk — who missed the biggest party of the year — to take care of her. And then he'd broken her heart, not that she'd ever let on that she had fallen so hard, so fast. But, now, in front of her stood the answer. A do-over. If things went well tonight, then maybe what happened between her and Jamie could finally be laid to rest. Brynn let her eyes fall closed while Spencer's lips brushed her skin, taking herself back ten years. *This was how that night should have gone.*

As she felt Spencer pull away, she opened her eyes again to his confident smile.

"I was hoping you'd be here tonight," he said, and her head spun, dizzy with possibility—or perhaps the aftereffect of a recent shot of Jack.

"Here I am," she said, then gave herself a mental eye roll. She needed another drink, fast, or else conversation would consist of Spencer speaking and Brynn doing no more than rephrasing his words.

"Here you are." Then he smiled again as the sound of a throat clearing interrupted the awkward moment, reminding Brynn they weren't alone. Not yet, at least.

She turned to see Jeremy holding out Spencer's name tag. This jolted her memory, causing her to look behind her to where Jamie still stood behind the bar. She bit her lip and smiled at him, a holy-shit-this-is-really-happening smile, and Jamie smiled back. It wasn't his real smile. She knew that. It was his I-kinda-hate-parties-but-will-only-do-this-for-you smile, and she made a mental note to thank him. Everything was on track, happening as it should, and she felt the tension release from her shoulders.

"Thanks," Spencer said, grabbing the laminated replica of his senior picture from Jeremy. Other than his hair being a little longer, wavier and more sun-kissed, he looked exactly the same. He pulled the lanyard over his head and looked down to where Brynn's rested on her chest.

"You look great," Spencer said. "Stunning, actually."

Brynn's whole core burned, and she felt the heat rise to her cheeks, a kettle about to blow.

"Um, yeah…" she mumbled, the English language seeming to evaporate from existence.

"Sorry." Spencer ran a hand through his hair, and she watched how the blond locks at his nape brushed the top of his collar. "That was maybe a little much. I just wasn't expecting…" He paused, his eyes drinking her in from head to toe. "I wasn't expecting *you*."

Yeah. That decided it. There would be a kiss tonight, and come hell or high water, something *after* that kiss. It hadn't just been a year since Brynn was in a relationship. It was also the last time she had been intimate with anyone other than something that required batteries, and frankly, as much as she adored the pulse setting, she had a feeling Spencer might have something better to offer.

"It's okay," she managed to say. "I guess I'm just not used to that word—stunning."

Sure, she'd put a little extra effort into how she looked tonight, but it's not like she was the antithesis of her everyday self. She'd been called cute, pretty, even beautiful by guys she'd dated. Then again, that was the job of the boyfriend, right? To see the beauty in his girlfriend. Holly calling her gorgeous didn't count. It was a sisterly obligation. But Spencer was just—Spencer. He wasn't her anything, yet he tossed out that word like it was the most natural thing for him to say.

He laughed then, like he didn't believe her, and she wasn't about to argue the situation even though she could do it and do it well.

No, really. No guy ever in the history of the world—or at least my existence in it—has called me stunning. I could probably get paperwork to back this up if you give me a business day or two.

She didn't say any of that, not wanting to spoil the moment. Instead she tugged at the lanyard around her own neck, needing something to do with her hand.

"Maybe we should grab a drink, catch up, mingle with the rest of the class," she suggested.

"I'm all yours," he said, and she led him past the bar where she swore Jamie was a minute ago. She'd probably find him on the party deck, where she and Spencer were headed now. That's all she needed, really, was to see him and know he wasn't alone—not that they were there *together*. But she wanted this night to be fun for him even if he'd rather be in his office color coding his calendar.

For now, she was on a mission—one that nothing would deter.

· · ·

"Seriously, Kingston? She's gone. You can come up now."

Jamie recognized Annie's voice, but her assurance of Brynn and Spencer's departure from the immediate vicinity did not make him want to come out of hiding. Not that he *was* hiding. That would be ridiculous. He'd watched the whole exchange between Brynn and Mr. California, rinsing their shot glasses in water hot enough to melt away a layer of skin, though he hoped he hadn't. He couldn't register something as mundane as water temperature when Brynn's dream guy was calling her stunning. He'd strained to make out the conversation, and he'd heard every word.

Is that all it took? The right compliment? How many ways had he told Brynn she was stunning in the past six years? Why did it mean something different when Spencer Matthews said it? And, Christ, why did it matter so much?

He sighed, knowing the answer to at least one of his own questions, the one he was willing to admit. Brynn saw him one way and Spencer another. That's how it was in high school, and that's how it was now. Save for the brief intermission in her Spencer Matthews crush, Jamie was the friend and

Spencer the potential more-than.

"I can see you, you know."

Jamie looked up from where he squatted to find Annie leaning over the top of the bar, so he stood to meet her snooping gaze.

"I was...uh...drying shot glasses and putting them away," he said, which wasn't *un*true. There just wasn't a necessity to dry said glasses at floor level rather than bar level, but he would keep that little tidbit to himself.

"You're an idiot," Annie said, and his eyes widened. It wasn't just *what* she said but the fact that it was *her* saying it. Annie was Brynn's closest friend other than him, but she was his friend, too.

"Excuse me?" he asked.

"I said you're an idiot," she repeated, as if that was the only thing standing in the way of Jamie's comprehension, *hearing* her.

"Yeah." His brows pulled together. "I heard you the first time. I'm kind of wondering *why* I'm an idiot."

He had plenty of ways he could answer this himself, but he was curious about Annie's opinion at the moment.

"You're still in love with her."

Just like that, she said it, point-blank and with no filter. And that word—*still*. As if it was a constant, had never gone away.

"Annie, I don't know what you're—"

"Ugh." She rolled her eyes, then sighed. "Come *on*. I'm not blind. I see you two together almost on a daily basis. And you forget I've known you *both* since high school."

He wasn't sure if Brynn had let Annie in on their *almost*. Once he told Brynn he needed her as his friend, she put the kibosh on ever bringing up their kiss again.

Jamie threw the towel over his shoulder and dropped the clean shot glasses on the bar. He needed both hands, needed to clasp them behind his neck and think.

He let out a long breath before speaking again. There was no hiding from Annie under the bar, and it looked like he couldn't hide anything else from her, either, though he swore he'd been hiding his feelings just fine from himself all these years.

"I'm seeing someone," he said, but knew that proved nothing. Not to Annie. Not to himself, though this was the first time he'd admitted it. "It's this night," he said as his shoulders sagged. "It's bringing up—*feelings*." He thought about telling her that it was just the environment, being around all these people. He was fine yesterday, and he'd be fine tomorrow. This was temporary. Or it was all bullshit. Maybe it was time to admit that, too.

"Am I that obvious?" he finally asked, and Annie's eyes softened, an unexpectedly sad smile taking over her features.

"To me and the rest of the world? Yeah. Probably. But you know Brynn. She won't let herself see. She's kind of stubborn like that."

Kind of stubborn. Ha. Brynn was a ten-story brick wall when she felt the need. He understood. She refused to discuss what almost happened ten years ago. Why the hell would she look forward and consider the possibility of a future between them? Shit. That's what he was doing, wasn't he? Imagining a future with her after bailing on that possibility ten years ago?

"I know," he said and pressed his palms flat on the bar. "Maybe I need to stop searching for what isn't there."

Shit. *Again.* He *was* searching. Annie knew it just by looking at him. It was like someone knocked him in the head. Sense memory his ass. What he felt right now—had been feeling since he showed up at Brynn's apartment—that was no memory.

It wasn't jealousy or memories that triggered these feelings, not even the alcohol. All it took was one person calling him on what had been there all along, drawing it to the surface. Saying it out loud was enough to make what he felt for Brynn more real than anything he'd experienced in years. If he was going to be perfectly honest with himself— and really, the floodgates were open now—he'd never fallen for another woman like he had for Brynn all those years ago.

He tried to come up with reasons to lob at Annie, reasons why adult Jamie was still listening to the teen version of himself. He couldn't come up with a single one. All these years he'd been protecting his heart, but the second he saw Brynn walk off with Spencer, he knew he was in trouble. The only thing he'd protected himself from was a chance at happiness.

It scared him. But, shit, Jamie wanted more than he'd let himself have. He figured the reason he hadn't truly fallen for Liz, or anyone else in his adult life, was because on some level he knew his feelings were never as real as they were that night on Brynn's couch. Real could be good—fucking terrifying, but good. That was the only explanation for what he decided. He should talk to Liz. She had a break at ten. Things were new enough with them that she'd understand. He shouldn't be dating her if he was reacting like this.

Then he'd talk to Brynn, lay his cards on the table, because he couldn't go another ten years pretending. And maybe she was pretending, too. Maybe all it would take was one of them manning up and putting it out there. After another shot of Jack—or seven—he'd have the balls to do it.

Annie shook her head, her short auburn bob brushing against her cheeks.

"Oh, it's there, Jamie. Maybe you just need to make her see what I do."

"What's that?" he asked.

She leaned across the bar, pressing her palm to his chest.

"Show her what's here," Annie said, and he sucked in a breath, the sharp stab of rejection threatening to pierce him where her hand lay. He'd pushed Brynn away once. What if she pushed him away now?

He was over the dissolution of his family, but he wasn't sure he'd ever recover if he lost Brynn. Could he risk it?

Annie looked down, nodding at the two shot glasses between them.

"You got something to put in there?" she asked.

He raised a brow. "Liquid courage?"

"Something like that."

"If I let you in on my secret stash, are you going to keep dispensing relationship advice?"

Annie shrugged. "Depends. Do you want to be happy?"

Well, that was a fucking loaded question.

He reached under the bar and produced the bottle of whiskey.

"That's quite the hiding place you've got back there," Annie said. "Any other surprises?"

He shook his head. "You know *all* my secrets now."

He poured them each a shot, and Annie held hers up to offer a toast.

"It's cuz your poker face sucks. Bottoms up."

Jamie laughed and threw back his shot. If that was the case, maybe it was time to come out of hiding.

Chapter Four

Brynn's eyes moved in a circle, taking in her surroundings. Pods of people dotted the upper deck of the brewery. She sat on a stool at the bar, ensnared in a group of old girlfriends, each one oohing and aahing over another's life milestones— new job, new husband, and, for a select few, new baby. She smiled and nodded, trying to ignore the disconnect between herself and people she considered friends years ago. Spencer stood nearby, his pod a little different than hers. Even though his book hadn't launched yet, the crowd around him seemed to be fawning. Spencer was the center of attention. Actually, pretty much the same as in high school. The difference was that this time she wasn't wondering if Spencer knew she existed let alone had a crush on him. Now, when her eye caught his, he smiled, and she raised her glass in response before taking a sip.

But even in her increasingly cloudy brain, the whole scenario made her think of Jamie. She knew the Spencer thing was, in some way, a sore subject for him. Then again, it was for Brynn, too. She'd made Jamie promise never to talk about what had happened between them, and here she was, getting the chance to wipe the slate clean. At least, that's what she hoped, that kissing Spencer would work like time travel, giving her the chance to erase a painful past. Because, try as she might, Brynn had never truly gotten past Jamie rejecting her. She'd forgotten all about Spencer the night Jamie took care of her. Tonight she hoped Spencer would finally help her forget how her best friend cracked her teenage heart wide open.

She finished her pint and slid off the stool, overtaken by a sudden rush of bravado and the need to get this whole turning-back-time thing underway. She marched over to the circle of people surrounding Spencer and inserted herself into the spot to his left.

"Hey," he said.

"Hey."

"Spencer was just telling us about his big launch party in L.A. in a couple weeks."

Stacy Fletcher, head of the reunion committee, let her hand fall on Spencer's chest as she said this, flirting with him like she was sure he was going home with her. Spencer smiled at Stacy, and Brynn took a mental snapshot of the two, their matching blond hair and overall look of having their shit together. Stacy was gorgeous, already a successful real estate attorney, and Brynn couldn't help but stare at the way Stacy's breasts bubbled over the taut material of her strapless navy dress. It was like they were trying to escape. Who knows? Maybe one would make a break for it at some point during the evening.

Brynn looked down at her turtleneck sweater dress. Maybe it did hug her curves in all the right places, but her boobs were no competition for Stacy's virtual waterfall of flesh.

"It's not a big deal," Spencer said, his modesty coupled

with a shy smile making Brynn's knees turn to jelly. "Just a small party at a local bookseller. If any of you are in town, you should stop by." He turned to Brynn then. "What are the odds of you making your way to L.A. in the next couple of weeks?"

An invitation, just for her. But California in two weeks? It wasn't quite within her budget, and what was she going to do? Travel across the country for a crush? Granted the crush was pretty severe, Brynn's seventeen-year-old fantasies rising to the surface. No. Spencer was more than a crush. He was the *answer*—the answer to the stagnancy in her life.

Brynn shrugged. "Not impossible," she said, and Spencer beamed. "Hey," she added. "Would you like to grab a drink— somewhere a little quieter?"

It was go time. If she was going to test the Spencer Matthews theory, it was high time she started experimenting.

He laced his fingers through hers.

"Excuse us everyone. We'll be back in a bit." Then he focused on Brynn. "Lead the way," he said, and she did. First stop, the empty bar at the top of the stairs. The bottle and shot glasses were still there, and now they were in her hands.

"I like the way you think," Spencer said, and she bit down on her lip, trying to contain her nerves.

"Here we are," she said as they stood in front of a closed door, one adorned with nothing but a small name plaque that read OFFICE. "I know the owner," she said. "We can hide out in here…if you want."

Spencer looked from the door to her. Then he licked his top lip, and Brynn almost lost it right there.

"Isn't Jamie Kingston the owner?" he asked, raising a brow, and Brynn nodded. "You two are still…close?"

Really? This was going to turn into a conversation about her and Jamie? This is supposed to be a do-over. Not a repeat of senior year. She rolled her eyes.

"What?" Spencer laughed. "You two went to every dance

together senior year. Everyone assumed you were together. *I* sure as hell did, especially when you never made it to Becket's party. I always figured I was crushing on another guy's girl."

Whoa. This was too much for Brynn to process—Spencer crushing on her *and* the thought of her being Jamie's girl…?

Time to get things moving.

She didn't respond but instead knocked softly, then tried the handle, and the door opened with ease. Spencer walked through first, and she followed, closing and locking the door behind her. She unscrewed the bottle and poured them each a shot. Time for a final toast, one to solidify tonight as a shift in her reality. Everything would be different after this moment.

"Cheers," he said.

"Cheers."

Brynn let the heat from the liquid permeate her veins, melting away the twinge of something she didn't want to recognize, an emotion she had no business feeling at a time like this. When Jamie was with Liz, he didn't feel like he was cheating on *her.* So why was her stomach in knots? Why did she need the liquid courage to do what Jamie had no problem doing every night he was with someone else?

No. No guilt. This is my *night.*

She slammed her empty glass down on Jamie's desk and giggled, the alcohol winning out over logic. *Jamie's desk.* Was she really going to do this here? Now?

"No time like the present," Brynn said aloud, answering her own question. And she pushed Spencer down into Jamie's chair.

. . .

Light. That was the only way to describe how Jamie felt as he headed back to the ale house. Like a weight had been lifted, like everything was going to be better from here on out. Not that things were bad. He hadn't been suffering or miserable or anything that made life less than okay. But that's just it. Things had only ever been *okay*. And he wanted *better*. No. He wanted *amazing*.

He still couldn't get over how easy things had been with Liz.

"It's okay, James," she'd said when he showed up in the ER waiting room an hour ago, asking to see her. As soon as Annie had forced him to admit what he felt out loud, he had no choice but to end things with Liz and tell Brynn the truth. "I like you a lot, but I knew you weren't in it for the long haul."

She knew?

"I'm not ready to settle down, and you've got that vibe, you know?"

Vibe? He asked the question only to himself, but Liz had answered.

"You're waiting for something. Not sure what, but I don't think *we* were it. No big deal, okay? It was fun."

Fun.

After their conversation, Jamie wasn't sure who broke up with whom. All he knew was there were no consequences. He was single, free, and not nearly as drunk as he planned on being when he set things in motion tonight. Either way, he knew this was the start of something, and as he hopped in a cab and headed back to the brewery, his thoughts went to one person—Brynn.

He went straight for the party deck, infiltrating every cluster of fellow grads as he looked for her. At one point, Stacy Fletcher grabbed his hand and tried to lead him to the bar for a drink.

"Teach me about your brews," she'd said, and despite how much he admired the skin pouring over the top of Stacy's dress, she wasn't the girl he was looking for.

"Sorry, Stacy. I have to—do something." It was a shitty exit but an exit nonetheless.

Brynn had made him watch *When Harry Met Sally* enough times to know that he was Harry at the end of the movie, in his big, New Year's Eve grand gesture scene.

When you realize you want to spend the rest of your life with somebody, you want the rest of your life to start as soon as possible.

Spencer Matthews wasn't the romantic lead. Jamie Kingston was, and Brynn needed to know that for him it had always been her.

Finally he found Annie talking to the asshole Ryan again.

"Where's the fire, Jamie?" Annie teased, but her expression shifted when he didn't return her smile.

He was buzzing with adrenaline and a sureness he hadn't felt since the night he'd kissed Brynn.

"Where is she, Annie?"

And just like that, he saw Annie go through three visible emotions in seconds. First the teasing, then concern, and now? He could swear her wide eyes and fallen smile spelled pity.

"Shit, Jamie." She gave him a once-over, noting his coat. "Where have you been? She just took off with Spencer."

Took off? Brynn wouldn't leave without telling him. They came here together, which meant the unwritten rule—they'd leave together.

"You didn't stop her?" His deep voice grew hoarse as panic set in, any hesitation he had about telling Brynn how he felt erased by the need to find her before he blew his chance.

Annie excused herself from Ryan and moved off to the side.

"Jesus, Jamie. What was I supposed to do? Tell her to wait because *maybe* you were finally going to make things right between you guys? I haven't even seen you since we left the front bar."

Her voice cracked, anger morphing to worry.

"It's okay," he assured her. "You're right. I'm just..."

He stuck his hand in his coat pocket, then patted the one in his jeans.

"I left my phone in my office. I'll call her. Or text. Or something. She can't be far, right?"

Annie shook her head, but he didn't wait for more confirmation. He raced to his office—to his phone—so he could catch Brynn before she did anything he wouldn't be able to get over.

He didn't remember locking the door, but he thought nothing of it as he fished for the keys in his pocket, remedied the situation, and burst into his office.

His heart sank, right to his toes and possibly through the floor. He swallowed back the burn in his throat that had nothing to do with Jack Daniels this time and braced himself against the doorframe. All those years of self-preservation, and Brynn was still able to demolish him in mere seconds. Because there she was, perched on Spencer Matthews's lap, one arm round his neck, the other poised to deposit an empty shot glass on his desk. Her seductive smile faded quickly.

Shit. She'd definitely never smiled like that for him.

He stood there, rooted in silence, waiting for some cosmic force to end this moment so he could get the hell out of it. An asteroid pulverizing Earth sounded pretty fantastic right about now. A Lake Michigan tidal wave? Bring it. The fuck. On.

Anything but this.

Brynn slid off Spencer's lap, and he stood, looking no worse for the wear.

"I'm going to head back to the party," Spencer said. "Great place you got here, Jamie," and he offered a hand to shake. Jamie had to do everything in his power not to say, *It's James, asshole.*

But Jamie shook his hand and forced a smile. As much as he wanted to blame the guy, Spencer had no idea what was brewing beneath the surface.

"See you in a bit?" he asked Brynn, and her face softened for a moment as her eyes fell on his. She nodded, and Spencer was gone.

"Dammit, James." The words fell out of her mouth, laced with bitter disappointment.

"Fucking hell, Brynn."

And that was that. Jamie accepted defeat.

Chapter Five

Holly and Annie ushered Brynn toward the Kingston Ale House entrance. Last night she'd practically strutted through the doors, but in the harsh light of morning, reality was not a pretty picture.

She'd *almost* kissed Spencer again. In Jamie's office. Talk about poor judgment. She could have found a more appropriate place, like the corner booth behind the stairs on the first level, or back by the pool tables, or a freaking bathroom stall. If she gave this one to her sister or Annie to analyze, which—duh—she was so not going to do, she knew exactly what they'd say. Holly would laugh and say I told you so while Annie would give her some big speech accusing her of taking Spencer there on purpose, secretly hoping that Jamie would catch them. Self-sabotage, Annie would call it, which was ridiculous, because Brynn wanted Spencer.

Not Jamie. Jamie had Liz and was happy. What happened in the past needed to stay in the past.

"I'm going. I'm going," she said after Holly gave her a good shove.

"I don't know why you're all bent out of shape," her sister said. "So you and Jamie had a little fight. Don't all married couples fight from time to time?"

Annie snorted. Brynn looked over her shoulder to give them both the stinkeye, but that only made them laugh more.

She was through the door now. The bar didn't officially open until 11:30, but the plan had always been for the gang to do brunch after the reunion before Jamie and Jeremy had to work the rest of the day and night and before Annie opened the store at noon. Brynn didn't work weekends, but the girls weren't going to let her off the hook for brunch. So here they were, at the ungodly hour of ten o'clock, and the horror that was last night punched her right in the gut.

Her stomach clenched. She and Jamie had fought before but never like that. Even that awful summer ten years ago hadn't been the result of anger. And as much as Brynn had been hurt by Jamie rejecting her after finally figuring out she had feelings for him, she knew in the back of her mind they'd get through it. They were kids. They had too much ahead of them not to find their way back to each other. But something about last night had a sense of finality to it that scared her.

"What the hell were you thinking?" Jamie had asked as soon as Spencer left the room. "In my fucking office? Did you *want* me to see? To make sure—in case I had any doubt—that I knew where we stood, where we *always* stood?"

Brynn had winced at those words, but the alcohol that had made her bold mutated as it coursed through her veins, putting her on the defensive.

"You're the one who decided where we stood, Jamie. A long time ago, so don't you dare try throwing that in my face." She'd been heaving as she spoke, not able to suck in enough air but knowing if she paused for even a second it all might backfire, and she might cry. But Brynn Chandler wasn't going to cry over Jamie Kingston again. "You want to know what

I was thinking? I was thinking that for once it could be *my* night. I was thinking that you wouldn't give a shit because you had a party to tend to and a girlfriend to go home to and—ugh! Why does this even matter? We're not a couple. We never were. It's time we stop *fucking* acting like it."

He'd stumbled backward when she said that, a small but noticeable step, and it tore Brynn's heart to shreds to hurt the person she cared about most. But that was it—what had been holding her back with Spencer even before Jamie walked in. They'd been each other's plus-one for years, but they'd never been together. He'd moved on from whatever had been there at one point. It was time for her to do the same.

"I'll take a cab home later," she'd told him.

"I know." Jamie had cleared his throat. "I'll ride with you."

"No. You won't."

And then, like a pro, she'd swallowed back all the residual hurt that had risen to the surface, strode past him, and returned to the party only to find that Spencer Matthews was minutes from leaving, taking a late flight home to L.A.

"I'd love you to come to the launch in a couple of weeks—if you happen to find yourself in California," he'd said. "Just wish we didn't have to cut tonight short."

He'd kissed her on the cheek, and she knew the restraint was because of where they were, of who owned the place. It was like Big Brother was watching—if Big Brother happened to be a brewmaster who didn't look kindly on people making out in his office. They'd exchanged numbers, and that was that. It would probably be another ten years before she saw him again. By then she could introduce him to her cats.

"Shit!" she heard Annie yell, bringing her back to the present.

"Whoops!" Holly added, then knocked into Brynn, launching her forward where she'd soon face-plant on the wooden stairs leading to the upper deck. But strong arms wrapped around her torso from the side, and she recognized the familiar scent of a cologne-free Jamie.

"Whoa there, Sleepy Jean. Don't want you ruining two years of perfect yet unpleasant orthodontic care."

She stiffened in his arms but didn't pull away. Because it was *Jamie*. Yet here they were—touching and at the same time miles apart. She waited until he loosened his grip, then righted herself.

"Sorry!" Annie blurted, running in behind Holly. "I tripped, knocked into Holly and, you know—domino effect. That's the first time I've seen it play out in real life, and I gotta say, the phrasing is spot on!"

Holly giggled but brushed past her and Jamie to their usual table in back by the pool tables. Annie followed, leaving Brynn to straighten and dust herself off before turning to meet Jamie face-to-face.

His hair was still damp, which explained the freshly showered scent, but he hadn't shaved. Instinct took over, and she ran her palm over his jaw. Jamie sucked in a breath, and she immediately pulled away. She wanted to tell him that she loved this look on him, when he let the shaving go for a day or two or seven, but it all seemed wrong now—noticing things like this. And after last night, saying anything to that effect felt like crossing a new boundary they'd both drawn.

"I don't *always* need you to catch me, you know," she said, defenses kicking in once again.

Jamie pressed his lips into a thin line, exhaling through his nose.

"Guess that's just for Saturday nights and Sunday mornings, then?"

On any other day this would have been Jamie making a joke. He and Brynn would have both laughed. But he wasn't even smiling. No, he was just reminding her that he was right and she was wrong. She'd needed saving last night and again this morning. Fine. That much was true. But as a general rule, Brynn Chandler did not need saving, and certainly not by Jamie.

"Let's just get this over with, okay?" she said, making a move to step past him. She spoke without malice, only exhaustion. She just didn't have it in her to do this right now.

Jamie opened his mouth to say something, so she hesitated. Maybe he had the solution, the correct thing to say to get them past this part. But when his eyes met hers, holding her there for a second longer, he simply closed his mouth and took a step back, giving her easy passage to the back of the bar.

. . .

Safety lay behind the bar, so that's where Jamie stayed. He sighed. The best brew for the drink was the one he hadn't added to his tap yet, one he hadn't even let Brynn taste, even though her palate would be the deciding one. His version of a witbier, the answer to Brynn's love of Blue Moon, was bottled and ready to go to Beer Fest in L.A. —*if* Jamie decided to make the trip. Which he still hadn't.

Jamie mixed a pitcher that was equal parts witbier and fresh-squeezed orange juice, the *beer*mosa. He poured a small amount into a pint to taste, then gave his head a shake. Good, but sweet. Too sweet for him. In a lone pilsner glass, he made himself a Red Eye—tomato juice and ale with a splash of hot sauce. Sure, it put extra hair on your chest and balls, but on a morning like this, it also gave him something to focus on other than last night.

"What's the holdup, big guy?" Annie hopped onto a stool opposite him.

He took another sip, then let out a long breath.

"It's probably better if I just hang here and play

bartender."

Annie pressed her lips together in a pout.

"I want your side of the story, now," she said. "Brynn told me what she could, but her arms were kind of flailing as she spoke, and I was more concentrated on not losing an eye than I was on the story."

He couldn't help but smile at the visual. He knew Brynn's unrestrained body language all too well. His hand instinctively went to his chin, the tips of his fingers brushing the small scar.

"I went to the hospital to break up with Liz," he said. Annie's jaw dropped, and Jamie nodded. "That's the only reason I left, and by the time I got back?" He shrugged. "It's my own fucking fault," he added. "I've kept her at arm's length this whole time, and it's not like she knew I was heading back here to tell her I've been in love with her since I was seventeen."

Annie sighed. "I can picture it, you know? How it should have gone — you storming back into the party, walking right up to her and scooping her into your arms like *An Officer and A Gentleman*."

He ran a hand through his hair. "I was going to go a little more *When Harry Met Sally*, but yeah, something like that."

She fanned herself with both hands, like she was trying to stave off tears.

"Are either of your brothers single?" she asked. "And are they at least half as romantic as you are? Because that would probably be enough for me."

Jamie reached for his pilsner glass, and Annie grabbed his hand before he could take a sip.

"You're going to tell her now, right? About Liz and the feelings and the loving her for a decade?"

She let his hand go, and he avoided immediately answering with a long, slow sip.

"She was straddling another guy — in *my* chair, Annie.

She doesn't want to hear about my feelings, and I sure as hell don't want to play runner-up."

Annie crossed her arms. She craned her neck to peer around the corner where Brynn, Holly, and Jeremy huddled in a booth nursing coffees and talking animatedly. Well, Holly and Jeremy were engrossed in conversation. Brynn just sat with her hands clasped around her mug.

"If she knew, she'd pick you," Annie said.

Jamie thought about this. She hadn't picked him before, not until he kissed her, and even then it was only because Spencer wasn't there. Yes, Brynn felt something in that kiss, too, but it never would have happened if she'd made it to the party. He wasn't going to be second choice again, or the person she chose because of proximity.

"What if I want her to pick me without knowing first?" he asked. "What if I want her to be sure who she wants before picking me?"

Annie narrowed her eyes at him and stood, grabbing the pitcher Jamie still hadn't delivered to the group.

"So you *want* her to go to California?" she asked, and his eyes widened. "That's right, loverboy. Spencer Matthews invited her to his book launch in L.A. two weeks from now, and she's already checking flights to see if she can afford it. If you are so sure about this picking you thing, then you'll be fine if she heads out to Cali to spend a weekend with the guy she almost kissed twice in ten years."

Jamie's jaw clenched. The thought was enough for him to grind his own teeth to dust. But as much as Annie was baiting him, she was also right. If Brynn wanted to see this thing with Spencer through, he had to let her go. He had to let her decide on her own who she wanted without him forcing the issue. As much as he hated this idea, it was out of his hands. Brynn had free will, and if there was anything still there on her end, she had to realize it on her own.

He drained the rest of his glass, the hot sauce blazing down his throat. His eyes widened, not from the heat but from either the most brilliant or absolute worst idea he'd ever had.

"Annie—" he started, knowing once he said it out loud he'd have to follow through if Brynn agreed. "Not only do I want her to go to L.A., but I'm gonna take her there."

She opened her mouth to respond, but Jamie was already making his way toward the end of the bar. He was done hiding. He could still make his grand gesture even if Brynn had no idea he was doing it.

This would be it, the trip that would fix them. All she had to do was choose Jamie before they got to L.A.—or else break them for good.

Chapter Six

Brynn jumped at the sound of Jamie pounding on the door, but her contact landed safely over her iris before she threw her hands up in exasperation.

"Holly! Can you let him in?"

Her sister popped out of her bedroom and poked her head in the bathroom door. "Will the extra thirty seconds make you *not* late?"

Brynn responded to her sister with a one-finger salute, which only made Holly laugh.

"Remember," Holly said. "Glass half full. This is going to be an epic trip no matter how it ends."

Brynn pouted on the way to her room, but Holly was already halfway to the door. She used to be the glass-half-full type, but it had been a long time since she'd seen the world that way.

Thirty seconds later, Jamie leaned in her bedroom doorway while she hopped on top of her suitcase, urging the zipper to do the impossible.

"I'm heading to work, you two." Holly ducked past Jamie

and into the room to give her sister a quick hug. "Text me every day. Send pictures. And if you find anyone about six feet tall, dark brown hair, and built like a pro soccer player, feel free to bring him back with you. Bonus points if he looks just as good in Armani as he does in L.L.Bean."

Brynn laughed and watched her sister poke Jamie in the abs and then leave, her eyes falling on his after Holly was gone.

Jamie stared back at her from under the bill of his worn White Sox baseball hat. He looked cozy in his gray hoodie, his dark jeans slung low on his hips—quite the opposite of how Brynn felt right now, which was nothing short of anxious. He raised a brow as she bounced on the suitcase, forcing the zipper the rest of the way.

"You got this, Sleepy Jean?" Though he didn't move to help her.

She slid off the suitcase and on to the floor, huffing out a breath. How did she answer that question?

Yes, her suitcase was packed. Yes, she'd taken two weeks of vacation. And yes, she was about to spend the majority of those two weeks driving cross-country—and maybe back—with one guy to go see another. Jamie's idea, not hers.

His easy smile relaxed her, so she said, "Yeah. Sure." Though at the moment she didn't feel like she got anything at all.

"What about you?" she asked. "You still want to share your precious alone time with me?"

When she initially suggested he go, she'd meant for him to take a solo trip. Now it was a road trip for two.

Again—Jamie's idea.

He took a tentative step forward, and when Brynn didn't budge, he pulled her into a hug. They'd spoken in the past week, but today was the first time she'd seen him since last Sunday's brunch. She'd thought they would avoid each other until it was time for him to get back behind the bar. Instead he'd strode over to the table with a pitcher of beer mimosa and a proposition—he'd go to Beer Fest, and she could ride shotgun, getting to L.A. in time to make it to Spencer's book launch. Holly had answered yes for her before Brynn could even open her mouth, while Annie hadn't said a word. So not like her. And because it felt like the olive branch they needed—without either of them having to discuss the reunion any further—Brynn had said yes. And as fast as her heart hammered at present, Jamie's arms around her felt good— something right when she was afraid it had all gone wrong.

"It was my idea. Wasn't it?"

She nodded.

"You need to see this thing through, B. I know you, and you'll always wonder." He cleared his throat. "And I need to spend a weekend with beer."

They both laughed, the first time they'd done that together since the reunion.

He was right. She needed to see what was there between her and Spencer. Preferably sober and without an audience. But that didn't change the tightness in her throat when she thought about her history with the whole Jamie and Spencer situation.

"I was going to take the trip anyway," he said, grinning. "I just needed a kick in the ass to get me out the door. Now I'll get us both out the door." He never officially said he was doing it to make up for walking in on her, but Brynn knew that's what this was. And she both loved him and wanted to smack him for feeling like he owed her. No matter how awful the reunion turned out to be, it was no one's fault. She wanted things to be right between them, but their smooth and easy friendship had torn at the edges last week, creating a distance she hoped could be repaired with a cross-country trek in Jamie's pickup truck.

She looked up at him, his blue eyes shadowed by the bill of his baseball cap. "I feel like I guilted you into this somehow, even though it was your idea," Brynn admitted, and she waited for him to protest. He didn't.

Jamie stood back, motioning between them.

"We need to fix this," he said. "And you didn't guilt me into anything. I need this trip, for a lot of reasons. Why can't one of them be us?"

Brynn interrupted. "We're fine, Jamie. I was drunk. And angry. But we're okay." She almost believed herself.

He smiled then, and she let the lightness of it fill her.

"Then getting you to the book launch in L.A. will just make us okayer. Won't it? I'm going at this point—with or without you—so you can get your ass in the truck, or you can stay here contemplating your choices." He adjusted the cap on his head.

She guessed he was right. Jamie wasn't even going to charge her for gas since he was making the trip whether she tagged along or not. Financially, it made sense. The trip wasn't in her budget to begin with. She'd pay him back, though. In installments or something. She wouldn't take advantage of her friend, only the fortunate situation.

"B?" Jamie's voice jolted her from her thoughts.

"Huh?"

"You ready to go?"

She took one last look at her bulging suitcase, then picked up the scarf from the edge of her bed and wrapped the featherlight fabric around her neck twice. She smoothed out her oversize sweater and nodded.

"Just need to throw on my boots and coat."

"Go ahead," he said. "I'll grab this beast." He nodded toward the suitcase, and she laughed.

"Thank you." She hoped he could feel the warmth of her tone, that he knew how much she appreciated this gesture.

"Anything, SJ. You should know that by now."

Brynn smiled, but with it she forced herself to swallow the lump rising in her throat. What if they wouldn't be *okayer* when they reached L.A.? What if last week was just the first in the start of a series of irreparable rifts? What if she and Jamie were reaching their limit—the limit of how far a friendship could bend before it finally broke? She couldn't take losing him again.

Glass half full. She listened to Holly's advice. Brynn would see the good in everything about this trip, including what it would do for her and Jamie. A week on the road together? They'd have to be closer after that.

"Okay, then," she said. "Let's go."

• • •

Jamie sat in the driver's seat of his pickup truck, waiting for Brynn to make one last bathroom trip.

"I don't want to be the one who slows us down because we have to stop at every gas station."

He had tried to explain to her that they had plenty of time. He'd mapped out the trip, planned it just right. It was only twenty-nine hours from Chicago to L.A. Even if they made a couple extra stops, they'd still make it in less than a week, have the weekend in L.A., and then a leisurely drive back. As long as he was there by Friday, he was golden. Still, she ran back up to her apartment to take care of business.

His phone buzzed with a text.

Annie: *You still an idiot?*

He laughed and responded. *Yep…who's into self-inflicted torture.*

Annie: *Tell her, James.*

Jamie: *I will when she makes her choice. If it's me, that is.*

Annie: *And tell her what you're really doing at your festival this weekend.*

Shit. Jeremy. Not like he'd forgotten he was meeting Jeremy in L.A., but he *had* overlooked the fact that he was Annie's brother and that Annie was suddenly his relationship therapist. Of course Jeremy told her everything about his last-minute plans to launch his new brew with taste-testers in L.A. God, he wanted to tell Brynn, but that would only take away her free will, letting her know the trip was always for her, whether she came or not.

Jamie: *She's getting in the truck. Good-bye, Annie.*

Jamie closed out of his texting app just as Brynn plopped down in the seat next to him.

"Who was that?" she asked, her voice nothing more than curious. He opened his mouth to answer, but she never gave him a chance. "One last good-bye to Liz?"

Right. Liz. He kind of maybe hadn't told her about the breakup. Because fucking up Brynn's reunion plans fucked up his own, and by now, after a week of keeping their distance between brunch and the trip, of Jamie realizing how much he needed to preserve their friendship and Brynn's freedom to choose, it seemed safer to let her think he was still with his girlfriend for now.

"Yep," he said, knowing he was a dick for perpetuating the lie. "One more good-bye. She's got a busy week."

Brynn clicked her seat belt in place and bounced in her seat. Jamie tried to ignore how much he liked the sight of her soft, dark curls against the cream sweater or how the deep red scarf brought out the pink in her cheeks. When he found himself staring, he cleared his throat and turned to face the road.

"Excited?" he asked, looking at her through his peripheral vision.

She caught herself before she bounced again, smiled, and nodded.

"Starbucks drive-thru?" she asked, and he let out a breath, his shoulders relaxing as he did. That's exactly what he needed, something normal and routine, like a cup of coffee. That would get rid of the unease.

"Hell yes," he said, turning the key in the ignition and shifting the truck into drive.

They made it just in front of the Starbucks down the road when they heard a pop followed by an immediate change in height of Brynn's side of the car.

She yelped, and Jamie swore.

"You've got to fucking be kidding me," he said, and he maneuvered the vehicle into a loading zone outside the coffee shop.

"What?" Brynn asked. "What was that? What happened?"

Jamie threw his head back against his headrest. If his initial unease weren't enough, this had to be some sort of sign, right? Not that he believed in signs.

"Flat tire," he said. Then he took off his baseball cap, raking his hand through his hair before putting it back on again.

That's when Brynn lost it. That was his only explanation for her sudden hysterical laughter. She'd cracked under the pressure, gone insane, and Jamie had literally driven her to the brink.

Still laughing, his now crazy friend undid her seat belt and turned to face him. She placed her hands on Jamie's cheeks, forcing him to look at her.

"Glass half full!" she cried, and Jamie wondered who he

should call first, the closest tire shop or some sort of doctor for Brynn.

"Are you…okay?" he asked, and she nodded, her laughter subsiding.

"God, I was so nervous about this trip. Were you? It's probably just me. I mean, look at you, the picture of calm. You're always the picture of calm. But Jesus, Jamie. I barely slept last night. And this morning when you showed up, I don't know. I guess I've been freaking out a little bit. Are you and I going to be okay? Are we going to kill each other on this trip? What happens when I actually get to L.A. and see Spencer again?" She paused only to catch her breath, and he just sat there and listened. "But this is it!" she yelled. "This is our sign."

He took her wrists in his hands, and she released her grip on his face.

"A sign that this trip will be apocalyptic? And since when do you believe in signs?"

She shook her head wildly.

"Not apocalyptic, silly! Don't you see? If we take the glass half full approach, this is it. We get our travel mishap out of the way before we even leave. We can relax, sip on a soy peppermint mocha…"

"Black coffee," Jamie interrupted, and Brynn threw her hands in the air, knocking her sun visor open and sending a small pile of paperwork straight into the side of her face. She laughed again. Regardless of this glass-half-full attitude she was adopting, neither of them were superstitious. And Jamie certainly wasn't going to interpret them *both* seeing this as a sign—even though their interpretations were polar opposites.

No signs!

"Whatever. You know what I mean. Better to get a flat tire now than on the highway, right? We're getting the hard part out of the way first. Nothing but smooth sailing from here on out."

She looked at him, eyes bright and earnest, and he couldn't help it. He agreed with her. That's what Brynn did. When her passion took over, she took him along for the ride. It was one of the things he loved most about her. And maybe she was right.

A nice, relaxing breakfast while they waited for the tire to be changed—that would get them past all the awkwardness that had built up in the past week. *The hard part*, he thought. They could get that out of the way.

He brushed a rogue curl out of her eyes, letting his fingertips linger behind her ear.

Heart hammering in his chest, he echoed her words back to her. "Smooth sailing from here on out."

Brynn held up her phone. "And a Monkees playlist."

Finally, Jamie laughed, too.

Chapter Seven

Brynn was right—it was smooth sailing all the way to their first sight-seeing stop, St. Louis. They'd left early enough—even with the quick tire change—that they could still make Tulsa by dark. And so far they'd managed to avoid talking about the reunion. Brynn wasn't sure if this was the best idea, pretending like it didn't happen when the fact that it *did* happen was the reason she and Jamie were in his truck right now. Aside from Jamie's insistence on *fixing this,* neither of them had mentioned that night again. Four hours, and the conversation never stalled, but it never went anywhere bordering on iffy.

Yep. Smooth sailing, all right. She wasn't going to count the last hour when Jamie had taken away her control of the playlist. Even she had to admit that after three hours, maybe it was time for something other than the Monkees. So she settled for Jamie getting his classic rock fix with a Pandora station she set up just for him.

"Name that tune?" she asked, hoping he'd play along.

He grinned. "You mean even if it's *not* all Monkees?"

She crossed her arms. "I do listen to other music. I just prefer Davy, Mickey, Mike, and Peter. A girl wants what a girl wants." She shrugged.

The muscle in his jaw ticked, but then he relaxed into a smile again.

"Okay," he said. "Best out of five?"

Brynn bounced in her seat and clapped. This was his favorite game. After the tire incident, she wanted to do whatever she could to assure him that the worst was over. That an amazing week lay ahead of them.

They waited for Eric Clapton's "Layla" to end, and she tried to clear her mind, to ready it for rapid song name retrieval. But Jamie was the master. It took one lick of the guitar for him to get the first song.

"'Shook Me All Night Long'!" he yelled, then slapped the steering wheel. "I can feel it, B. I'm gonna stay undefeated. You sure you don't wanna just throw in the towel so you don't embarrass yourself?"

She rolled her eyes. "Ha. Ha. Ha. Maybe I have a strategy. Did you ever think of that? I could just be waiting for the perfect moment to throw you off your game. You won't even see it coming."

He laughed softly, and they both broke into their best AC/DC impressions, singing along to the rest of the song.

When Lynyrd Skynyrd's "Sweet Home Alabama" began, Jamie called out the song title in what Brynn swore was the silent pause before the song started.

"You're cheating!" she whined.

His shoulders shook as he laughed.

"How can I cheat at the game *you* started?"

She examined his phone.

"I don't know! Maybe this is some secret playlist."

"It's a classic rock station, B. The app plays what it wants, not the other way around."

She stared straight ahead, watching the road roll out in front of them as she sulked through a song she usually enjoyed. So when the next song started, she hadn't cleared her mind. In fact, she was still sulking when the guitar intro ended and Van Morrison started singing the first verse of "Brown-Eyed Girl."

Yet Jamie said nothing. *Nothing.* Even though she knew *he* knew the song on the first note.

Her brows pulled together, and she turned to him, the suddenly stoic driver with his jaw clenched.

"Are you *letting* me win?" she asked. "Because this isn't how I wanted things to happen, you throwing the game on what I know is your favorite song." She batted her lashes. "Come on, James. I thought *I* was your brown-eyed girl."

She'd meant to tease, but as soon as the words left her lips, they felt all wrong.

He cleared his throat.

"Not cheating, B. Just zoned out."

Gone was his easy smile and his take-no-prisoners attitude. As quickly as the game had begun, it ended, and Brynn somehow knew not to ask any questions.

So they listened to song after song in what was otherwise silence.

She took the current tune, Tom Petty's "Mary Jane's Last Dance," to steer the conversation in a new direction.

"Did you smoke in college?" she asked. "It's funny, but of all the things we've done together, we never got high."

"You don't get high," Jamie said, eyes still on the road.

"I tried it once," she countered.

He smiled at this. "Yeah, but it's not your thing."

She thought about this for a second, not sure why she felt defensive. After all, he was right. It wasn't her thing. She hated it the one time she tried it, but somehow him making this assessment of her college self, one he saw much less often while they spent four years at different schools, put her on edge.

"You didn't answer my question," she continued.

"Which was…?"

He seemed to be enjoying her agitation, the visor of his baseball hat doing nothing to hide the crinkled lines at his eyes that accompanied his grin.

"Did you smoke in school?"

At this Jamie full-on laughed. "I brewed beer in my living room. I had to while away the days of waiting with *something*," he said with a chuckle. "That was it, though. Only college. And even then, never on the regular." He let go of the wheel with his right hand and placed it over his heart. "Once I became a brewmaster, I had no choice but to pledge my life to the barley and hops. Anything else would be sacrilege."

Brynn slapped him on the shoulder.

"Hey," he reprimanded, though his smug grin never left his face. "No beating the driver."

She crossed her arms over her chest. "Why didn't you ever do it with me?" As soon as the words left her mouth, she rolled her eyes at herself and groaned under her breath. "Smoke, I mean. Why didn't I know this about you?"

It was a small detail, a tiny pocket of his college life she wasn't aware of, and she knew it shouldn't bother her. But she thought she knew everything about the guy sitting next to her. The whole best-friend thing meant no secrets, right? It's not like she hid anything from him. Except for stuff that dealt with *feelings*. Ugh. Stupid teenaged Brynn. And stupid teenaged Jamie. They were both just so…stupid.

Jamie shrugged. "It's not like I was some big pothead. And you for sure weren't, so…I don't know. No biggie." He paused. "It's something we don't do together now, so why does this matter?"

Brynn's lips pursed into a small pout. Why *did* it matter?

"It doesn't," she said. "I guess I'm just learning there's stuff I don't know about you, James. I never took you for a man of mystery, but maybe I was wrong."

Jamie adjusted his hat, pulling the bill down lower, but it did nothing to hide his raised brows, and Brynn wondered if he liked the idea of her seeing him like this—a man with a secret or two up his sleeve. And though she wouldn't admit it out loud, the answer was yes. She kind of did like seeing him this way, like a part of the lens she looked through had always been smudged, and only now was she starting to clean it off and see what had been blocked from view.

Right now it was not-a-pothead Jamie, but who knew what else lurked beneath that lowered bill? She had several days to find out.

. . .

Shit, Jamie thought. He should have told her about Liz, well, that there was no Liz. Maybe he should right now. She was already being all weird about the smoking in college thing. He reasoned she'd move beyond weird if she found out he was flat-out *lying* to her about something. He never lied to Brynn—unless he counted that whole year in high school he was punch-drunk in love with her but never said a word. Or when he finally had the balls to kiss her and then told her he couldn't be with her after his parents split. But that wasn't really a lie—at the time he needed her friendship to get through it all, and he couldn't chance losing her. The full truth was he feared loving her and watching whatever ate away at his parents' relationship do the same to them. He kissed Brynn and awakened something in her he couldn't believe was there, and then he ended things before they had a chance to start. He loved her more than air that day he shut her down, but he never let her know.

Maybe he hadn't thought this through the right way—what it would do if she didn't pick him. The bravado he had when he proposed the trip to Brynn was starting to be overshadowed by the voice inside his head that began asking what the hell he thought he was doing.

You're bringing her to another guy, dipshit. Some grand plan you put together.

"Fuck off," Jamie said to himself under his breath.

"What?" Brynn asked.

"Huh? Oh, nothing. I think this is where we get off…our exit, I mean." He cleared his throat. "You wanted to see the arch, right?"

Her eyes lit up, and suddenly that asshole voice of reason was squashed like a bug. How could he question what he was doing when *he* was going to be the one to experience this with her? No one else. Whatever happened at the end of this trip, they'd have these days together, an experience that couldn't be replicated. It was all just a matter of timing now. Walking in on the girl he loved straddling another guy? Epically bad timing. But somewhere in these next several days, he'd get it right. If he didn't, then he deserved what waited for him at the end of this trip—letting her go. But it wouldn't be for lack of trying. Not this time.

Chapter Eight

Maybe it was the fact that they were a few hours south, or maybe it was just the mood of the early afternoon, but the sun was warm on Brynn's face when she stepped out of the truck. Eyes closed, she tilted her head up to the sky and let the heat soak into her skin. She took off her coat but kept the scarf. Jamie, who never seemed to get cold, wore only the hoodie and a T-shirt underneath, so he left that on. He met her on her side of the vehicle and smiled.

"What?" she asked.

He shrugged. "I like seeing you excited about something."

Could he feel the energy brimming inside her? Because she *was* excited. She could have let her chance with Spencer pass her by—thrown her hands in the air and said *Forget it*— again. She could have stayed mad, blamed that night on Jamie. But that wasn't fair. After all, it was *his* office, and Jamie was never one for big parties. Of course he'd want to hide out at some point that evening. Maybe if she'd had a little less to drink, she would have taken Spencer someplace less likely to be invaded. But she'd been tipsy, so she hadn't been logical, and what happened, happened. This time she wasn't going to make excuses. She was going after what she wanted, like she used to, before rejection by the person she trusted most took away her confidence to do so.

Spencer hadn't rejected her. They just had bad timing. Twice. And really, it all worked out in the end. She still had her best friend, and now she had not a second but a third chance to see, once and for all, if Spencer was the guy—the one that got away.

Yeah. Brynn *was* excited about something.

Then she looked up, and her smile quickly faded.

"B?" Jamie asked, but she didn't answer.

It wasn't that she didn't hear him, but her palms grew as sweaty as her mouth was dry. She cleared her throat and tried to swallow. Were her tonsils swelling?

"B?" This time he waved his hand in front of her face. She blinked and focused on him rather than the monstrosity they were about to approach.

"It's—high," she said, her voice a hoarse whisper.

Jamie laughed. "Uh, yeah. Pretty sure I read it's the highest man-made monument in the nation. Six hundred thirty feet at the top."

She lost her footing and staggered back until she bumped the passenger door. So much for smooth sailing.

Jamie shook his head. "Uh-uh. You are *not* afraid of heights, Brynn Chandler. Your family went to Florida every winter throughout middle school and high school. You've been on a plane more times than I can count."

She nodded. He was right, so she could understand his logic. But he'd never been with her on one of those planes.

"Dramamine," she said, finding her voice again.

Jamie's gaze went from the Arch back to her. "What?"

"Dramamine," she said again, this time louder and more insistent. "I took Dramamine before every single flight."

"Since when do you get motion sickness?"

She shook her head.

"I took Dramamine because it made me drowsy. I always fell asleep before takeoff."

Jamie flipped his baseball hat backward and crossed his arms over his chest. God he looked so young like that, like the guy who dragged her to countless Sox games when they were teens, when his dad had season tickets. After his parents split, Jamie stopped going to the ballpark, but he never stopped loving his team.

"Are you going to lecture me?" she asked, trying to reconcile his boyish look with his authoritative stance.

"Let me get this straight," he said. "You've never actually experienced a flight. You slept through them all?"

She nodded.

"Because you're afraid of heights."

Brynn nodded again.

"But how do you know you're afraid of heights if you've never been conscious in the air?"

Well, putting it that way, it did sound a little ridiculous, and she hated sounding ridiculous.

"See? This is why you never knew. You can't logic your way out of a fear, Jamie. It's not like it kept me from living my life. I found my way around it through simple, over-the-counter medication. Problem solved."

He raised his brows.

"What about *that*?" He pointed to the Arch, and Brynn's gaze followed his outstretched arm.

Her knees buckled, but she righted herself just as Jamie reached for her.

"Forget it," he said. "We're not going up."

"Yes we are," she countered, her voice emitting the hint of a tremble.

Jamie was holding her now. Somehow she hadn't realized

this.

"Told you I'd always catch you," he whispered in her ear. "You don't have to do this. We came. We saw. We can get back on the road."

But Brynn pushed him away. She brushed out nonexistent wrinkles from her jeans and mustered up as much conviction as she could.

I don't need saving. She could save herself from her fear.

"You're right," she said. "I never experienced those flights because I let the fear win. I let the possibility of Spencer slip away senior year because I was scared that missing the party meant I missed my chance." She stepped away from the truck and passed Jamie. Then she turned to face him. "I need to stop using fear as an excuse."

She'd played it safe for ten years. When she applied and got into her safety school, she went without question. When Annie opened the store and offered her a job, Brynn didn't care that she could make more money working for a big firm. The bookstore was safe. Working with Annie was safe. And when she needed a plus-one for a wedding, she always brought Jamie rather than going it alone. Enough was enough already. She could take this step, stare down one of her fears all by herself. Or with Jamie by her side, but it would still be *her* doing. Not his.

"Don't you get it?" she asked. "If I can do this, without the help of over-the-counter drugs, I might add, I'm that much closer to doing—other things."

She let out a long, slow exhale. Maybe she had inadvertently kept this little phobia from him. But it wasn't her fear of heights taking center stage. This was all a prelude to a kiss, one she'd convinced herself would make all the difference.

Jamie took a step toward her, his exasperation melting into something softer.

"You're scared," he said, realization in his voice, and Brynn knew he understood. "This trip scares you."

She sighed, relief washing over her.

"God, yes." She laughed now, grateful that she wouldn't have to hold this in all week. "I'm driving across the country because of a *kiss*. One that didn't even happen. Twice. That's insane. But doing nothing would be worse. I don't want to wonder what might have happened or to regret not finding out. Even if this trip doesn't end how I want it to, I won't have to wonder anymore."

She twisted a curl around her finger, and Jamie smiled. He tugged at one of her spirals, too, making her laugh. Then he turned, walked back to the truck, and reached into his bag. When he returned he was holding something silver in his hand.

"What's a beer man doing with a flask?" she asked.

"Best man gift from Ben's wedding."

Ah, yes. Now she remembered. Both of Jamie's brothers were married now, leaving the baby of the family the last bachelor standing.

"Still doesn't answer my question."

He unscrewed the top. "Well, I figured we might need to toast something at some point. Didn't realize it would be this early, but here goes." Jamie held up the flask. "To saying *fuck you* to fear and going after what we want." He took a swig and handed it to her.

Brynn smiled. Leave it to Jamie to know exactly what to say and exactly when to say it.

"Fuck you, fear!" She brought the flask to her lips, knowing what was inside. The Jack Daniels burned hot as it traveled down her throat, but she welcomed the sensation. "Wait," she said, handing the flask back to him. "You drove with this? Isn't that…?"

Jamie cut her off, producing a miniature bottle of the whiskey from his pocket. An empty miniature bottle.

"No open alcohol in the vehicle." He smiled. "I work in a brewery. I know my alcohol laws. Missouri, by the way, not so strict. Not that it will matter because I'm assuming we just finished what little we had."

Brynn shook the flask and confirmed his guess.

"You're full of surprises today, Mr. Kingston."

He took the flask from her, capped it, and tossed it back in the truck.

"Maybe I'm just prepared," he said when he was by her side again.

"Such a boy scout."

He raised a brow. "Not sure they give badges for bringing alcohol on a road trip."

Brynn laughed, the adrenaline mixed with the shot making her feel light and giddy and ready to take on a six-hundred-thirty-foot monument. Maybe. She hoped.

"Thank you," she said, then kissed her friend on the cheek. She may have lingered for an extra second or two, taking in his scent. "David Beckham?" she asked, her Christmas gift to him in 2012.

He shook his head.

"Justin Bieber?"

He laughed. "Wrong again."

"Which one is it?" She couldn't place the celebrity scent, but whoever it was—Antonio Banderas, maybe—suited him. He smelled *good*…and somehow familiar. Even after four-plus hours on the road.

The alcohol must have been getting to her. One shot could do that, right?

"It's just me," he said. "Showered, shaved, and out the door. Sorry to disappoint."

"Huh," she said as they started walking. "Just you. Me, too," she added. "Just me."

Brynn watched the smile move along Jamie's profile. And though she didn't say it out loud, she allowed herself the thought.

No need to apologize. I'm not disappointed at all.

Chapter Nine

Fuck you, fear. How about, *Fuck you, Jamie the hypocrite*? Because toasting to their fears — or to staring them in the face, *that* would be the perfect time to throw in, *By the way, I broke up with Liz because I've loved you since I was sixteen.*

But he didn't say that. He let Brynn think the moment was all about her, and maybe that was okay. She needed this, and she needed him to help her through it. To drop the bomb on her now would be to steal her thunder. There was no rush. Heck, he'd been holding it in for eleven years. He would find a way to ease into telling her how he felt. After all, hadn't he learned his lesson from the reunion? Surprising Brynn when she was drunk was *not* the way to go. Not that she was actually drunk right now, but the speed with which she walked — and talked — made it clear that Brynn *was* under the influence of something. Blame it on the alcohol, the setting, the adrenaline most definitely coursing through her veins, but she was on a mission, and he was not about to derail said mission for his own selfish gain.

Besides, didn't he want her to choose him of her own free

will? Placing his cards on the table now would only put her on the spot, and that wasn't how this was supposed to go down.

"You're totally right," she was saying as they trekked toward the entrance. "I slept through my fear. Like, literally. And you know how much I hate when people use the word literally...but, Jamie..." She shook her purse, a large bag slung cross-body down her torso.

He had to focus on what she was saying and not on how the strap bisected her, pressing firm in the spot between her breasts, accenting both as her sweater pulled against them. God, couldn't she adjust her scarf or something?

"I've got some right here. Literally!" she continued, and he forcibly cleared his throat, then shook his head so he focused on the *right here* of the purse she was shaking and not the *right here* of the place where his eyes were naturally drawn. "If I popped one of these suckers, I'd be out in twenty minutes. Tops. In fact..." She stopped midstride, unzipped the bag, and rummaged through it until her hand emerged with a small cylinder of the motion-sickness pills. "I'm entrusting these to you, in case I want to bail on the whole experience before we're halfway up. Even if I freak out, don't let me have one of these unless you want to carry me to the truck afterward."

Jamie laughed, but Brynn's face was intent, brows raised in earnest. She was dead serious.

"Are you going to have a panic attack or something? Maybe we should rethink this. I mean, I'm all for conquering your fears, but this seems like a giant leap where you maybe should take baby steps."

She grabbed his wrist and placed the tube of pills in his palm, curling his fingers tight around it. Her hand was warm, fever hot, even, and he knew what this was—Brynn on fire. Determined and headstrong, even if she was about to do something incredibly stupid. It brought him back ten years to when she was ready to attend that end-of-year party with a fever and glands so swollen she couldn't swallow without tears spilling from her eyes. And then he'd kissed her and messed everything up, almost ruining their friendship when he needed her most. It was hard not to feel like he was to blame for some of the fire going out of her, and damn if he didn't love seeing it now. Even if it meant he risked being trapped with her, and a couple of strangers, six hundred thirty feet above the ground with the possibility of a major freakout.

"I'm twenty-seven, Jamie. Twenty-seven and stuck. I need something bigger than baby steps."

He nodded because, whether she knew it or not, she was talking about both of them. Jamie thought he'd moved on these past ten years. He'd dated plenty, and a couple of times he came really close to falling in love. But close wasn't a step in the right direction. He hadn't moved forward at all. Only sideways. And now his path intersected with hers again.

"Bigger than baby steps." He echoed her words and slid the Dramamine into his pocket. "If things get ugly up there, just remember that I'm with you. I will never let you fall."

Brynn took in a long breath, then let it out, slow and controlled. He knew she was preparing herself for the giant leap she was about to take.

"I know," she said, her voice soft with recognition. "I know."

Then she bounced onto her toes, spun his baseball hat around, and tugged the bill down over his eyes. There was something intimate as well as silly about the gesture, but it meant she was standing close enough for him to catch her scent. Among the dewy grass and earthy aroma of wet, fallen leaves, there it was. A mixture of coconut from her hair and the eucalyptus body wash he knew she loved. He loved it, too. No celebrity scent to cover what didn't need covering. Just her, Brynn, his Sleepy Jean.

But she was wide awake and ready to take on the world, and he let the sweet smell of her wake up his senses, too.

He held out his hand, and she laced her fingers through his. This was nothing new for them, but for Jamie it felt like more than habit. It was a beginning.

He took the first step, and Brynn followed suit.

Forward, he thought. And they moved toward the Arch.

• • •

"Maybe you were right."

Brynn whispered the words to Jamie as she leaned back against the wall of their…pod? Compartment? Coffin? Oh God. She was going to be buried with Jamie, a young mother, and the woman's small child when the bottom dropped out of this monstrosity and they plummeted to the earth.

"You're okay, B."

Jamie's voice was calm but far from soothing. He squeezed her hand, and if she wasn't sure she only had minutes left to live, Brynn would have been mortified by her sweaty palms. But what was a little sweat between friends when she was ready to head toward the light?

"We're almost at the top," he said, his voice smooth and soft, though Brynn could swear she detected a smile. She wouldn't know, though. She stared straight ahead at the tiny, white elevator-like doors illuminated in an eerie, sterile white light. She ignored Jamie in her periphery as she held her body rigid against the back of her chair in the…was it a cubicle? What the hell was this thing called?

"When the capsule gets to the top, in about seven more minutes, we can get out and go to the observation deck."

"Capsule!" she said, her volume far and away too much for the cramped space.

"Mommy, why is da wady wif da big eyes so loud?"

This got Brynn's attention, and she let her gaze fall on the fair-haired preschooler seated on her equally fair-haired mother's lap.

The woman smiled apologetically at Jamie, and he shrugged. *Kids*, they seemed to say without the words, and Brynn was not amused.

Her eyes did feel a little dry now that she thought of it, but she didn't have enough elbow room to fish her contact solution out of her bag and, clammy hands or not, she was not letting go of her death grip on Jamie's hand. The little girl would just have to spend the next seven minutes with Brynn in wide-eyed revelation that she was, in fact, in a *capsule*.

"I can't do it," Brynn said. "I can't get out. Give me the pills. I'll take one or seven, and we'll call it a day. You can drag me to the truck and get us back on the road. I don't even need to eat."

Jamie narrowed his eyes at her.

"*I* need to eat," he argued.

"So eat! Who's stopping you from eating? I'll be asleep."

He sighed. "You *can* do it. You already *are* doing it."

She wanted to argue with him, to tell him that the only thing she was doing was exactly what he predicted she would do—freaking out.

"I'm not afwaid," the young girl said. "I was, but I'm not anymore."

Brynn sighed, and her shoulders relaxed at the sound of the little girl's voice.

"You're not?" she asked as she leaned forward, resting her elbows on her knees as she waited for the sage wisdom of the three- or four-year-old girl in front of her.

The girl shook her head.

"Mommy said I'm always safe when I'm wif her, and I believe Mommy. She said it's 'cause I...what's da word,

Mommy?"

"Trust," the woman said, and the girl beamed.

"Twust! It's 'cause I twust Mommy."

Brynn craned her neck to look at Jamie, who was so close she had to lean away just to see his face next to hers.

"Smart girl," he said, and now Brynn not only heard it but *saw* his smile. He wasn't making fun of her or teasing her, just smiling.

"I used to be the smart girl."

Brynn pouted, not feeling anything along the lines of smart. Put her in front of a computer and tell her to make sure accounts payable and accounts receivable added up correctly, and she could do that. Do your taxes? Sure! No problem! Leave her alone too long on the second floor of Two Stories, and she'd create a display that highlighted her favorite period romances or the best young adult trilogies. Give Brynn Chandler something visual to organize, whether it was books or numbers, and she was the smartest girl around. But ask her to organize her life, to know the difference between false bravado and honest-to-goodness paralyzing fear, and she was not to be trusted.

But Jamie—there was a guy she could trust. A friend who'd never let her fall.

Brynn's eyes widened again, but this time it wasn't the frenzied look of fear. It was something else—something like realization.

"I'm not going to fall," she said, her words directed at Jamie. What if she did have someone there to catch her when she needed catching? Was that so bad?

"Not while I'm around." His smile broadened. He knew he'd broken through, and as much as she didn't want to give him the satisfaction of being right—of winning, essentially— she smiled back at him.

"I trust you," she told him, and he let out a breath, his

shoulders relaxing.

Geez, he had been as tense as she was, but he hadn't let her see it. He hid that for her, and she trusted him even more now because of it.

"It's about freaking time," he said, and Brynn realized her palm wasn't the only one sweating. He'd been this nervous *for* her. God, she had to loosen up or he was going to give himself an ulcer getting her across the country.

"Always," she said. "I will always trust you, Jamie."

The capsule shook and then stopped. The blond little girl giggled and looked over her shoulder at her mother. Brynn, on the other hand, slammed her foot down onto the floor as if she were stepping on some emergency break.

"What was that?" She started to transform into the Brynn of ten minutes ago, the one ready to throw in the towel as long as it meant she didn't have to experience this.

"You did it, SJ. You made it to the top."

The capsule door slid open, and the woman and her little girl shuffled out first.

"Don't be afwaid," the girl said to Brynn. "I'm not so big, but I did a big girl fing, and now I'm not so scared to do more big girl fings."

Brynn *was* afraid. It's not like years of programming could be deprogrammed within minutes. But she wasn't doing this alone.

"I made it to the top."

Jamie nodded. "And we can wait right here for it to start up again. Ten minutes, and we're on our way back down."

She shook her head. "It would be a really crappy leap if I stopped in the middle of it. Wouldn't it?"

"You still made it to the top," he said. "That's a big step, if not a leap."

"Let's go take a look," she said, and Jamie waited as she pushed past him and out of the capsule. She offered him a hand, and he grabbed it, letting her pull him on to solid ground—solid ground that was six hundred thirty feet up in the air.

"You sure?" he asked when he was standing next to her.

She shook her head. She wasn't sure at all. But she wasn't stopping, either, not when she had come this far.

"Do you feel safe up here?" she asked.

"Yes." Jamie didn't hesitate with the word, not for a second.

"Then I trust you," she said. "In the grand scheme of things, this *is* a baby step. The giant leap will be L.A."

She put one foot in front of the other, knees threatening to buckle with each step, but she kept moving.

If she made it through this, it would be a sign, something foretelling of the rest of the trip, just like the flat tire. If she could do this, she could justify traveling across the country for a guy who *might* be the one. Because if she could follow through with conquering one fear, she could do the same with the rest.

Solid ground awaited, and so did Spencer Matthews. She hoped.

Chapter Ten

"Truth or dare?" Brynn asked, and Jamie chuckled softly.

"What kind of a dare can I do when I'm driving? You *do* want to make it to our next destination, don't you?"

His smile didn't falter, though. Jamie liked this, the ease of being with Brynn and playing silly games. When he wasn't fixating on her *giant leap* in L.A. or how he felt, along with how he would tell her, the two fell into a rhythm that was effortless, like nothing had changed. That's because maybe for Brynn, it hadn't. *Jamie* was the one with a realization the night of the reunion. Not her.

Time. He had time. For now he could push his fixation into a corner of his mind, lock it away until the time was right. On this leg of Route 66, the two of them could just *be*.

"I'm still waiting," she said with exaggerated impatience. "And I promise not to jeopardize our safety. I'm not going to risk my life after conquering the Arch."

A self-satisfied smile spread across her face, and he decided to let her bask. He could mention her bursting into tears when the capsule reached the ground again, but he was proud of her and wanted her to have her moment.

"And I'm still thinking," he mused, dragging out the seconds just to annoy her. "Fine. Dare."

Jamie allowed himself a quick glance before settling his gaze back on the road. Brynn's brows shot up before she went all contemplative. She tapped her finger against her pursed lips, and he just kept driving, his smile lingering. Whatever she had to throw at him was better than opening himself up to questions he had to answer 100 percent truthfully.

"Sing me the chorus to your favorite Monkees song."

Jamie let his head thud against the headrest, eyes rolling in time with the movement.

"Seriously?" he said. "*You* have favorite Monkees songs. I'm just the guy who humors your strange musical fixation. One, I might add, that I kept a secret all through high school for you."

Brynn blew out a breath and crossed her arms defiantly over her chest, though he wasn't sure what she was defying other than good taste in music.

"You chose *dare*, James Kingston. I don't remember there being any sort of request for personal insult. *This* is the reason for going underground with my Monkees love after middle school, you know. Reactions like yours. Well, guess what? I'm out of the musical closet now, so you can't bring me down, mister. Now stop stalling. You've heard all the songs. There has to be one you like better than the rest."

He *had* heard all the songs, over and over again. It's not like Brynn didn't listen to any other music, but the Monkees were always the go-to when she needed something to make her smile. He couldn't argue with that, and because he chose *dare*, he also couldn't argue with the request. Though he promised no guarantee the act would not endanger their lives or the lives of others.

"I didn't mean to insult…" he started, but she cut him off.

"Still stalling," she said, her tone haughty. "Come on, James. I've heard you sing. You're not too bad. Now just prove to me you know the words, and we can both put this behind us."

So he did it—belted it, actually. Jamie Kingston didn't *just* sing the chorus to "I'm a Believer." He sang the whole damn song, finishing just as they came to their exit in Galena, Kansas. He pulled into town and then into the parking lot of the historic Cars on the Route service station.

"I gotta piss," he said, throwing the truck into park and holding back a smirk. Brynn sat, mouth agape, silent through his whole performance and silent still. When he opened his door and hopped out, he heard her clear her throat behind him.

"That was...um...good," she said. "I didn't know you could sing like *that*," she added softly. But he didn't turn back. The disbelief in her voice was enough. Plus, he didn't want her to see how much he beamed with satisfaction as he strode toward the station.

Let's see Spencer Matthews do that, he thought.

Then he hummed what he supposed *was* his favorite Monkees song the rest of the walk to the door.

He'd make a believer out of her yet.

• • •

What the hell was that?

Brynn braced her hands on the side of the sink, uncommonly clean for a gas station bathroom. The white porcelain sparkled, and the end of the toilet paper was folded into a triangle like they do at fancy hotels. Chalk it up to the place being a historic landmark or to the tourism in general, but the Cars on the Route bathroom was one of the cleanest public restrooms she'd ever seen. Hands-on-the-sink clean.

Brynn blinked, her dry eyes already irritated. So she pulled her contact case and solution from her purse and decided to give her lenses a little rinse.

Her mind went back to the question at hand. *What. The hell. Was that?*

She'd expected Jamie to scoff at her dare request. She'd expected him to comply, begrudgingly, of course. What she hadn't expected was the entire song, or how freaking good he sounded singing it. He didn't sound like Mickey Dolenz or Davy Jones. He didn't sound like a Monkee at all.

He sounded *good*. Better. Sexy.

When had he learned how to sing like that? Or was that another part of her friend she'd never been privy to before?

She tried to reconcile the Jamie who just got out of the truck—the one who sang with abandon and pretty much blew her mind—with the reserved guy who preferred hiding out on his own to mingling with their fellow graduates at last week's reunion. She thought back to that night, to how much she'd wanted to, at the very least, make eye contact with him before she left with Spencer. But he was MIA until he came barging into his office.

Huh. Brynn saw it more clearly now compared to then, when she looked at Jamie with inebriated ire. He *had* barged, like he was in a rush or on some sort of mission. Did he have to start an emergency Oktoberfest batch? It was too late for that. Maybe he'd suddenly realized a color-coding error on his dry-erase calendar. That would have needed immediate attention. Whatever it was that had kept Jamie hidden before Brynn snuck off with Spencer had also sent him back to his office anxious and agitated, and she'd never asked him why.

Why, Jamie? Why, when she decided to take him up on his offer, had she thought the trip would be simple until they reached L.A.? Why, instead of relaxing in the comfort of being with someone she'd known for more than fifteen years, had she been surprised at every turn, wondering if she ever really knew the man she was with the way she thought she did?

She knew part of the answer lay in what happened ten years ago. She'd never admit it to Jamie, but she had held back, kept a safe distance since he put a crack in her vulnerable teenaged heart. At first the distance between them was fueled by anger—anger at him for making her feel what she didn't even know was there and then squashing any sort of possibility with his own fear.

But Brynn knew fear, too—fear bigger than a six-hundred-thirty-foot arch—and she let that fear keep her from fighting for him when they were teens. She let it keep her safe for ten long years, reminding herself that if they ever crossed that boundary again, losing him a second time would hit her harder, that the damage to their friendship would be irreparable. They were kids then. When the heart was young and strong, it could bounce back from breaking. But she and Jamie were all grown up now. Wounds didn't heal as quickly as they used to, and it had taken them four years to make their way back to normal last time. So Jamie sounding sexy singing his heart out in the truck could be nothing more.

She sighed at herself in the mirror—though all she could see was her blurry outline while her lenses soaked in their case—mustered up a small helping of that fear, and used it to bury any sort of delight she took in Jamie's recent performance. They had less than two hours to go before Tulsa, their resting spot for the night after nearly eleven hours on the road, but her eyes were begging for relief now.

She unscrewed the lid labeled L and quickly deposited her contact back into her left eye. There. So much better. She was about to do the same with the right, but the knock on the door startled her, her hand jerking toward her face, and the contact toppling from her fingertip…into the too-clean sink and down the drain.

"B? You in there? I went back to the truck and didn't see you…"

"SHIT!" she yelled. What was it with Jamie and his goddamn timing?

"What's wrong? Are you okay? Let me in, Brynn!"

Jamie's voice was strained and insistent, dripping with worry. So Brynn unlocked the door, ready to drown his worry in venom.

He barreled into the bathroom, and she stumbled backward both with déjà vu and the dizziness associated with being extremely farsighted while wearing only one contact. Jamie caught her before her back hit the sink, and she threw her arms around him, holding herself up. For a moment they lingered like that, but she quickly remembered why she was dizzy in the first place.

"You!" she yelled, pushing herself from him and trying to focus with her good eye. "It's always *you*!"

Brynn closed the eye without the lens and watched as Jamie looked from her to the sink and then back again. She'd left the contact solution on the corner of the sink, and he must have seen it, because recognition and guilt bloomed across his face.

"You've got to be kidding me," he said. And then he started to laugh.

She swatted at his chest but missed, and he only laughed more.

She didn't join him. In fact, she had to hold her breath to keep from bursting into tears. Jamie had to have seen it in her expression because his laughter ceased the second his eyes focused on hers—her opened eye, that is—again.

"Don't even tell me," he said, but Brynn nodded.

He figured out exactly what she just realized only moments before. When she rummaged through her bag for the contact solution, she became aware of the one necessity she forgot to pack—her glasses.

This wasn't how the first day was supposed to end, not when there had been signs—the flat tire, conquering the Arch.

"Smooth sailing," she insisted and realized the tears came anyway. "It was supposed to be smooth sailing from here on out."

She sniffled and faltered in her footing again, this time burying her head in Jamie's chest.

"I can't wear just the one," she sobbed. "I'm dizzy enough already. It'll make me sick if I keep it in."

Jamie rubbed her back and rested his chin on her head.

"I'm sorry, B." His voice still carried the hint of a chuckle, but he was no longer laughing. "I guess we've never really had good timing."

She sniffled again. "What am I going to do?"

"I'll take care of it," he said. "Let's get you cleaned up and back to the truck, and I'll fix this."

She nodded against him, but she had to ask.

"How?"

"I've already got the hotel in Tulsa booked. I'll call Holly, have her overnight your glasses to the hotel, and you'll have them before we head out tomorrow. Until then…"

He hesitated because they both knew what *until then* meant.

"I'm legally blind," Brynn said.

He took in a deep breath, then sighed. Her head rose and fell with the action.

"Do you still trust me?" he asked, and she let out a bitter laugh.

"To not also take away my hearing? That would make this trip a double bummer."

"To make sure you don't miss a thing," he said. "I'll be your eyes for the rest of the evening and until the glasses arrive in the morning. And I'll cover whatever it costs for Holly to get them here by then."

Brynn righted herself and held a hand over her contact-free eye.

"I'm still mad at you."

"As you should be."

"But it's a nice gesture. Very gentlemanly."

A small smile formed on his lips.

"I'm glad you think I'm a gentleman."

She shook her head. "The gesture was that of a gentleman, but you are still the pain in the ass who blinded me."

He laughed. "Noted. Should we salvage the remaining lens and get you to the truck?"

"Lead the way," she said, and gestured toward the sink. Of course she misinterpreted the depth of space and smacked her knuckles against the porcelain. "Dammit!"

Jamie grabbed her hand and placed a soft kiss against the throb of pain. The hairs on the back of her neck stood up, and she yanked her hand away, hastily removing the contact from her eye, dropping it in its case, and shoving both that and the solution into her bag.

Then she let her arms fall to her sides, lest she knock loose any more bone fragments from her most likely bruised hand.

Jamie linked his arm with hers and turned her toward the door. At least she thought they were facing the door.

"Shall we?" he asked.

"You're not going to mess with me and put me in someone else's car, are you?"

"I hadn't thought of it until you mentioned it," he said, amusement in his tone.

"Forget I said anything, then."

"Forget what?" he asked.

"Exactly," Brynn said, and bit back the beginning of a smile.

Chapter Eleven

Brynn's phone made a tweeting sound on the nightstand, but she didn't move. Jamie watched her from his bed as she lay across hers, eyes fixed on the ceiling.

"Do you want me to answer that for you?" he asked, but she waved him off.

"That's Holly texting even though she knows I can't read it." She didn't turn to him when she spoke, just stared straight up. "I can see a crack in the paint ten feet above me," she said, "but I can't read a freaking text."

She hadn't told him to read the text, but then she hadn't told him not to, so he made the decision for himself.

"Holly says that we're lucky it's a weekday because the courier doesn't overnight on weekends. The courier takes payment on delivery only, but since I already gave her my debit card number, she's going online shopping with it, and your glasses will be here before noon tomorrow."

Jamie put the phone back down next to their stacked room-service plates. Brynn wasn't much in the mood for sightseeing, especially since it was nearly dark when they arrived. Since she couldn't really see the sights anyway, she'd insisted they just eat in the room in case she made a mess of herself, which she hadn't.

Jamie carried the plates from the room, placing them on the floor in the hall of Oklahoma's Campbell Hotel. His intent was to surprise Brynn on their first night away with a place well above motel standard. Instead he'd surprised her in a Kansas gas station bathroom and cost her the luxury of vision for the next eighteen hours.

When he stepped back through the door, Brynn was lying on her side facing him.

"Stop," she said, so he halted just inside the room. Then Brynn smiled, and he realized he hadn't seen this expression on her since they'd played Truth or Dare.

"Hi," she said to him and offered a small wave.

Jamie slid down the door so he was sitting against it. He understood.

"You can see me," he said, and she nodded.

"You're a little fuzzy around the edges, but I can actually tell your nose from your chin now."

He laughed. "I actually feel a little fuzzy around the edges. This is a good distance?"

Brynn nodded. "Far enough away for me to see you but close enough to know you're still here."

Jamie knew she was talking about her vision, but she may as well have been talking about them and the unspoken distance they'd created in the last ten years. Despite staying friends, there'd been so many times he'd wanted to address that summer, to tell her again how sorry he was. But she made him promise not to bring it up again, and the least he could do was keep his word, even if it meant this thing was always hanging between them.

But something felt different now, like being on the road suspended them in an alternate reality or a parallel universe.

Maybe here he could break the rules and get away with it.

Now, Jamie. Tell her now. She just gave you an opening.

But he paused a second too long, and Brynn took the initiative to fill the silence.

"Think Spencer will like me in my specs?" she asked. "That was my last pair of contacts, or I'd have had Holly send those, too," she said. "I don't get it. I'm an excellent packer. For me to not only forget to order new contacts but also neglect to pack my glasses? It's not like me."

Jamie knew this was the place where he was supposed to say something comforting, reminding her that she'd be in great shape after her glasses arrived, but he was having trouble getting past her first question. *Think Spencer will like me in my specs?*

Spencer was human, and Brynn was Brynn, so of course he'd like her in her goddamn specs. Jamie *loved* Brynn in her glasses, because something akin to a transformation took place when the contacts came out and the glasses went on. Brynn morphed from her day-to-day, high-strung self to someone almost relaxed. *Almost.*

"Jamie? Did you hear anything I just said?"

His gaze met hers, and he realized he'd zoned for longer than he thought. He reminded himself this was about choice — *Brynn's* choice. And so far, she hadn't chosen him.

"Huh? I mean, yes. Of course he'll love bespectacled Brynn. He writes books, right? You'll look more…readerly."

Readerly? Shit. Things were bad when he started making up his own vocabulary. It was either that or tell her that even though the lenses of her glasses were thicker than a Coke bottle, she looked more herself when she wore them, more comfortable in her skin. And when Brynn was comfortable in her skin, she was stunning.

But he wasn't about to call his best friend stunning, not now that Spencer had used that word for her, and especially not when she was concerned with what some other guy thought of her looks.

"Readerly, huh?" she mused, then sat up. "I know I should be tired. I mean, it's been a long day…"

"It's only nine o'clock," Jamie interrupted.

"Are you tired?" Brynn asked. "You did all the driving. I can drive some of the way tomorrow if you want. Once I'm bespectacled."

While Jamie could appreciate the sincerity of the offer, he also knew that Brynn was confident he'd never let her behind the wheel of the truck. Just because she somehow passed her driving exam didn't mean anyone should willingly let her out on the open road. She wouldn't argue this, either.

"You know I like to drive," he said. "I'm good to keep going."

"Oh, thank God," she said, and they both laughed.

"And I'm not tired, either," he lied. If he got back on that bed and put his head on the pillow, he'd be out until morning. The driving, the drama, the energy it took to keep everything he was really thinking and feeling bottled up—it all took its toll, and he wanted sleep, welcomed it even, but not at the price of losing time with Brynn.

"Well," Brynn said. "Watching a movie is out. Although I *could* listen. We could play more Truth or Dare…"

She broke off in mid-thought. Jamie figured if he was going to stay awake, the only thing that would help was something cold and on tap.

"There's a bar on the main floor. Buy me a beer?"

She swung her feet over the side of the bed and planted them on the floor.

"Only if you buy me one," she said.

He strode to her side and helped her put on her boots.

"How do I look?" she asked.

Her hair was up in one of her messy buns, and the day had

worn away any makeup she'd been wearing.

"Perfect," he said, and felt something in his chest constrict at the word. "You look perfect."

"Good answer, Mr. Kingston. Now let's go have a pint."

• • •

When they made it into the Campbell Lounge, Jamie uttered a low "Whoa" under his breath.

"What's up, Keanu?" Brynn asked, her hand linked with his as he led her through the door.

"I've read about some nearby breweries, and it looks like the tap beers here are local brews."

Well, Brynn thought. *That settled it. Jamie was never going to leave this place.*

"A kid in a candy shop," she said. "Okay, expert. You get to pick what I drink."

"I have a better idea," he said, and he led her the rest of the way.

Brynn perched atop a stool at the bar. It was Jamie's idea to sit up close because then Brynn couldn't cheat, not that she would. But whatever. She'd humor him.

"A blind taste test, huh? I feel like you're taking advantage of my situation, James. How do I know you won't have our friend Tim here put Tabasco in my glass or make me drink some other patron's leftovers?"

Tim was the bartender, and Jamie had introduced himself as a brewmaster the second they sat down. Now the two were practically besties, and Jamie was behind the bar with Tim instead of on a stool next to her.

"It's not like this is a fraternity prank," Jamie said. "But you have given me some good ideas, now, if I decide to go that route. And it's not a taste *test*. It's an experience. You can interact with the brews from a completely different perspective. A more sensual beer-tasting event."

Brynn raised her brows, and Jamie and Tim both laughed, a duet of maleness that was maybe a little bit sensual.

"Head out of the gutter, Chandler," Jamie said. "Sensual as in senses—as in using your *other* senses to enjoy the experience."

She knew the definition of the word and was ready and willing to argue her point, but before she could, Jamie grabbed her hand and placed it on a cool pint glass. Brynn assumed she knew the rules and immediately raised the glass to her lips.

"No!" Both men yelled in chorus, and her hand stopped mid-tilt, beer dribbling over the rim and on to her hand.

She rolled her eyes and groaned. "Am I not supposed to *drink* it? Maybe I should have had you clarify *sensual* a little better."

"She's funny," Tim said to Jamie.

"Difficult is more like it," Jamie mumbled, but Brynn caught the words just fine. Maybe her sense of hearing was sharpening now that she was virtually without sight.

"I'm right here, guys. Hello?"

She set the glass back down, and one of them handed her a napkin. She couldn't make out which.

"Thank you," she said.

"You're welcome." The voice definitely belonged to Jamie. Okay. She'd give him a point back for politeness, but she was going to file away *difficult* for the next time she wanted to throttle him.

"Can we try again?" he asked. "This time with clearer directions?"

She crossed her arms and waited.

"Just put your hand on the glass first. It's dry, by the way."

Brynn sighed but did as she was told, allowing Jamie to guide her hands so there were no depth perception incidents.

Jamie and Tim were silent, and she was a tad creeped out

without anyone talking to her.

"Um…is there a chant or something I'm supposed to say before I sip? What happened to my clear directions?"

A curl fell free of her bun, landing over her left eye. She blew it out of the way more on ceremony than anything else. Not like it was blocking her vision. But it flopped down again. She wanted to reach for it, but something told her she wasn't supposed to let go of the glass, not after Jamie had so carefully placed her hands on it.

And since Jamie could probably hear her inner monologue, she wasn't surprised when his fingertips brushed her forehead and then her cheek, tucking the rogue curl behind her ear. At least, she hoped it was Jamie. Because if it was Tim, that would just be weird.

It was definitely Jamie. She could smell that *just him* scent on the sleeve of his hoodie as it, too, tickled her cheek.

"Sensual experience," she muttered and cleared her throat. "Directions, please?"

"Just tell me about the glass," Jamie said.

"Jamie," she whined. She just wanted to drink the damn beer.

"Brynn?" He drew out her name, his tone reminding her she'd agreed to play along.

"It's cold," she offered, but Jamie didn't respond. While his shape was unclear, she could tell he was close, leaning on the bar in front of her, that scent of his lingering. Fine. The faster she got through this, the faster she could drink and drown out the *just him.*

"The glass is perspiring," she continued, "so that already rules out stout because you would never serve me a chilled stout."

Someone whistled his approval, and then she heard Tim's voice.

"Your girl knows her brews."

Brynn smiled at this, and okay, maybe she even puffed up a bit with pride. Jamie had been putting his scientific brilliance to this kind of work for almost a decade now, and she hoped he was just as proud at how much she'd paid attention. Of course, there were times he'd gone on for far too long about the IPA he was trying in any given year, and Brynn would zone understandably. A girl doesn't want to get attached to one ale only for him to never make it again. But the passion with which Jamie did his work—that was contagious. Mellow and even on all other counts, his spirit ignited when he talked about what he loved.

"She certainly does," Jamie said, and Brynn beamed. Jamie didn't correct Tim about the *your girl* comment, and she decided to let it go as well. No point in steering the conversation in that direction when they were just starting to have fun.

"Do I get to taste it now?" she asked, the moisture from the glass making her mouth water.

Jamie put his hands over hers, guiding her to lift the glass. *Finally*, she thought, but the motion stopped when her hands were just in front of her face.

"What do you smell?"

Brynn sighed. At least the glass was closer to her mouth. Baby steps, she supposed.

She sniffed and was transported to a memory. Barely more than a year ago, the Fourth of July. Brynn had just gotten out of a relationship—her doing—because after six months there weren't any fireworks, so the last thing she wanted to do that night was *see* the evidence of what was missing from her life. She boycotted the Fourth and holed up in her apartment by herself until Holly, Annie, Jeremy, and Jamie brought the anti-party to her. With a half barrel filled from the ale house, the five of them drank their fill with the shades drawn and the Monkees blaring. Not one firework was seen or heard, and

Brynn relived this scene simply from the scent of citrus.

"Orange," she said, grounding herself back in the moment with the sound of her own voice. "With maybe a hint of grapefruit. Or lemon. Something tart."

"Dude," Tim said. "Do not let this one go."

This time Brynn and Jamie responded in perfect unison.

"We're not together."

Brynn's version was emphatic, Jamie's hesitant, but their words were the same nonetheless.

"Then will you marry me, Brynn?" Tim asked in earnest.

Brynn flushed at the compliment, sure both men could see the evidence of it on her pale skin, but she didn't care. It felt nice to have this part of her brain admired—the beer part. Maybe she'd call it her beer cortex.

"Haven't tasted it yet, Tim," she said. "A girl's gotta drink her beer *before* she marries the guy who poured it."

She stuck her tongue out, ready to lap up the fragrant liquid.

"You're killing me," Tim said.

"Dude, I poured it," Jamie argued under his breath, and Brynn wondered if the remark was for Tim-the-bartender or her. This blindness thing was heightening her other senses all right, and she didn't like it. Because heightened senses made her think. And overthink. Hell, she did that on a normal day. Right now she just wanted to forget thinking altogether and drink her beer.

"Can I taste it, now?" she asked, sure that as soon as the liquid passed her lips, she'd probably down the whole glass. It was turning into that kind of a night.

"One sip," Jamie said. "One sip and then initial reaction."

She stuck her tongue out again, partly because she liked the idea of Tim-the-bartender thinking it was hot. She didn't do things like this, acting playful and sexy with a perfect stranger. But blind or not, Brynn felt sexy in this moment, and she dipped the tip of her tongue into the head of the beer.

"Jesus."

The word was soft, under his breath, but Brynn's sense of hearing was sharper this evening, because the word did not escape her, nor did the recognition that the voice belonged to Jamie and not to Tim. She reminded herself she was playing at sexy for the complimentary bartender and swallowed the bit of foam on her tongue. Then she laughed softly, the tickle of the carbonation lingering.

"I can name that beer in one sip," she said.

"Don't rush," Tim told her. "I've got all night."

"Actually, do it, now," Jamie said, and for the first time tonight she wished she could read the expression that went with his words.

Instead she sipped. One long, slow gulp.

"It's a Hefeweizen," she said, then rested the glass on the bar. "A close second to my favorite, which is a Belgian white, though this one hasn't brewed me one yet." She nodded toward where she thought Jamie was. Who knows? It could have been Tim. Heat coursed through her, and she closed her eyes. She saw no fireworks, but it was most definitely the Fourth of July.

"Game over," Jamie said.

"No way, dude. We're just getting started," Tim insisted. "Drinks are on the house the rest of the night. What can I get you?" he asked Jamie, and Brynn listened to him sigh.

"You got any Jack?"

Chapter Twelve

Jamie woke with a start. The room was pitch black, and it took him a moment to get his bearings, to remember he wasn't in his apartment but instead in a hotel in Oklahoma. He grabbed his phone from the nightstand and checked the time. It was just after nine in the morning. His brows furrowed. He couldn't reconcile the darkness of the room with what his phone was trying to tell him, and then it happened again, the noise that must have woken him. A sharp knock at the door.

He climbed from the bed, eyes straining to make out Brynn's form in the bed across from his. She was still asleep.

There had been Jack at the bar last night, but he only drank one shot, regardless of how many times Tim insisted he have one more. He knew Brynn would want to get on the road as soon as her glasses arrived. While Tulsa was their planned first stop, they weren't doing much of the tourist thing like they had in St. Louis. Last night was simply to rest—and to see a side of Brynn he never knew was there. Sure, he'd always found her beautiful, but she had never let on that she knew it. That's one of the things he loved, how unassuming she was.

But last night she floored him, and thank God she couldn't see the look on his face when she dipped her tongue into the foam of that beer. Her hair in a haphazard bun atop her head, eyes closed in concentration, recognizing the beer before she officially tasted it. Nothing had ever turned him on more.

As he approached the door, he finally took note of his attire—shirtless but jeans still on from last night. This was a good thing, because imagining what Brynn did at the bar had the same effect on him as watching her do it in real time, and his erection strained against the denim.

One more round of knocking sounded before he reached the door.

"Just a sec," he said, his throat dry and hoarse.

When he opened the door, a young woman stood there. She wore an unzipped fleece jacket, under which was a green T-shirt, the image of Yoda dead center on her torso and the letters OOYL stretched across her chest.

"That's funny," Jamie said.

"You're half naked," she responded. "And you owe me two hundred fifty bucks."

"Excuse me?"

The question came from behind him. Brynn.

Why was it so dark in here? He turned to face Brynn.

Her hair was crazy. There was no other way to describe it than tornado-like. Creases from her pillowcase lined her cheek, and she squinted either at the light coming in from the door, or to try to make out the scene before her, or both.

It was *her* T-shirt, though, that caught his eye. Her Chicago Cubs shirt, the one she'd had since high school. Brynn wasn't even a Cubs fan, but she bought the shirt to wear to school for a team-themed spirit day, and when Jamie asked why she didn't borrow a Sox shirt from him, she claimed she didn't want to wear a shirt two sizes too big.

Why hadn't she bought herself a Sox shirt? he'd asked,

and her only response was that she wanted something with a little color. She wouldn't get rid of the shirt, so Jamie made her promise she'd never wear it when she was out with him. He guessed this was her way of bending the rules since they weren't technically *out*.

As much as it should have been the team represented by the shirt that got Jamie's attention, it was the realization that he hadn't seen her *in* the shirt since high school. And that maybe the shape of her upper body had changed since they were teens. And maybe—just *maybe*—now would be a good time for her to put on her bra.

"Ahem." The sound came from the girl at the door.

"Who is it?" Brynn asked. "What time is it? And why is there, like, zero evidence of daylight in here?"

Jamie looked from girl to girl, only sure of one of the answers. He opened his mouth to speak, but the girl outside the door's threshold beat him to it.

"I'm Lauren. It's nine fifteen. I heard this place has some sweet blackout shades. And I have a package to deliver to a Brynn Chandler."

Finally, Jamie thought. *Answers.*

Brynn clapped her hands together and squealed. Then she leaped at Jamie, depth perception be damned, and flung her arms around his neck.

"My glasses! You did it! Oh my God, thank you."

She squinted hard toward Lauren, no doubt Brynn's new best friend, and reached for the package Jamie hadn't noticed in the girl's hand.

"I need you to sign and pay first," she said. "Two-fifty, and I forgot my scanner, so I hope you have cash. Otherwise I gotta drive an hour there and back again."

Jamie found his wallet on the dresser and counted out its contents. Two hundred and seventy-five bucks, enough for the glasses, a small tip, and a little left over for housekeeping.

They'd have to hit an ATM on their way out of town.

"Here you go," he said, and then signed for the glasses since Lauren wouldn't hand them over until he did so. As soon as she relinquished the item, he thanked her and closed the door.

"Open it, Jamie. Open, open, open!"

He laughed as he freed the item from inside the box and then placed the glasses gingerly on Brynn's face.

She crinkled up her nose.

"Is that what you've always looked like?"

He crossed his arms over his chest.

"Very funny."

Then she caught a glimpse of herself in the mirror, and Jamie's eyes lingered on the snug Cubs T-shirt.

"Shit," she said. "I need a shower."

Jamie felt himself pressed firm against his jeans and knew he had to take evasive action.

"Me first!" he said, and like a bratty child, hopped into the bathroom and slammed the door shut behind him. "Don't worry," he called out to her. "I won't use all the hot water."

In fact, he didn't use any hot water at all.

• • •

Is that what you've always looked like?

That's the best she could do? What else was she supposed to come up with when after a day without sight and a night like last night the first thing she sees is Jamie, hair rumpled with sleep, and the whole no-shirt-with-jeans thing happening.

These *ways* she'd been seeing him since the trip began... it was just projection. She was projecting her feelings about Spencer—about the possibility of Spencer—on Jamie. That had to be it.

She spun slowly, taking in the room's polished wood

floor, its four-poster wooden beds and ornately patterned wallpaper. This was no motel, and Brynn knew it wasn't a place Jamie would have stayed alone. Then there was the situation of the glasses. She blamed him again, guilted him into paying for the courier, and now on top of whatever this room had cost him, he just dropped two hundred fifty dollars cash so she could see.

She flopped down on the bed and listened to the shower water run, going over their pattern for the past week. It seemed Jamie was always opening doors at the wrong time, and Brynn was always losing something when he did—a contact, Spencer, a contact again. For two people who were supposed to be the best of friends, they had a shitty rhythm. She didn't want to blame Jamie when things got thrown out of whack, but he always seemed to be there when they did.

Yet he always picked up the pieces when she couldn't. Contact in her apartment sink? Jamie to the rescue. Spoiled kiss (second attempt in ten years) with Spencer Matthews? Jamie brings her to California. Contact lost in a Galena, Kansas, gas station? Jamie gets her glasses to her by morning. Maybe he had some work to do in the opening doors department, but he did pretty well with the friendship.

Brynn sighed, and then she felt the urgency that came with waking up—the urgency to pee.

She popped back up and padded to the bathroom door. A light knock.

"Jamie? Can I come in to pee?"

He didn't answer, so she knocked harder and then cracked the door open.

"Jamie?"

"Yeah?"

His one word dripped with exhaustion, and she wondered if she should offer to drive again even though she knew what his answer would be.

"Can I sneak in to pee?" she asked.

"Sure."

She opened the door wide, expecting to hit a wall of steam, but the air in the bathroom was as cool and clear as that out in the bedroom.

"Don't listen," she said as she slid down her shorts and underwear. "And don't peek, either."

"Wouldn't think of it."

She expected him to tease her, but his words were clipped and compliant.

"I'm gonna flush, okay? Just warning you."

He didn't respond, so she assumed he was enjoying his shower, waking himself up for the long day ahead.

"Thank you, by the way."

Brynn decided this was as good a time as any to have a chat, especially since she didn't have to see him and think about him shirtless in his jeans. Because now he was naked in the shower and, oh God, she needed to keep talking and stop thinking.

"Thank you," she started again. "For my glasses, for bringing us to this nice place last night, for the fun with Tim in the bar." She took his silence as permission to continue. "I know I can be difficult when things don't work in my favor, like yesterday. And last week. But you never lose your patience with me, Jamie. You should, but you don't. So—thanks. I'm going to pay you back that two-fifty when we get to an ATM. That part's not on you."

He remained silent, and she hoped she hadn't misread his smile when he gave her the glasses. Although, if he was angry with her, she wouldn't blame him. Maybe this trip wouldn't exactly be glass-half-full the whole way through. But she promised herself this—for the rest of the journey, she was going to go with the flow. Roll with the punches. Take whatever came at her and make the best of it. That was how she'd get to the finish line and guarantee that when she arrived at Spencer's book launch, she'd be in the best place—in her head and in her heart—for their reunion.

She headed for the bathroom door and was almost out of the room when Jamie popped his head around the shower curtain.

"You're welcome, Sleepy Jean," he said. "I just—need a few more minutes to wake up. Order us some coffee?"

She smiled at him. "Sure." She pulled the door closed behind her and filled her mind with thoughts of steamed milk and caffeine, certainly not with what lay behind the shower curtain.

Chapter Thirteen

Jamie hadn't charged his phone since they arrived in Tulsa. His mind seemed to be constantly preoccupied with things he wanted to put off, but undealt-with thoughts liked to creep up when he least expected them—like when a certain girl licked the head off a draft beer or when that same girl wore a baseball shirt that made him crazy. So when he finally plugged his phone into its car charger as they readied themselves to leave Tulsa, of course there was a text waiting from Annie. No, it wasn't waiting. It was taunting. Goading. Reminding him that two days into their trip, he was no closer to telling Brynn the truth as he was running out of time before handing her off to another guy.

> Annie: *Are you two engaged yet? If not, did you at least do it?*

Do it? Jamie was sure his cold shower this morning was pretty much the opposite of *doing it*. Not that he wasn't thinking about, well, *it*.

He texted back:

Plans delayed due to temporary blindness but getting
back on the rails today.

Then he turned his phone to silent and locked his screen.
He didn't have the energy to explain any further, so he put the
truck in drive and pulled up to the lobby door where he'd left
Brynn waiting with her suitcase.

He hopped out of the truck to grab her stuff and toss it in
the back of the cab.

"James Fenimore Kingston, have you seen this hotel?
It's gorgeous. I can't believe I missed it!" She looked over her
shoulder at the hotel as Jamie ushered her to the car.

He opened the passenger door for her and rolled his eyes.
"My middle name isn't *Fenimore*."

"It should be."

"I have a perfectly adequate middle name," he told her.

This argument wasn't new. At some point it would take
effort and research for her to keep up with the replacement
middle names, but his grandfather's name, David, never
seemed to do when Brynn wanted to hyperbolize. And
"Hyperbole" was *her* middle name whenever she was over-
the-top excited. Just plain James meant she was pissed, but
throw in another famous James's name, and the moniker took
on a whole new tone. Regaining her sight and seeing the hotel
he wished she could have seen last night was one of those
instances.

James Fenimore, James Byron, James Augustine—he was
pretty sure he was the only person he knew, next to Brynn,
with the knowledge of James Joyce's full name. It was the
day they both graduated college, and though they hadn't seen
each other since the Christmas before, when Brynn called
him on the phone, it was like he'd just left her house after a
late-night *SNL* viewing.

"James Augustin Aloysius Kingston. You are graduating

college today."

He had been nervous that morning. Nervous and excited and clueless and all-knowing at the same time. But Brynn's voice, and her welcomed teasing, grounded him in the moment.

"I am," he'd said. "And so are you."

"I think this means we have to be grown-ups now. Did you get a manual? Because I didn't get a manual."

He knew Brynn had called for him—to ease *his* mind about that day—but the tremor in her voice said she needed him, too.

"No manual," he'd told her. "I think we just figure it out as we go."

"Figure it out together?"

"Deal."

That had been it. While they'd stayed friends, best friends, throughout college, there was always that undercurrent of strain. College gave them the physical and emotional distance they needed, and Jamie was sure they were stronger for it. When she called him that morning, addressing him with one of her too important middle names, Jamie knew they were back—picking up the pieces of where they were when this thing between them almost broke.

They were stronger that day, Sleepy Jean and Jamie, and had grown stronger ever since. Now he wanted to cross that uncrossable line, which could be great, but it could also break them completely.

"Yes," he finally said, wondering what else she might see more clearly after a day of blindness. "The hotel is pretty nice."

He closed her door and made his way to the driver's side of the vehicle. He took a deep breath.

See it, B. See us.

Jamie wasn't practiced in the art of telepathic suggestion, but he thought he'd give it a try. Because shit, this would be so much easier if Brynn would just realize she felt the same about him as he did about her. Fucking doubt. It ate a hole in his insides. He never doubted anything—not his work, not how the women he dated felt about him—and he was beginning to understand why.

His job was the easy part. He was good at what he did. Science came naturally to him, and the science of brewing even more so. And women? Well, his social life wasn't lacking. But connection—something was missing there. He couldn't remember the last woman he truly connected with enough that when the relationship ended he regretted its ending. They all just seemed to run their course, or in the case of Liz, run completely off track when he finally saw what was right in front of him—what had always *been* in front of him, but he'd been too scared to act. Too scared to lose. Because regret would not be enough when it came to losing Brynn.

"Hey, sweetie. Aliens take possession on your walk around the truck?"

He looked at Brynn, who was sitting next to him in the vehicle, the one he hadn't remembered entering. His left hand gripped the wheel, and his right was at the ready with the key slotted into the ignition.

"Shit," he said under his breath. And then louder. "I was just thinking."

She nudged his shoulder. "Can you think and drive? Because I'm a little worried about your multitasking abilities right now."

She slid her glasses to the tip of her nose and inclined her head toward him, looking over the top of her frames. He let out a laugh, one that broke whatever spell he was under for the moment.

"Can you even see me when you do that? You're just south of making eye contact, you know. But my nose will take your look into account."

She sighed, resituating her glasses and then, proving Jamie right, readjusting her gaze so they were eye-to-eye.

"Got you to laugh, Mr. Serious. What's up with you, anyway?"

He started the truck. He *could* multitask. There was no question about that. But he sure as hell didn't want to tell her what was up, at least not when it felt so one-sided.

"Ready to hit Amarillo?" he asked, and she settled into her seat and nodded, not pressing him to answer her question, and so he didn't. "I've gotta fill up first."

At that, Brynn began rummaging through her bag, and when her hands emerged, she thrust two twenty dollar bills at him. Jamie took the cash, looked at it, and then tucked it into the center console cup holder so he could shift into first and stop blocking the hotel's entrance.

"What's this for?" he asked.

"Gas," she said. "I didn't think I had any cash left. But sometimes I have a few bills in one of the credit card slots in my wallet."

Jamie raised a brow, and she continued.

"Whenever someone gets mugged in a movie, they always make them open up the cash pocket so they can see the contents, make sure they're getting it all."

He nodded, a slow smile spreading across his face.

"And you want to outsmart all those muggers trolling the hipsters in Lincoln Park."

She crossed her arms. "If they take everything, how will I hail a cab for help?"

Jamie scrubbed his hand across the stubble on his chin.

"Cabs do take credit cards."

Brynn sighed and opened her mouth to reply, but he cut her off.

"And what if they take the whole wallet?"

"Then I guess they'll get a little surprise after I cancel my credit cards." Brynn rolled her eyes. "You're making fun of me, but if I didn't hide my emergency cash from the muggers, we'd have none right now."

Jamie pulled into the first gas station they came across, one that housed two pumps and a pay hut that looked like it had room for no more than the person who sat in it along with his cash register. Jamie shook his head as he eyed the sign in the small window: COMPUTER DOWN. CASH ONLY.

A self-satisfied grin greeted him when he turned to face Brynn.

"You're welcome," she said.

He put the truck in park and killed the engine.

"You know, for someone who makes her living working with numbers, you have a pretty twisted sense of logic."

"All part of my charm," she said. And she was right.

Jamie grabbed the forty bucks, grateful he had just half a tank to fill, and decided that when they actually did find a working ATM that he'd grab an extra twenty and slip it behind his debit card.

Chapter Fourteen

"Tell me about the bar. It's the only part I didn't get to see for myself."

Brynn closed her eyes, waiting for Jamie to launch into a description of the place where she had the most sensual beer drinking experience she could remember. But remembering the way she tasted the foam somehow brought her to thoughts of Jamie this morning as he popped his head out from behind the shower curtain. And then her mind conjured images of Jamie from last summer, trim and tan, playing volleyball with his buddies at the beach. Only the net and the volleyball quickly disappeared, and the image of him wearing nothing but his swim trunks augmented the quick glimpse she got of his covered-with-beads-of-water torso. Her breath quickened, and she opened her eyes just as he gave her a sideways glance.

Brynn took off her glasses and kept her eyes open.

"Didn't we just blow all our remaining cash so you could get those back?"

She nodded but looked straight ahead, no farther than what was right in front of the windshield, the blurry sight of the road her main focus. Sure, it made her dizzy, but not half as much as the bewilderment she felt when thinking of Jamie naked in the shower. Because she *never* thought of Jamie naked in the shower. And shit. *Naked in the shower* were the only words attaching themselves to the idea of him at the moment, so the blurry street it would be.

"I want you to describe the bar to me, and I'll concentrate better if I can't see anything else."

Jamie seemed to believe the half-truth because he launched into his recollection of the Campbell Lounge almost immediately.

"The lights were pretty low," he started, and she nodded.

"I could tell. Felt cozy." A small smile settled onto her face, and tension she didn't know she was carrying ebbed out, her shoulders relaxing and her eyes falling shut once more. Her mind played no tricks now as she concentrated on Jamie's voice.

"It was. Lots of dark wood from the floors to the bar top."

"Mmmm hmmm." She produced the image in her mind's eye, a floor planked with dark hardwood, stools lining the rustic-looking bar. She had no idea if the picture in her head fit what Jamie actually saw, but it felt nice, thinking of the two of them—and Tim, of course—in a place like that.

Jamie cleared his throat, the sound jarring her so that her eyes opened with a start, and she put her glasses back on. When she looked at him, he opened his mouth to say something, but her phone chirped with a text notification, and she dug in her bag to see who it was.

"Oh," she said, eyes on the phone's screen.

"Holly?" he asked, his voice tight, and Brynn had a momentary urge to lie. But she didn't lie to Jamie, or to anyone for that matter. Even if she did, he'd see through her. The point was that she had the urge, irrational as it was, *not* to tell Jamie who had sent the text.

"It's Spencer," she said, forcing a cheery nonchalance to her tone and then immediately regretting doing it. Why? Spencer Matthews, soon-to-be-published author and senior year crush, just texted her to say he was thinking about her, that he was looking forward to seeing her again.

This was good news—all the encouragement she needed after wondering if she was making a fool out of herself for taking this trip. When she told Spencer she was coming, he'd acted pleased, but he could have just meant to be polite. Now he texted her with no prompting, *thought* about her, and she had to remind herself that this was what she wanted—the plan finally coming to fruition.

Yet, at the same time...

"You should get some sleep or something," Jamie said, interrupting her thought. "We have a long drive, and the rest of it's going to pretty much look like this until we hit desert."

Brynn peered through her thick lenses out onto the rolling green earth passing them by. Trees lined the rural expanse, and other than the thin cloud wisps stitching the sky above, the trees rose into what looked almost like a sea overhead.

They'd slept until nine, but Jamie's voice was tight, the suggestion evidence that he no longer wanted to discuss last night—or anything for that matter. Her breath hitched, and she wanted to say something, that it was all wrong for the day to look like this and Jamie to write it off as not worth the view. They should stop, take a picture. Or better yet, she *should* close her eyes, but not to sleep. She could take off her glasses again and ask him to narrate the scene, because something made her want to see it through *his* eyes.

"I'm not tired," she said, mirroring the words she said last night, the ones that led to their beer-tasting escapade and a night that was perfect other than temporary blindness.

"I just concentrate better when we're not talking, and I didn't want you to be bored," Jamie countered. "So if it's all the same to you, I'm just going to pay attention to the road for a bit."

"Maybe we should chill and have a leisurely breakfast," she said, ignoring the coffee cups in the cup holders between them. "That got us off on the right foot for the first leg of the journey." If you didn't count the flat tire that forced them to do so.

"I'm fine."

"I could drive, even, if you want to take a break from concentrating today. For real. It's all highway, so your transmission should be safe."

She offered a weak smile, but Jamie didn't take the bait. And while she wasn't sure she wanted to ask, she knew she should. Because the Spencer thing couldn't still be an issue. Brynn had gotten past the kiss. Jamie should have gotten past whatever he felt about her and Spencer. Because if he hadn't, he'd tell her, right?

"James Earl Jones Kingston, is everything…"

"I said I'm fine, B. Just practicing safe driving."

Yet no hint of a smile, even when she pulled out the James Earl Jones. In fact, he wouldn't even look at her when she spoke. *Safe driving.* That didn't mean he couldn't throw her a glance or offer a quick grin. But she wouldn't push it.

Jamie nodded in the general vicinity of the radio, and she knew the conversation was over when he gave her control of the tunes.

She scrolled through the music files on her phone, but somehow "Daydream Believer" didn't feel quite right. So she played with the tuner until a local station came in with minimal static.

Old-school hair-band music, Jamie's favorite next to classic rock. But just as Motley Crue's "Kickstart My Heart" blared from the speakers, Jamie hit the power button.

"Headache," he said.

"I've got ibuprofen," she said.

"I'm fine." He leaned in to the driver's side door, as if he didn't have enough room in his seat.

She gave up and closed her eyes, resting her temple against the cool glass of the window and sliding to the edge of her seat as well.

Maybe she was tired after all.

Chapter Fifteen

What the hell had he been thinking taking Brynn with him on this trip?

Safe driving his ass. Jamie couldn't keep his eyes on the road for long, his head constantly drifting to the right to see if she was still sleeping. He wanted to brush the curls out of her face, skim the back of his fingers over her cheek. Instead he gritted his teeth and white knuckled the steering wheel, berating himself for thinking this trip would be anything more than what he offered her.

If it had been just him in the truck, cruising along Route 66 (or, technically, I-40) for the last five hours, he'd have filled at least four of those hours with the recent *Brew Strong* podcasts he'd missed. He'd have appreciated watching the trees lining the route slowly morphing to those impressive yet mildly freaky white windmills that now seemed to be judging him and his life decisions. And instead of pulling off on to the frontage road from mere obligation, he'd be marveling at the Cadillac Ranch art installation in the cow pasture he was now standing in as he wondered if his passenger would wake up or miss the stop completely.

It didn't help that he hated himself a little more with each mile for putting his ego and his heart through such torture—and also for deceiving Brynn. He wasn't one for half-truths. Nor was he an ulterior motives kind of guy. Yet here he was, his agenda for this trip a far cry from hers.

He shook the can of black spray paint as he stared at the line of graffitied cars half buried in the dirt at angled nosedives. He'd come prepared. He wasn't sure what he'd have wanted to add to make his mark if he'd been here alone, but when he decided to take Brynn with him, he was sure they'd be doing this together, contributing something that signified their often zigzagging journey to what should have been a happy ending. But all it took was one damn text to remind him that while his agenda had been to finally make things right with Brynn, her agenda was someone else entirely. Annie was right. He was a fucking idiot. But then again, he always had been when it came to Brynn. Why this surprised him now, he didn't know.

"Welp…" He heard her voice from behind. "If anyone needs a lesson on how to freak a girl out, leave her asleep in a vehicle on the side of the road and let her wake up alone."

She was out cold when they'd pulled up, and at the time he didn't see the sense in waking her. He was going to do his thing with the spray paint and be back in the car before she knew they'd stopped. In hindsight, he could see how maybe it wasn't the best decision to leave her on her own in the truck in such a strange place.

Jamie opened his mouth to apologize until she strode up next to him and he laid his eyes on what she was wearing. The weather had warmed the closer they got to California. This afternoon in Amarillo it was a sunny eighty-three degrees, a far cry from the wet and windy autumn they'd left in Chicago. Brynn had apparently layered in anticipation because, instead of the jacket she'd had on when she got into the car in Tulsa,

she now wore only a simple white button-down with jeans.
The light cotton was wrinkled from the hours in the car, but
that's not what caught his eye. It was the one-too-far she'd
gone with leaving the top unbuttoned. In fact, he was sure she
hadn't meant to show him the cream-colored lace of her bra,
let alone the pink flesh of her nipple that peeked out of the
demi-cup.

Yes, Brynn and Annie had schooled him on bra cup
definitions when they were freshmen in high school, when
he was still too squirrelly to know the difference between
being horny all the time and being in love with his best friend.
But fucking Christ on a cracker, he knew the difference now,
and he could safely say that at that very moment he was
experiencing both.

He didn't have to say anything because Brynn followed
his bug-eyed stare right to the source, and she barked out a
laugh. Her skin turned as pink as the part he wasn't supposed
to see, and she quickly buttoned not only the one that had
come undone but one more above it for safe measure.

"I guess it's a good thing it's just us on the side of this
creepy little road, right?" she asked, crossing her arms not-so-
nonchalantly over her chest. "Is it legal to do that?"

She nodded toward the can of paint he'd forgotten was in
his hand, and Jamie cleared his throat. He'd been doing a lot
of that lately.

"It's kind of an unwritten rule that tourists can, um,
contribute...to the art." He gave her a quick explanation of
Cadillac Ranch, the art exhibit turned collaborative tourist
experience.

Brynn walked up to the car closest to them, reading some
of the inscriptions already on it.

Kisses and hugs to our fam + friends.
Jack was here.
Randy 08.

"Well," she said. "I don't think you can top *Randy 08*. We might as well just go home."

Jamie laughed. He'd been choking on bitterness for five hours, the taste of it burning a hole in his stomach, yet all she had to do was say something so simply Brynn, and he laughed. No matter what his feelings were for this girl—this woman—she was the friend who could always make him smile, and maybe that didn't have to change. He got over her once before, didn't he? Enough to live his life without pining, at least. He could do it again if it meant they'd always have this.

She walked around the half-buried car, running her fingers along the undercarriage before ending up back where she began, facing him.

"Are you still *fine*?" she asked, her eyes hesitant behind their protective glass. And his gut twisted at the way he'd treated her when she'd received Spencer's text. She didn't deserve his jealous reaction or the way he froze her out after that. He wasn't alone on this trip, but for the past five hours he'd acted like he was, and the only person he had to blame for missing out on actually spending that time *with* Brynn, instead of alongside her, was himself.

He closed the distance between them but stopped short of his usual gesture, a kiss to the top of her head. Instead he used his free hand to tug on one of her curls.

"Better than fine, Sleepy Jean."

At this she laughed. "I can't believe I passed out for... how long has it been?"

He spread his arms wide as if greeting her.

"Welcome to Amarillo."

• • •

Brynn toed the dirt at her feet with the worn white rubber of her favorite gray Chuck Taylors. She'd missed the whole day? She'd roused a few times from her slumber, but she couldn't bring herself to cut through the tension that filled the space between her and Jamie in the truck. So she'd chosen more sleep each time instead of making the first move.

She could feel it now, the clearing of the air between them, but it also felt like something had shifted. An acceptance, almost, coming from both of them. But an acceptance of what? His smile, the way he wrapped her hair around his finger and gave it a playful yank, was an apology of sorts. Jamie didn't need to say it, because she felt it.

Now, when she swatted his hand away and poked him in the belly—were his abs always that hard?—she hoped he read that as her *I'm sorry*. Brynn wasn't sure what she was sorry for or if she even owed him an apology, but as much as she wanted this trip to have the ending she'd been waiting for, she wanted to know that she and Jamie would be okay when it was over, too. And right now she was pretty sure they would be.

"Do you want to do the honors?" Jamie held the can of paint in her direction, but she shook her head.

"This is your trip, James. I'm just a stowaway. Do whatever you would have done if I weren't here."

Jamie shrugged as he walked toward the car and then shook out his arms in exaggerated preparation, and she watched his black T-shirt sleeves pull taut against his biceps. She was grateful his back was to her now so he couldn't see her involuntarily lick her lips, an action she rationalized as a response to the dry Texas heat and not the warmth pooling inside of her.

He stood facing the roof of the buried car and then in one leap was standing on it right where it framed the back windshield.

"Jesus!" Brynn blurted the word, her heart leaping as Jamie faltered for a millisecond and then righted himself. She had lurched forward with the word and then laughed at the ridiculous gesture. It's not like she could have caught him if he fell. No way in hell. Instead they would have both lain in a broken heap until another car full of tourists with spray cans showed up.

Jamie winked at her, and this time the voice in her head was the one to scream *Jesus*!

You know I'll always catch you, right?

Those were Jamie's words, the ones he'd spoken to her the night of the reunion when she almost bit it on the sidewalk outside her apartment and again the next morning when he'd kept her from face-planting on the wooden stairs before brunch. She'd been so focused on *not* needing saving that she couldn't see past her own stubbornness, the fear that made her unwilling to let him back in.

But holy fucking shit. She got it. Maybe they'd both crack wide open if he fell and she tried to catch him, but oh my God. She wanted to be the one to break his fall.

Damn it.

Damn it. Damn it. Damn it. Damn it.

Jamie was dating Liz, and she was on her way to Spencer, and *now* was not anywhere near the right time for—for—these *feelings*. Not halfway between Chicago and L.A. with him almost killing himself while spray-painting his version of the White Sox logo on a half-buried Cadillac. And certainly not ten years after her teenaged self went down this road only to have him slam on the brakes before they got past their first kiss.

Nope. Nope, nope, nope, nope, *nope*. You don't just fall for someone in a single moment of time. A millisecond doesn't even qualify as a moment, does it?

This was not part of the plan.

Damn it, James Van Der Beek Kingston. What the hell are we supposed to do now?

Chapter Sixteen

Jamie had planned to drive one more hour through Amarillo and on to Adrian, Texas, the true midway point between Chicago and L.A. But they needed gas. And food. With Brynn sleeping the whole way from Tulsa he hadn't stopped, not until Cadillac Ranch. Now the truck's gas light was on, and his stomach was growling. He was pretty sure he heard Brynn's stomach protest as well, but she was quiet in the passenger seat, which, for an awake Brynn, was on the strange side.

"How about we eat, find a gas station, and then get back on the road for one more hour? I have a reservation at a Holiday Inn just outside Adrian."

Brynn didn't answer at first, so he pulled into the first restaurant parking lot he saw, the Coyote Bluff Café. He didn't need any convincing that this small white shack of a restaurant was the right place for him. The green frame of one window was painted with the word BURGERS. The other said BEER. Jamie nudged her and said, "Food," and Brynn snapped into focus from wherever it was she had been.

"Yeah," she said absently. "Sounds good."

Brynn squinted at the sign, then looked at him.

"Cash only," she said, and Jamie groaned as his eyes found what hers had already seen, a sign on the door that confirmed her words.

He put the truck in park anyway and hopped out, slamming the door behind him. He paced a couple of times, muttering to himself as he threw his arms in the air. He would have found an ATM first if he knew burgers and beer could only be obtained with actual bills in his wallet.

His stomach growled again. This had to be a joke. Or maybe some new reality show that followed unsuspecting road-trippers who were out of cash to see if they could MacGyver their way to a free meal. On one of his paces back toward the truck, he saw Brynn had gotten out, too, so he made his way over to her side where she leaned against the passenger door.

"Any cash left from when we filled up in Tulsa?"

Jamie shook his head. "Not enough for *both* of us to eat." He pulled a quarter out of his pocket. "Heads I eat. Tails you do."

She narrowed her eyes, and this at least let him ease into a smile. Whatever had gotten under her skin at Cadillac Ranch seemed forgotten. He'd wanted to ask her about it, but she seemed so lost in thought when he hopped off the roof of the car that he was afraid to disturb her. It was like one of those days in late March when he'd bring her lunch so she could eat while working, always in the zone as it got close to filing Annie's taxes for Two Stories. When she fixated on something, it was as if Brynn were in a parallel universe, existing on another plane. Physically, she was there. But mentally, she was unreachable. Somehow she would still be able to eat whatever he brought her, even if it involved chopsticks, but other than that, she was aware of one thing only—her spreadsheets and tax programs.

That's what the ride to town had been like, though Jamie was pretty sure she wasn't doing taxes in her head. She was back now, and that's what mattered. He had someone to commiserate with him in his insatiable hunger that would not be filled at the Coyote Bluff Café.

He tossed the coin. "I'll take heads."

Brynn pushed off the side of the car, reaching to catch the coin before he did.

"Let's just get gas and find an ATM first, Mr. Hangry," she said, but they were both distracted from the task at hand when a crowd of people poured out of the shack and took up residence in the dusty dirt of the parking lot. Jamie blinked and did a double take, not sure how the amount of people that just exited the building before him could have possibly fit inside unless the Coyote Bluff Café had the same properties as a circus clown car.

There were hoots and hollers as the door swung open again, and Jamie and Brynn watched as a woman with long auburn hair and even longer denim-clad legs emerged onto the small wooden step. In addition to her formfitting jeans, a white halter tank top pulled tight across her, well, the only way he could describe her breasts was huge. They were, in fact, probably the biggest tits Jamie had ever seen, and he'd seen his share. But in his experience, breasts that size weren't usually so…buoyant…in a top that clearly made wearing a bra impossible. Even Jamie knew that.

"For fuck's sake, James." Brynn was next to him now, and she knocked her hip into his. The tone of her voice told him the gesture was one of reprimand rather than something playful.

"What?" he whisper-shouted, feeling like they were intruding on whatever the spectacle before them was.

"You know they're not real, right?"

"How do they do that?" he asked, unable to look away

but knowing he should. "I mean, it's like they're floating."

Brynn backhanded him in the gut, and he caught her hand. On instinct he kept hold of it and then, for no explainable reason, threaded his fingers with hers and squeezed. Her hand flexed and then relaxed into his, and he felt that weird shift between them again, though what direction it went he had no idea.

"Y'all ready?" the woman yelled, and that's when Jamie noticed what else set her apart from the crowd other than her — halter. She was wearing a veil, and in her raised hand was a small bouquet of white roses.

"Are we crashing a wedding?" Brynn asked under her breath.

"I think we are."

And then the bride turned her back on the crowd and tossed.

Maybe if she'd been a righty, things would have gone differently. Or maybe if Jamie had parked on the other side of the lot, they could have just gotten back in the truck and sneaked away and found a freaking ATM or a restaurant that took debit cards.

But Jamie hadn't parked on the other side of the lot, and the well-endowed bride was a lefty who tossed the bouquet just kitty-corner enough that it bypassed the three women, who seemed to be in a game of tackle football, and now resided in Brynn's free hand.

In a flurry of motion the two were whisked inside the café with the momentum of the crowd, the place obviously closed for the wedding party's exclusive use. They eyed the small buffet of Texas barbeque, and then they eyed each other and grinned.

Jamie grabbed a paper plate and handed it to Brynn. Then he grabbed one for himself.

"Now," he said. "*Now* we're crashing a wedding."

They still had no cash, but that didn't matter.

The food was delicious.

. . .

Angie and Dean were the lucky couple, and they welcomed them to their celebration with open arms, the whole crowd too nice or too liquored up to care when they realized Jamie and Brynn were strangers.

Speaking of liquored up, this wedding clan sure as shit knew how to party. Brynn could hold her own with a few beers. Hell, even with a shot or two of Jack thrown in. But they were in Texas now, and the Coyote Bluff Café had ten kinds of tequila behind the small bar, which meant this wedding party was getting ten kinds of plastered.

Brynn stared at Jamie who shook his head slowly at her, but his grin stood at odds with the gesture. Did he want her to do this shot or no?

She lifted the small glass, and someone at the table shouted, "She's going for number three!" The bride and groom joined in, clapping as everyone cheered her on.

Was this really her third shot? Because she felt fine. Totally fine. She felt great, actually. She realized now that Jamie's smile was more of a smirk, challenging her. And she wanted to smack that smile off his face—if smacking meant licking it.

Wait. Did she just think about *licking* Jamie's face?

That was enough for her to throw back the potent liquid without another thought. If this *was* her third shot, it would be enough to wipe out all tendencies to lick or even think about licking the man sitting across from her. When she slammed the glass on the table, everyone cheered again, and she searched for her lime. When she tilted her head up, her eyes met Jamie's.

"Looking for something?" he asked. The rest of the party's attention had gone back to the bride and groom who were getting ready to cut their cake, and Jamie and Brynn had a rare moment of privacy at a table full of strangers.

"My…" But then she saw his hand, palm up on the table, her lime wedge resting in it. He raised his arm and changed his grip so he was pinching the fruit between his thumb and forefinger, and he reached it toward her mouth.

Her teeth pierced the lime's flesh, and then she sucked. Jamie's finger rested on the corner of her mouth, and on the other side, his thumb. She could almost taste his skin if not for the sweet bitterness of the lime. Before he lingered at her lips too long—and really any amount of time was too long—she gripped his wrist and pushed it away as she released his offering from her lips.

"Foggy," she said, and Jamie's brow furrowed. "S'foggy in my head," she explained and hoped he'd be able to translate whatever she was thinking into something that made sense. "You gonna drink that?" she asked, and reached for the full shot sitting on the table in front of him.

With blinding speed he downed the shot himself—completely ignoring the lime.

"You, Sleepy B, have had enough."

"Jean," she said.

"Who's Jean?"

She shook her head. "I'm not Sleepy B, silly."

Jamie chuckled. "I'm sleepy," he said, his voice soft and warm, like Brynn could snuggle into it.

"Mmmm…" she said. "I wanna snuggle with your voice."

Wait. What?

"You're hammered," he said, laughing again.

"You're screwed," Brynn countered, and then she laughed so hard she snorted. "Do you get it? Hammered and screwed? Now someone just needs to get nailed."

More snorting ensued as Jamie's eyes widened. She *was* hammered. Plastered. Screwed. Nailed. All of it—three sheets to the wind plus a pillowcase and maybe a duvet. She knew because even with her glasses on, Jamie was fuzzy around the edges. She *knew* because she didn't normally say things about snuggling with his voice, and she certainly didn't have a habit of sucking fruit from between his fingers and wanting to devour him in the process.

So this was how it was going to be from here on out? Alcohol working as some sort of truth serum? Well, she was going to do something about that, and by something she apparently meant vomiting out more truth.

"James?" she asked, doing her best to fake composure. Because this was important.

"Sleepy *Jean*."

He nodded, seeming proud of his ability to overcome his own tipsiness to call her by the correct nickname.

"I think you should know that, mostly against my will, there were a couple of times in the past two days when I maybe, kind of, probably thought you were sexy."

Good Lord. She was Mr. freaking Darcy.

"Wait," she said. "I didn't mean it like that."

Jamie leaned back in his chair and crossed his arms. Oh crap. While Brynn apparently couldn't fake composed to save her life, Jamie had just done his best version of measured calm with a tiny dash of smug. He was eating this up.

His eyes raked over her, and his grin stretched wide. But he didn't say anything, not for several seconds.

"You," he finally replied as he leaned across the table, his voice deep yet noticeably unsettled, "are the sexiest woman I know."

She stared at him. Speechless. This was the part where she was supposed to ask how he could say that to her when he was dating someone else. But the tequila wasn't making her wish for that kind of honesty. Instead she smiled and tried to ignore how shallow her breathing seemed to be. But with each inhale, the oxygen in the restaurant grew thinner.

She grabbed her bouquet and stood up.

"I need some air."

Brynn's pushing away from the table did not go unnoticed.

"Y'all leaving us already?" This came from Angie, the bride, who proved to be as sweet as her boobs were huge.

"I think so," Jamie said, answering for Brynn as he joined her in standing. "But thank you for everything."

Brynn nodded in agreement with Jamie's sentiments, and after a flurry of hugs and thank-yous and pats on the back, they were out the door.

The only difference between being in the Coyote Bluff Café and outside of it was that now Brynn was drunk in broad daylight.

"Maybe we should stay here tonight?" Her statement came out as a question, the three shots of tequila—and whatever else came before that—giving her the liquid courage she had hoped for. Because finding Jamie sexy wasn't the only thought she needed to get off her chest. She had to tell Jamie about her Cadillac Ranch epiphany.

But even in her state she couldn't help thinking how shitty it would be to tell a guy who was in a good relationship, one that seemed to make him happy, that you might be in love with him.

Oh shit. Oh shit. Oh shit. Was she in *love* with him? That was the epiphany—her *feelings*. Now wasn't the time to figure out what she felt. Not when she ran the risk of saying it out loud.

"Saying what out loud?" Jamie asked, and Brynn wanted to strangle her internal monologue for going all external on her.

She started walking down the sidewalk, swaying as she

passed a small strip of retail shops. Jamie kept pace with her.

"I *am* hammered," she finally said.

Jamie slung his arm around her shoulder, steadying her into his side.

"I'm not in any condition to drive. That's for sure," he said.

Oh, how she wanted to burrow into him and take in his scent while she had him this close. But wanting to smell him and lick him and tell him things that he probably didn't want to hear—this was not part of the plan. And Brynn liked plans, especially when everything went according to them.

But everything she thought about this week had just gone topsy-turvy, and only part of that was because of the tequila.

"We'll lose our reservation," Jamie said. "And they might charge me for the night anyway because of the online discount code I used. It was kind of an all or nothing type deal." They were supposed to stay in Adrian, Texas, tonight, a town about an hour west and the true midpoint of Route 66. But waiting out their inebriation would mean getting on the road after dark.

"You're right," Brynn blurted. "It's a dumb idea. We'll just go when you're good to drive. I just—I don't know—I kinda like this place is all."

And then he dropped his arm from her shoulder and did that thing again where he linked his fingers with hers. They'd done it before, hundreds of times, but it all felt different today, and she found herself trying to read something into a gesture that had always been second nature for them.

"I kinda like this place, too," he said.

That's when the first raindrop pelted Brynn in the back of the head. At least that's what she thought it was, but with one hand in Jamie's and the other gripping what he was calling her lucky bouquet, she couldn't check to see if it was water or something worse, like some sort of karmic bird making her pay for the free barbeque and tequila. But then Jamie's free hand flew to the back of his neck where he wiped away what was clearly a drop of water.

And then it was pouring, the truck that now neither of them could drive was in one direction while they ran in another, seeking shelter in the first place they could find. After a couple of blocks, someone beckoned to them from the screen door of a house, and neither questioned the other as they sped up the sidewalk and under the roof of the covered porch.

"Look at you kids," an older man said from inside the opened door. "You're soaked. Come in and dry off, at least until the storm passes."

They didn't argue. Despite the warm desert air, the quick burst of rain had quickly chilled her to the bone, and when they got inside, a plump woman with chin-length gray hair approached her with an afghan and draped it over Brynn's shoulders. Then the woman's hand went to her chest as she inhaled, swelling with a smile.

"Frank, look. They're newlyweds. No one's booked the cottage for tonight…"

Frank, tall and lanky but for his paunch of a belly, scratched the back of his salt and peppered head and then clapped his hands together as if just then realizing what his wife had said.

"The cottage! Of course, Dora." Frank turned back to the soaked and hammered Brynn and Jamie. "Let it be our wedding gift to you two."

Brynn's brows pulled together. She was still shivering, which made it harder for her to focus on the conversation. Okay, the alcohol might have had something to do with her focus as well. When she looked at Jamie, his hair dark with rainwater and his black T-shirt plastered to his form, he shrugged and half whispered, "Lucky bouquet."

Oh my God. This was no karmic bird shitting on her head. It was a karmic joke, this lovely couple who seemed to be the proprietors of a B&B were offering them a room as a wedding gift. For their *wedding*. Because obviously, a girl in a white shirt and jeans holding a bouquet in one hand while her other was linked with the man's next to her *must* be a bride.

"What do you think, sweetie?" Jamie asked, and a feeling of sheer terror shot through her. He was playing along.

"I…" Her mouth hung open. "We had that reservation in Adrian," she started, and Dora tsked before waving the idea away.

"Y'all are not driving to Adrian in this." She gestured outside. "We don't get much rain around here, but when the sky decides to open up, she gives us everything she's got."

Brynn couldn't argue there. She'd never expect Jamie to drive in this even if he did sober up, and a free night in Amarillo would make up for the charge Jamie would most likely incur for canceling his reservation so late. Brynn rationalized that they wouldn't be taking advantage of this nice couple since karma would win out in the way of them still paying for a room, even if it wasn't the one they were staying in.

"Come on in the kitchen, and we'll fill out some minor paperwork before we get you checked in. And this is a community residence, so don't be shy around us." Dora nodded to Brynn's hand, still resting in Jamie's. "I remember what it was like when we first got married. Couldn't keep our hands off each other. A little kiss here or there won't get anyone's panties in a bunch."

Dora smiled, and Brynn forced her expression to mirror the other woman's despite the fact that she'd just said the word *panties*. But Dora didn't move or say anything after that. She just—waited. And when Brynn's eyes locked on Jamie's, she saw that his were wide with recognition.

It had been ten years. Ten years and five months, but who

was counting?

Brynn. Brynn was counting. Because it had been ten years and five months since she had thought she was going to kiss one boy but ended up kissing another. And here she was, about to do it again.

She pulled the afghan tighter, but the shaking wasn't caused by her cold, wet clothes. Not even by the tequila still coursing through her blood. In fact, she wasn't shaking at all.

She was trembling.

Chapter Seventeen

He could do this. For a free room, and probably a really nice one at that, he could give Brynn a quick peck and be no worse off. He did it all the time. Sure, it was usually on the forehead or the cheek, but this didn't have to be any different just because they were playing bride and groom and had enough tequila and beer in them to last the rest of the evening.

He just had to stop thinking about it. Because they had a small audience now as some of the other guests started filing toward the door to see what the fuss was all about. An audience waiting for a show from the newlyweds, and they were failing miserably at playing the part.

Yet he hadn't forgotten Brynn's admission—finding him sexy on more than one occasion, which meant not just today and not just because of the alcohol.

Damn, even in his state he was still hesitating, still trying to figure her out before he made any sort of move. He had to stop worrying about what would happen when he hit the ground and just fucking leap already.

So he did.

It was meant to be quick. They'd pass it off as being shy in front of the onlookers. He even half expected Brynn to flinch when he lowered his head toward hers, deer in headlights as she was. But she raised her chin, a tacit agreement that they were going to do this. A wet curl was plastered to her cheek, and he hooked a finger under it, tucking it behind her ear.

She shivered as his hand came to rest on her neck. It had to be from the cold. But the hair that stood on end on Jamie's arms? That had nothing to do with temperature. There was no turning back now that he could feel the warmth of her breath on his face. And when he leaned in to make contact, he heard her breath hitch, and he was sure of one thing—this kiss was going to ruin him.

The first thing he felt was water. Brynn's hair was so wet, it was dripping down her face, her bottom lip catching the most recent drop, and Jamie had to steel himself not to flick out his tongue and lick it right off. This was his best friend, the girl he had loved since he was sixteen, and she was on her way to another man regardless of any admissions she made under the influence. His mouth would stay closed, and closed it was when he kissed the girl he pushed away so many years ago.

It was Brynn who did the unthinkable. She returned the kiss, soft and sweet. But when she should have pulled away, taken a bow because *Show's over, folks*, she parted her lips instead and waited for him to join her for what must be the grand finale.

He only had so much resolve, and she had cracked right through it.

Yep, this was going to ruin him, but he was going to enjoy the short ride while it lasted.

Jamie's tongue dipped inside where it met hers, and damn it if she didn't let out a little moan. His eyes flew open long enough to see her drop the bouquet to the floor, and then her arms were around his neck, and she was kissing him like she did that night on her couch senior year, but this wasn't seventeen-year-old Brynn emerging from a fever haze. This was grown-up Brynn, a woman who knew exactly what she was doing and who, with each flick of her tongue against his, was taking his long-protected heart and trampling it to dust. Everything he wanted—everything he'd been afraid to want for ten fucking years—was in his arms right now.

It was the applause and catcalls that reminded him that what was probably the biggest moment in his life was being shared with a group of total strangers, and the two of them parted.

Brynn's cheeks were flushed. Her chin was pink from where his stubble had scratched her skin, and Jamie held his breath for the second it took for her expression to register. She was biting back a smile.

"Hooo-ey!" Frank yelled, clapping his hands together. "Now that's what I call just married." He grabbed Dora by the hand and tugged her close. "After I get these two to the cottage room, I'm gonna remind you that we used to kiss like that."

He gave her a quick peck and then smacked her on the ass, and Dora yelped with laughter.

"Don't you kids have any luggage?"

Jamie ran a hand through his still-damp hair and sighed, reality interrupting fantasy once again.

"We were taking a walk. Left the truck down the road at the Coyote Bluff Café."

Frank's gaze left Jamie's as he glanced outside.

"Should blow over in a few if you want to wait it out. Or I could give you a lift. Was just thinking you might want to get out of those wet clothes. There are robes in the room."

He raised his eyebrows at Jamie who stole a glance at Brynn.

"I'm freezing, Jamie. I'd love a hot shower…"

She trailed off, and he wasn't sure how to proceed. Of course he couldn't drive the truck back here, but what was the other option? Pacing their room in his soaked clothes, waiting for Brynn to warm up and say something about that kiss? Or did she want some time to herself, to remind herself why she was on this trip in the first place—to once and for all make things happen with Spencer Matthews?

"We've uh..." Jamie started, and Brynn hiccupped and then giggled where she stood.

Frank nodded. "Ahhh...of course. You two have been celebrating. If you give me your keys, the wife and I will grab it for you. You don't want to leave it unattended overnight."

Jamie opened his mouth to protest, but Dora cut him off.

"We insist," she said. "Now you two go get warmed up."

"Thank you," Jamie said, then turned to Brynn. "How about you go have that shower, and I'll wait here for the truck and our stuff?"

She nodded and let out a shaky breath, and Jamie knew he'd chosen wisely—deciding to hang back and give her some space.

"I'll get the bride to her room before we leave, and then we'd love to have you join us and the other guests for dinner at seven. Frank's chili is the best in Amarillo, and I've got my blueberry cobbler for dessert. Say you'll join us. All included in the newlywed package."

Dora winked, and Jamie didn't know if he should wink back, if there was a private joke he was a part of but didn't know the punch line yet. Instead he deferred to Brynn again, and she shrugged and nodded.

"We'd love to, Dora. Thank you. My name is Brynn, by the way." She held out her hand to shake Dora's. "And that's Jamie." Jamie smiled when Brynn pointed to him. "Thank you so much for taking good care of us."

Dora threw her hand over Brynn's shoulder and started

leading her away from the entrance. "Sure thing, honey. A lot of newlyweds come through here, but they're not all the real deal. I know the real deal when I see it, and it warms my heart to play a tiny part in you two starting your new life together."

It must have been Jamie Dora had her eyes on during that kiss because yeah, that *was* the real deal. It was Brynn who was putting on the stellar performance, wasn't she? Sure she was drunk, but that kiss felt too real. In her inebriated state, was she finally starting to *see*?

· · ·

Brynn didn't pace. Wild gesticulation—that was her thing. But this pacing? This frenetic energy made it impossible for her to stay in one spot, let alone concentrate enough to get out of her wet clothes and into the shower that just minutes ago was the only thought that kept her jelly legs from collapsing underneath her.

But now that she was alone, her only thought was that kiss—Jamie's lips on hers like he was claiming her. What the hell kind of performance was that? Because that's what it was, right? Jamie was with Liz. Even if he wasn't, he had pushed her away the last time this happened, and she'd made him swear to never talk about it again. He had yet to make a real commitment to any woman, insisting his indefinite bachelor status meant he'd never end up like his parents did, and maybe she'd always taken a secret comfort in watching him stay unattached. But Liz—she'd lasted longer than the rest, and Jamie seemed happy. Maybe this was it. Maybe Brynn had realized too little too late, and that show they put on in the entryway of this adorable B&B, where a garden apparently exploded in the aptly named Garden Cottage, was just a show. A drunk, silly show.

Her phone buzzed and she jumped, having forgotten it

was in her back pocket. Thank God for her waterproof case.

It buzzed again as she pulled it out, and she stared at the two text notifications before she opened them up and read.

Spencer: *I was just thinking about you. Are you on the road? Will I see you before the launch?*

Jamie: *Truck's here. Be there in a minute.*

Brynn let out an exasperated sigh, wishing she could flip-flop the names that went with the texts. But Jamie didn't say things like that to her: *I was just thinking about you.* He was thinking about the truck. And she—she was still thinking about that kiss.

A knock sounded on the door.

She lost her footing and staggered back, catching herself against the floral bedspread of the Garden Cottage bed.

It's just Jamie out there, she told herself. *I can do this—whatever this is.*

Her free hand fisted the bed covering while the other threatened to crush her phone.

So she let it drop from her hand as she took a deep breath and moved toward the door. When she opened it, Jamie stood there, his blue eyes a gray storm of emotion, a look she'd never seen on him before.

"I wasn't pretending, B." He let out a long breath while Brynn seemed to hold hers. "I don't know what that means, but if it means anything to you at all, please…tell me."

She let herself exhale, a trembling release of breath, but she felt light-headed nonetheless.

She hadn't been pretending. *He* wasn't pretending, either.

The boy who called her Sleepy Jean. The man who claimed her with his kiss.

She stared at him, at his questioning eyes, at the bags on

the ground beside his feet. Yep. The bags would definitely have to wait.

She touched the tips of her fingers to her own lips and then to his. He kissed them, but that was it. He was waiting for her.

There was something she had to ask him. Something important, but she couldn't remember now. The only thought in her head after his admission was, *God, how long we have waited.*

She slid her hand higher, her palm resting on his cheek, yet he remained still. He said the words, and now she had to respond.

And then Brynn Chandler rose on her toes and kissed Jamie Kingston.

No audience, no pretense, and certainly no lucky bouquet.

She hooked her finger in the belt loop of his jeans and pulled him over the threshold, pushing the door shut behind him.

"I wasn't pretending, either."

Chapter Eighteen

Brynn's finger was still attached to his belt loop, and Jamie was feeling dizzier by the second. He looked down at her hand and then into her glassy brown eyes behind her lenses.

"You...you weren't pretending?"

He felt it in the kiss, enough to give him the balls to say the words. But now he needed to hear her say it again. And maybe one more time after that.

She bit her lip and shook her head as her finger curled tighter on his pants.

"Look," she said, then nodded toward the ice bucket on the dresser. "Dora grabbed it on the way to the room."

Champagne. Because they were newlyweds, of course.

"We should toast," she said. "To...a change of plans!"

She was too adorable when she was excited, and shit... was she really excited about him? About them? What about how she felt a week ago? Jamie didn't want to go back to that night, to him throwing open his office door and finding Brynn straddling another man in his fucking chair.

Pain ripped through him at remembering the sight, and

he tried to shut it out, because he was not going to let one stupid memory ruin what was about to happen.

She handed him the champagne.

"Are you sure?" he asked, and she nodded.

Brynn yelped with laughter as he popped the bottle open, and Jamie thought there was no better sound, especially when that smile was for him. Two plastic flutes sat next to the ice bucket, and he filled them with the sparkling liquid.

"To a change of plans," he said, handing her one.

"To a change of plans."

They tapped the glasses together and then sipped. At least Brynn sipped. Jamie drained his, sure that everything happening right now had to be some sort of alcohol-induced hallucination. Too perfect and too right, he didn't want to take a chance they'd break the spell. As if she read his thoughts, Brynn followed suit, emptying her glass, too, giggling when she pulled it from her lips.

And that was all he could think about after that—her lips and what it would be like to taste them again.

"I really wasn't alone in that kiss, was I?" she asked. "That was both of us. And I've never felt...I never...I mean, what are we even doing?" She threw her hands in the air, her right one clocking Jamie in the chin. "Shit!"

Jamie swiped a finger over the scratch, but he was laughing. He knew if they crossed this line he'd end up getting hurt. He just hadn't anticipated she'd actually draw blood.

"Oh my God, my ring. Jamie, I'm sorry." But the champagne still had a hold on her, and she let out another giggle. "I'm, like, dangerous around you."

He dabbed at the skin with the hem of his T-shirt. The wound was superficial, the location right where she'd gotten him with the letter opener months earlier.

"Can we try to keep the stabbings to only one a year?" he asked, and she groaned.

"Maybe you should run while you still have the chance."

He shook his head. "No way, Sleepy Jean. I'm exactly where I want to be."

She touched him, gently this time, a hand on his chest. And though his shirt was damp and cold, heat radiated from her palm and through his veins. How had he ever thought he could be okay with just her friendship? And what would he do now if he lost it? He'd lose her forever.

Right now, though, in this room and with the magic that was Amarillo and tequila and lucky bouquets, she was his.

"Maybe you should kiss it and make it better." He touched his chin again, and his fingers came away clean.

Brynn mirrored his action, but her skin was like satin compared to his own rough touch. And the heat, again he felt it from the pit of his stomach to the nerve endings in his fingers and toes. He felt everything when she touched him, and when her lips took the place of her hand, all reason went out the window.

"Like this?" she asked, her voice breathy and sweet and like nothing he'd ever heard from any other woman.

His eyes fluttered shut. "Yes."

"And this?"

He opened his eyes to watch as, standing on her toes, she peppered his neck with kisses.

"Mmmm-hmmm."

He raked his fingers into her hair, and she looked up at him.

"You know we're going to see each other naked, right?" Jamie chuckled.

"It's kind of what I hoped."

"What if you laugh?" she asked.

"I won't laugh."

"What if *I* laugh?" she asked, her cheeks growing pink, and shit she was adorable when she was nervous.

He took off his shirt, and Brynn sucked in a sharp breath.

They'd seen each other at the beach. This wasn't anything new. And yet it was miles away from the boundaries of friendship.

"You're not laughing," he said, and she shook her head. He liked seeing her speechless. He liked being the one to *make* her speechless. "Now you," he told her, his voice gentle as he tried to ease them both into the unknown.

Her fingers fidgeted with the top button of her shirt, but she couldn't quite get it open. Jamie's hands covered hers, steadied them, and they undid the buttons together. She let the open garment fall from her shoulders, and there she stood, the cream lace of her bra against the flushed pink of her otherwise pale skin.

Jamie wasn't laughing, either. In fact, he had to remind himself to breathe so he had enough oxygen to formulate any sound at all, because her hands moved to the front clasp of her bra, and yep. He still wasn't breathing.

"What?" she asked, pausing to look at him.

He pulled her hands down to her sides before she completed her task.

"You don't want me to…" she started, but he shook his head.

"Seventeen-year-old me is out of his mind with how long he's wanted to touch you like this. He needs a second to collect himself."

Brynn giggled, but he didn't consider this laughing. It was sweet and sexy, and he inhaled slowly, preparing himself for everything that would follow this next moment. She took his hands in hers and placed them on her breasts, her nipples peaking against the lace, and Jamie felt his erection strain against his jeans as his heart hammered beneath his ribs.

"Are you sure?" he asked, bringing his hands to her cheeks. He may have had as much as she did to drink, but he knew enough to ask this question. "I don't want this to be something you regret later."

Her eyes met his in a moment of clarity, and she nodded.

"Yes, Jamie. Yes. I want this. I want *you.*" She clasped a hand around his wrist, directing his palm to the spot between her breasts, where the last barrier separated him from seeing her as his best friend and oh-so-much more. "You do it," she said, and he did—flicked open that clasp and pushed the lace cups away from her skin.

Forget logic or sobriety or collecting himself because instinct and need and ten years of loving this girl took over.

He rasped out a breath as he dipped his head into the crook of her neck where he kissed and nipped. Brynn responded with a soft hum as she arched into him, pressing her breasts against his chest as his arms encircled her, and he led her to the bed.

"There are a *lot* of flowers in this room," he remarked as he eyed the bedspread, the wallpaper, and even the curtains.

"Garden Cottage," she said, pulling him down to her as she fell flat on her back.

"Noted," he said, looming over her on all fours. "You're perfect."

"Jamie…"

"You're beautiful."

"Jamie…"

"I'm in love with you, and I just thought you should know."

He didn't let her respond, because he wasn't ready to hear it either way. If she loved him, too, he supposed that would ease the tiny voice in his head that kept telling him to ask the question, like why she was heading to L.A. if that was the case. If she didn't love him, and he knew that was a possibility, he didn't want her to say anything she didn't mean just to protect him. Instead he leaned down, flicked his tongue against her nipple, and then sucked. She gasped.

First her hands fisted the bedspread, but then she ran a palm up his thigh. He groaned against her as the tip of her thumb grazed his balls, aching against the denim of his jeans. She palmed his erection, and he hissed in a breath as he kissed a trail from one breast to the other, licking and nipping and sucking the left as he had the right.

Brynn's hands worked at his button and then the zipper. She pulled the hem of his boxer briefs over his tip, swirling her finger in the wetness.

"Jesus, Brynn." Something about all of his nicknames for her didn't fit. Those were the endearments of a friend, but this—this wasn't friendship. They were in undefined territory.

• • •

Brynn stared at the beautiful man in front of her, his blue eyes dark with need. She stroked his erection from root to tip, feeling him pulse in her palm, and she knew she loved him. This beautiful, infuriating, stubborn man who could have had her ten days ago—hell, ten *years* ago—if he hadn't been so damn careful with his own heart. Didn't he know she'd never hurt him? Didn't he know, in one way or another, she'd loved him for more than half her life? He didn't have to protect his heart anymore, now that he'd trusted it to her.

She was ready to tell him, the words poised to spill from her lips: *I love you, too.* But then he did that thing with her breast, and her brain went to mush, and she was just happy she could remember her own name. So she followed the direction of her body, letting her actions do the talking for now. There'd be time after to explain, to apologize for not knowing sooner that it was him. It was always him, and she almost let him get away.

She pushed him gently to his back and removed the rest of his clothing.

"Oh my God," she managed, and he chuckled. "Shouldn't you have a beer gut or something?"

She didn't wait for an answer. Instead she sent her jeans to meet his on the floor, leaving her lace bikinis on until they were ready for that final step. She straddled him, slid up his thighs, and rubbed against his shaft until she cried out, the agony exquisite and at the same time almost too much.

Is this what sex was supposed to be like? Hadn't she been in love before? Or was her love for Jamie what intensified the experience? The thought scared the crap out of her, but his thumb pressed on her swollenness. Her eyes rolled back, and she arched into his touch.

Jamie slipped a finger through the side of Brynn's panties and plunged inside her. She gasped and slid to her side next to him, giving him a more advantageous angle and sending her very near to the edge.

She faced him, stroked him again, and he crushed his lips to hers. Nothing about their movements now was careful. Every touch and kiss spoke of insatiable need.

Two fingers were in her, pulsing before they slid out and around her clit. She writhed against his hand, her body begging him not to stop and at the same time lamenting that this soon would end.

"Is this really happening?" he asked in a low whisper. He entered her again, and she gasped.

"Yes," she whimpered. "It's real," she added, begging him to understand what she meant, what she had yet to say. "Jamie, I…"

But he stopped her again with his mouth, the kiss deep and slow as she rode his hand until she thought she might burst at the seams.

"I'm on the pill," she said, knowing he'd seen her swallowing the oral contraceptive last night yet never saying a word about what that meant for her intentions with Spencer. *Shit.* Spencer. She'd deal with that later. Right now she *needed* Jamie.

His fingers dove deeper, and she shuddered against him.

"Now, Jamie. For the fucking love of God, get inside me now."

He smiled against her and slid his hand out of her panties, helping her wriggle free of them. She didn't wait another second. Instead she straddled him and slid up his length, this time unfettered by the thin lace barrier. She watched his Adam's apple bob as he swallowed. Then she kissed him and urged him inside, buried him to the hilt, and there it was— fireworks, "I'm a Believer"—and her heart cracked wide open for the man she'd been too stupid to know she loved with every fiber of her being.

He rocked inside her, every thrust solidifying that her journey was over. She didn't need L.A., and she wouldn't have to adopt a litter of kittens after all.

The second thought made her laugh quietly.

"What?" he asked, his voice hoarse in her ear.

"You're perfect," she said.

"Brynn…"

"You're beautiful," she added and watched his eyes widen with recognition of what was coming next. He didn't stop her this time. "And I'm in love with you and just thought you should know."

She let him kiss her then, surrendered to him as he rolled her to her back, all the while keeping himself deep inside her. He plunged in and out, slow and achingly sweet, his eyes on her until they both were so close. Jamie's movements picked up momentum, and with his thumb circling her just above where their bodies joined, he made sure she came apart both inside and out. And if the other B&B patrons had any doubt as to their supposed newlywed status, all of it was wiped away as Brynn let out one last cry, and Jamie hissed her name before collapsing against her.

He twitched inside her, and she drew in a breath. Then

he brushed a curl off her cheek and pressed his lips to her forehead. All she could think was *Thank the stars for crashing weddings and October rain in Amarillo.*

"Fine," Brynn finally said when she'd regained the ability to form coherent speech. "It was a lucky bouquet."

And they both began to laugh.

Chapter Nineteen

After slipping back into his almost-dry jeans, Jamie dragged their bags in from the hallway. He'd insisted that Brynn have the first shower. With an hour before they had to show up for their "newlywed" dinner, he wanted her to take her time. Not that he hadn't thought about joining her, but he needed some time to think.

She loved him. There was a sobering thought. She'd made her choice, and he was still wrapping his brain around the fact that it was *him*.

He tried to free her from the obligation of those words, only wanting her to know he wasn't entering this situation lightly, that he'd never let happen what just happened—and, holy shit, did something happen—if he wasn't sure how he felt about her.

He could forgive himself for being a scared teenager, watching what he thought was his parents' perfect marriage dissolve in front of him and not wanting to see him and Brynn go down that road. What he couldn't forgive was holding on to that fear for so long, doubting that he could have meant something to her then—that he meant something to her now.

Neither of his brothers had it easy on the other side. Ben and Theresa separated for six months but were trying to make it work. His mom let it slip that Denny and his wife were in counseling. He got it. Marriage was hard. But he and Brynn were only pretend married. Otherwise, what were they? What did this all mean, this loving each other at the strangest possible time? He wanted to rationalize that it would be easier for them because they were Jamie and Brynn. She was his ridiculous Sleepy Jean, belting Monkees tunes from the shower as he sat on the edge of the bed trying to make sense of it all.

His phone buzzed on the nightstand, and he wasn't sure he was ready to spill the news to Annie if she was texting to goad him again. But when he looked at the screen, he realized it was Brynn's phone he grabbed instead. The screen woke, and though it was locked, he could still see the first line of the text and who it was from.

Spencer: *If you make it by Friday, our room is booked…*

He dropped the phone back on the dresser, face down. This was way out of line. Thinking it was his phone was one thing, but reading any further was definitely another. Obviously she'd been talking to Spencer since the reunion. He couldn't fault her for that.

He tried to swallow back a bitterness rising in his throat. But she was, after all, on her way to him. To Spencer. Who had a room booked for the two of them. Together. And Brynn was on the pill.

He shook his head and groaned.

She said she loved you, asshole.

He had to give her—them—the benefit of the doubt. She could have said what she said because of the whole about-toorgasm thing. Shit. That would suck. But Jamie knew how *he* felt. If she really did love him, that text would prompt her to tell Jamie she was calling things off with Spencer and staying with him for the remainder of the trip. And then they'd go home, together, where they'd figure out the rest.

He flopped back on the bed and closed his eyes, ready to surrender to the utter physical and mental exhaustion that was this trip. When he heard the bathroom door open, he left his eyes closed, not ready to enter reality.

The bed dipped next to him, and he knew she was sitting there, but he waited. Soft lips brushed his collarbone, and he sighed, letting the tension out of his shoulders.

"This is totally weird, right?" Brynn asked, but she didn't wait for him to answer. She just kept kissing his skin, and he thanked himself for not throwing on his shirt. "I mean, I never would have thought I'd be in Amarillo, Texas, doing what we just did…" She was kissing across his chest now, her lips and tongue pausing to pay special attention to a nipple that never saw it coming. Jamie groaned and buried a hand in her wet hair. "And wanting to do it again."

Jamie's eyes flew open.

"Again?"

Brynn lifted her head, her eyes meeting his. She bit her lip, smiled, and raised her brows.

"We have to be downstairs in, like, twenty minutes."

She pressed a firm palm against his zipper. "Are you saying you don't want to?"

Jamie glanced at her hand. "I think it's pretty obvious I want to. But B, I haven't even showered yet." He couldn't believe he was arguing the point, but these people were giving them a free room for a lie they weren't correcting.

She stood then and untied her robe, letting it fall to the floor. Well, then. If this was how she wanted to play, he could get used to these rules.

He got up from the bed, cupped her cheeks in his hands, and teased her with a sweet kiss. Then he skimmed down the length of her body, lowering to his knees as he did.

Her breath hitched. "I was going to say we could kill two birds with one stone if you let me shower with you."

Jamie wrapped his hands around her thighs and looked up at her startled expression.

"Oh, I'm going to let you do all sorts of things to me in the shower, but first…"

He spun her so her back was to the bed, hoping she wouldn't be able to stand much longer. When he leaned forward and swirled his tongue around her clit, he felt her knees buckle as she fell to the mattress. Mission accomplished.

"Do you know how long I've wanted to taste you?" he asked before his tongue plunged deep in her folds, and she writhed against him.

"Oh my God. Jamie."

Oh my God was right. In some way he knew no other woman would measure up to what he tried not to want with her. But now that it was a reality, forget it. He was a ruined man, and he would go down in one hell of a blaze of glory as long as it was Brynn setting the fire.

And yeah, they were going to be late for dinner.

• • •

Thankfully, Texas time worked much differently than Chicago time. Brynn and Jamie made it to the dining room at twenty after seven, and no one was even sitting yet. As soon as he saw him, Frank handed Jamie a bottle of Shiner White Wing, and Jamie beamed at the man.

"You just made a friend for life," Brynn said, laying a hand on Jamie's chest. "My guy here is a brewer."

Frank immediately stole Jamie away to talk beer,

admitting to dabbling in home brewing himself, and Brynn had to collect herself after the whirlwind that took her from kissing her best friend, to the last couple hours in the Garden Cottage, to the words *my guy* falling from her lips like it was the most natural thing to say.

"You got the look, honey."

Dora was next to her now, and Brynn realized she hadn't taken her eyes off Jamie as he walked away with Frank. She turned to the woman next to her.

"What look?" Brynn asked. Maybe Dora could explain to her what she was feeling and how to take in this surge of emotion that was ten years in the making.

"Like you believe he'd lasso the moon for you if you asked him to."

That was the thing. Even before today, she kinda believed he would.

"I probably wouldn't even have to ask," she said, a lump rising in her throat. If a stupid, lucky bouquet hadn't brought them to this house, to strangers insisting that they kiss, would Jamie have done it otherwise? Would she?

As the realization of her feelings settled in, so had something else—something that had wrestled at the back of her thoughts, masked by tequila, adrenaline, lust, and—well—love.

It was guilt. Jamie was in a relationship. *Oh my God*, she thought. *I'm the other woman.*

Her phone buzzed in her pocket, and she excused herself to the hallway to check who it was. Holly. But when she unlocked her screen she saw she had more than one text waiting. Holly was just checking in, but the one before had come from Spencer. She looked at the time of the text and knew that he'd sent it while she was in the shower. Had Jamie heard the notification?

Spencer: *If you make it by Friday, our room is booked at the Sunset Tower, close to the bookstore where we're doing the launch. If you don't get in until Saturday, I'd love you to stay at my place. Looking forward to reconnecting, Brynn.*

"Trying to ditch me already?"

She jumped at the sound of his voice as her phone dropped to the floor. Jamie bent to grab it, but, being lower to the ground already, she beat him. Thank God.

"Everything okay?" he asked as he offered her a hand and pulled her up.

"Yeah. Fine. Everything's fine." She waved her phone, an exaggerated gesture that almost sent the thing sailing to the floor again, but this time she caught it. "Just Holly checking in. I'm gonna text her back to let her know we're headed out tomorrow. Right?"

Jamie eyed her warily and nodded. "Yep. Holbrook, Arizona, tomorrow. Second to last stop before L.A." He took a deep breath and let it out slowly. "Are you sure everything's okay? You know you can tell me anything, don't you?"

"Of course," she said.

There was that lump in her throat again. And the guilt? It blanketed her now. Because not only had she turned Jamie into a cheating man and let alcohol cloud her moral judgment, but she just lied to him, and why? They were in uncharted waters here, and the one person she could talk to about anything was suddenly the person she feared talking to most.

Jamie loved her? If that was how he felt, what was he even doing with someone else? And what the hell was he doing taking her to Spencer? She had fantasized about Spencer Matthews since the beginning of their senior year of high school, and now he had a room for them at what was sure to be some swanky boutique hotel. All she had to do was text him and tell him she wouldn't be making it to L.A. after all, but there should be some sort of discussion with Jamie first. They would have to have *the talk*, the one that used the word *relationship* and *future*. *How could you cheat on the nice doctor who stitched up your chin?* And, holy shit, she needed a minute.

"I'll be right back," she said, and rose on her tiptoes to give him a quick kiss.

Something in his expression fell, but he masked it just as quickly. Not before she noticed, though.

"I'll save you a seat," he said with a smile that didn't quite reach his eyes. Then he turned back toward the dining room.

"Jamie?"

When he turned to face her, eyes expectant, she wanted to tell him everything, to put it all out there—how amazing the day had been and how scared she was for what it meant. She wanted to tell him that Spencer texted and ask him what she should tell him. What should she say to Holly? What would he say to Liz? Was this just the magic of the trip, and Jamie would return to his life when they got home?

What are we now, Jamie?

But fear got the best of her.

"Grab me a beer? I'll be there in a minute."

Not that she needed any more alcohol. She wanted to think clearly now, but it was something natural for her to ask and something he would be happy to do. If anything, it bought her time.

"Sure thing." He didn't smile at all this time, and she let him walk out of the room.

She ignored Spencer's text for now and replied to Holly:

I slept with Jamie and I'm a horrible person because he's with Liz.

Brynn knew better than to head back into the room without waiting three seconds for Holly to reply.

It only took her two.

Holly: *I KNEW IT.*

She couldn't help it. Despite her warring feelings, Holly's response made her giggle.

Brynn: *You did not.*

Holly: *I SO DID, AND YOU KNOW IT.*

Brynn: *Stop yelling at me!*

Holly: *YOU SLEPT WITH JAMIE. I WILL NEVER STOP YELLING.*

Brynn: *I think I might be in love with him.*

Holly: *OF COURSE YOU ARE IN LOVE WITH HIM YOU FREAKING IDIOT.*

Her eyes watered as her laughter continued, and while she was grateful for Holly giving her conscience a momentary reprieve, she had to stifle herself before her emotions got carried away. Her eyes watered when she laughed, but she could feel the torrent building, the threshold where hysterical laughter turned to sobbing tears, and she was one more giggle—maybe two—away from the waterworks.

Brynn: *Did you miss the part about me being a home wrecker? This is a mess with Liz and the trip and Spencer, who still thinks I'm coming, btw.*

Holly: *Does Jamie think you're "coming"? LOL.*

Brynn: *HOLLY.*

Holly: *Okay. Sorry. Home wrecker. So…that part is maybe not so good? But Jamie's relationships always seem to fizzle eventually. Maybe this is just a bigger fizzle?*

Brynn: *I'm a horrible person.*

Her stomach lurched, and she had to look down to see if the floor had dropped out from beneath her. Nope. She was still standing, regaining her balance and perspective. This was not how she wanted to fall in love, the moment—the whole day even—tainted by the fact that what she and Jamie had done would hurt someone else.

Her phone vibrated, but it wasn't a text this time. Holly was calling.

"Hello?" Her voice trembled a little, but it was enough for Holly to recognize.

"You're overanalyzing, big sister." Holly knew her so well. "Maybe things with him and *Elizabeth* aren't that serious."

She let out a bitter laugh. "He's been with her for months, Holl. *Months.* Yet he said he loved *me.*" Her palms were sweating, making it harder to hang on to the phone. She felt a familiar panic, not unlike her behavior in the St. Louis Arch capsule. Except this time she wasn't afraid for her life. She was afraid for her heart.

"God," she continued. "It's not like I'm any better. I'm traveling across the country for one guy, and I just slept with another."

"Hey," Holly said. "You are not a cheater. Whatever

might happen with you and Spencer, it hasn't happened yet. *You* did nothing wrong."

But she had, hadn't she? She knew Jamie was with someone else, yet she let it all happen. And as angry and confused as she was, she couldn't help the way her body reacted to thoughts of what she and Jamie had done less than an hour ago. Yes, she let it happen, but it was the best *happening* she'd experienced. Ever.

Brynn shook her head. "I did," she said, her voice flat.

Holly sighed. "This is you and Jamie, sis. *Jamie*. I know I've given you shit for years, but that's only because nothing is more right than you two. Yes, you may have gotten off to a messy start. But think about what you found today. You've both just been too freaking stubborn to see it."

Or blind, Brynn thought. Quite literally, until this morning. Now that she saw what had been in front of her the whole time, she could only fixate on what it would be like to lose it. But she smiled at the tenderness in Holly's voice, something she knew didn't come easily for her snarky little sister.

"Everything just happened so fast today. I need time to think. I need Jamie to give me some sort of explanation that will make this somehow okay. So…we'll talk, I guess. Right?"

"Atta girl!" Holly said.

Brynn took in a deep breath and let it out slowly. Time to walk into that dining room and face her fake husband/ adulterous lover and a bunch of strangers head on. Piece of crashed-wedding cake.

"Love you, Holl."

"Love you, Brynn. I'm gonna text Annie now and tell her everything."

"Holly, wait!"

But she was already gone.

Chapter Twenty

Jamie sipped his beer slowly and plastered on a smile as Dora scooped a helping of chili into his bowl. The storm had passed, and the evening chill filled the room through opened windows, perfect weather for a warm meal. But Jamie felt chilled to the bone after watching Brynn lie to him.

Maybe it wasn't an out-and-out lie, but it was one hell of an omission. He was positive she was in the hall texting Holly. They'd talked every day of the trip, sometimes more than once. But if she was texting Holly, then she also saw the text from Spencer and said nothing. He would wait her out. It wasn't his place to bring it up and not just because he'd look like a jealous teenager. They were in public — with a bunch of strangers. He'd cut her some slack for that. But Brynn had to make a choice, which meant telling him about Spencer and what she'd decided. When they got back to the room, she'd come clean.

"Thank you," Jamie said, as another guest — a woman his mother's age, maybe — handed him a basket of corn bread.

Brynn walked back in the room, her eyes finding his and,

man, it was hard to hold on to his doubt when she looked at him like that, like she was finally seeing what had been there between them since they met in middle school. Even when he didn't know he loved her like this, he knew their friendship was unlike any other he'd experienced. It took puberty and a bit of wising up for his head to figure out what his heart had known all along. Then it took another decade of thinking he could protect that heart from what it felt right now.

She sat down beside him, and he smelled the clean soap mixed with her skin. All their years giving each other celebrity perfumes and colognes for Christmas, he wasn't sure he knew what *her* scent was before this week. Now his sense memory was all her—the sight of her looking at him in a way that made his heart stop, the touch of her skin against his, the taste of her on his tongue. He felt consumed in a way that brought him to life and at the same time paralyzed him with fear.

The table was buzzing with conversation, which meant he could steal a private moment with Brynn.

"Everything good in Hollyland?" he asked, trying to keep his voice even.

She nodded but didn't say anything. His instinct was to lean in and kiss her, but she backed away. The movement was slight but perceptible enough for him to notice, and doubt reared its ugly head again. After what just happened in their room, this was not a good sign. And, unfortunately, he was starting to believe in signs.

No one else seemed to notice the awkwardness between supposed husband and wife. Instead the group welcomed Brynn to the table, and she smiled at the new faces.

"How long have you two been together?" This came from the corn-bread woman.

"Did you elope?" This from Dora.

Frank chimed in. "Are you going to be making as much of a racket tonight as you did during that storm?"

Jamie was about to swallow a swig of beer but choked it back into the bottle after that one.

He threaded his fingers through Brynn's under the table. When she didn't retract her hand, he took it as encouragement and decided to go for broke.

"Actually," he said, bringing her hand to his lips for a quick kiss, "we met in middle school."

Their table mates *oohed* and *aahed*, and Brynn stayed silent, so Jamie continued.

"She was listening to the Monkees, and I thought she was insane, and that was pretty much it. Best friends ever since."

She didn't smile or squeeze his hand or anything that gave him the thumbs-up. It was like she was waiting for something, so he kept going, wanting her to know not only did he love her now, but it had always been her.

"I was an idiot for a lot of years, but when we were juniors in high school, that's when I fell hard."

"What?" Brynn's voice cracked on the word, and there was no going back now. He was going to lay it all out there because how could he not? "You were with Stephanie Delaney when we were juniors."

Her eyes were wide, and maybe this was too much too soon, but he felt the clock ticking. In two days they'd be in L.A., and what happened then banked on what happened now.

"I wasn't in love with her. It took being with her to realize that I was already *with* the person I loved most. She just didn't know it."

Her eyes welled with tears, and he wasn't sure if that was a good sign or not.

She looked at him, at their small audience, and then at him again. He watched her piece it together, willing her to speak.

"I thought…" she finally said. "*I* asked *you* to kiss me."

He reached for her cheek with his palm.

"No," she said, her voice cracking. "No. We figured it out together. Just like today."

He shook his head. "I figured it out at the reunion," he admitted. He knew they were blowing their cover, but he didn't care. She needed to know everything now. "I tried to tell you, but there were you and Spencer in my office." Her eyes widened, but he kept going. "And I thought I was too late, so this trip was my last chance to tell you how I feel—to see if you might choose me, and—"

She pulled away from his touch. Okay *that* was a bad sign.

He watched her eyes grow distant.

The table was silent, and Jamie now wished he'd saved this conversation for when they were alone in the bedroom disguised as a garden, but he had to make it to the end of his story, or his beer was going to get warm and everyone's chili cold.

"You lied about the trip? About wanting to take me to the book launch?" She trembled as she spoke. "You let me go on about facing my fears, about going after someone else so I could have a chance at the same happiness you found, and the whole time you've been plotting to get me off course? Why wouldn't you just tell me how you felt?"

She pushed her chair from the table and stood.

"I'm sorry, Dora. Frank." Brynn forced a quick smile, then left the room.

Whoa. This was so not going at all where he thought it would. Jamie's brain tried to think of a means for damage control, but all it came up with was *Go after her,* so he did. When he made it to the hallway, Brynn exploded.

"You already messed with my heart once," she admitted. "For a decade I've watched you go through relationship after relationship, and now that you finally realize I'm the one you want, you don't even say anything?" She sucked in a long breath and let it go. It killed him to hear the tremor in that sound. "If I hadn't gotten sick that night ten years ago—if I hadn't asked *you* to kiss *me*—would you ever have told me how you felt? Or was it all bullshit?"

"Hey," he interrupted, anger and pain warring in his tone. "That wasn't bullshit. Jesus, Brynn. I watched you pine for Spencer for a year. You didn't quite give me an opening to spill my heart. And then when you finally did, I was fucking terrified of losing you after I lost my goddamn family. I needed the one thing in my life that was stable, that wouldn't change or pull the rug out from under me. And that was you…my best friend."

She paced as she spoke. "I get that. It took me a long time to understand, but I swear I do. It doesn't change the fact that you broke my heart, Jamie. It doesn't change the fact that you buried those feelings again for ten years, saw me with another guy, and then just *had* to have me even though you were with someone else." She crossed her arms, hugging herself like he wished he was doing. "The secret agenda is one thing, but doing it behind your girlfriend's back? If I hadn't chosen correctly, were you going to go home to her like nothing happened?"

Oh shit. He hadn't told her about Liz. Fucking shit. He thought he was pulling out the big guns, revealing his undying love for her and how long he'd felt this way. Instead he'd just dug himself into one hell of a hole because the way she spat those words at him—the way she saw things—it made him look like one hell of an asshole.

"Brynn." He reached for her hand, and she stepped away. But she couldn't escape his gaze. "*Brynn*." He moved forward and cupped her cheeks, and she squeezed her eyes shut, forcing the first tear to fall. "I broke up with Liz the night of the reunion. I would never— I can't believe you would think that of me. I wasn't thinking clearly, especially after kissing you, or I would have told you before we…" He was starting to panic, the words pouring out of him as fast as they could come, but none of it sounded right. None of it seemed to change the look of betrayal in her eyes. "As for ten years ago, Jesus. I was a fucking kid. A *scared* fucking kid. That's not me anymore." He kissed her forehead. "That's not us." She opened her eyes, and Jamie motioned between them. "*This* is us. Right here. Right now. Everything that's happened today has been real."

She took a step back.

"Real or not, nothing has changed. You've had almost two weeks to tell me how you felt, but instead you're more worried about protecting yourself. You're *exactly* the same guy you were ten years ago. You may be keeping yourself safe from getting hurt, Jamie, but all you're doing is breaking my heart again. I thought I'd made you a cheater. I thought you'd made me a home wrecker." She took in a long breath and let it out. "I *get* how scared you were then. I really do. But this is now. We're adults, and I don't want to play games anymore. What does it matter how we might feel if you can't be honest with me?"

Gasps came from the dining room, proof that what couldn't be seen could still be heard, but the show went on. They were nearing the end of the act, and Jamie knew it was going to be one hell of a climax.

"Brynn, don't."

Then she asked the question she must have been asking herself all afternoon, the same one that gnawed at him every time he tried to analyze their situation.

"If today hadn't happened…if there was no *lucky bouquet*—just like if there was no mono senior year—would we even be having this conversation? Or would we be winding down before the last leg of the journey, before you handed me off to another man?" She swiped at a tear, and his heart sank to his feet, maybe even out of his body and through the floor completely. "The day we left, you told me you were texting Liz good-bye. You wanted me to believe you were still with her, which means you had no intention of telling me you weren't."

Jamie felt the oxygen in the hallway thinning, or maybe Brynn's line of questions had just knocked the air out of him. There was more for him to say, but it was time for the lights to come up. The show was over, folks.

When he hesitated too long before answering her questions, Brynn backed out of the hallway, her hand over her mouth.

"Well, damn, son. You got yourself a fiery little wife there."

Jamie spun to face Frank, Dora standing next to him. He let out a long breath. No more lies.

"We're not married," he said. "That's the woman I've been in love with since I was sixteen, but she's not my wife. She was my best friend up until today, but now we're probably not even that. I'm sorry we took advantage of your kindness. I'll pay for the room, the meals—all of it. I'm just—sorry."

He didn't wait for a response, deciding to wallow in his own self-pity while he looked for Brynn. And because timing was everything, Jamie's phone buzzed with a text.

Annie. Which meant Brynn told Holly everything.

Annie: *Tell me you've got good news!*

He wished he could.

Jamie: *Actually, pretty sure I fucked up. I think I already lost her.*

Annie: *Impossible. I just talked to Holly. That girl loves you. You just need to iron out the wrinkles.*

Jamie: *I know. I love her, too. But that might not be*

enough.

Annie: *Ugh. Such a crock. Love is always enough, because if you love someone then you fight to make it work.*

Jamie smiled at this. He wanted to believe her, and he wanted to fight for Brynn like he should have ten years ago, like he should have ten fucking days ago. But she had to fight for them, too, and he was afraid Brynn had already given up.

Jamie: *Afraid it might be a one-sided battle.*

Annie: *Good. Odds are in your favor, then. Wear her down so she has no choice but to fight back. You could tell her about L.A., you know.*

He ignored that last part. He wasn't going to throw some idiot grand gesture her way now. It would only show he'd been keeping something else from her. Still, Annie's confidence buoyed him enough to continue.

Jamie: *You really believe in this?*

Annie: *For fuck's sake, James. Holly and I already have a deposit on a DJ and a balloon artist for the wedding. There's more riding on this than you think.*

He chuckled—he couldn't help it—and the small release felt good. He could do this. He could wear her down and make her fight back.

Jamie: *You're crazy.*

Annie: *And you're crazy about my best friend, so go*

fix this. Then tell her to text me everything. And I mean everything, James.

He laughed and took that to be the end of the conversation. She was right. It was time to fix this. He just hoped he could.

Chapter Twenty-One

"You didn't exactly make it hard to find you."

Brynn pulled her coat tight across her chest and burrowed into the corner of the bench in the B&B's garden.

"I wasn't exactly hiding. I just needed a minute."

Jamie nodded toward the spot beside her, and she shrugged. She'd only noticed now that he'd abandoned his usual travel attire of a T-shirt and a hoodie for a fitted khaki button-down and dark jeans. A smile tugged at the corners of her lips. He dressed up for her. But then she remembered he lied to her about Liz and his motivation for the trip. And teenaged Brynn let everything she thought she'd tucked away for all those years rise to the surface, and it was all too much.

He sat down, his knee bumping hers, and for a minute they just stared at the small pond in front of them. It was dark now, but the low lights by the water illuminated Jamie's profile, and she peeked at him from the corner of her eye, watching his chest rise and fall.

Even though they'd grown up together, a part of her always saw him as the goofy skater boy from middle school. Never mind that the summer between freshman and sophomore year had been quite the transformation for him, a growth spurt combined with the added muscle mass he'd gained playing volleyball at the beach or pickup baseball games with his buddies. Jamie wasn't a star athlete in high school, but he was good enough to hold his own in any sport he played. He just played for fun rather than to win, something she now saw as kind of noble. And sexy. But she hadn't seen it then, or maybe she hadn't let herself. She realized that hanging on to her initial vision of Jamie's preteen self was *her* safety net. Not noticing him the way other girls did meant she wasn't jealous, didn't feel like she was missing out, because she had the part of him that mattered most.

"Why, Jamie? Why weren't you honest with me?" she asked.

He put his arm across the back of the bench. Not around her, though. For how close they were sitting, both were noticeably trying not to touch, and her stomach twisted.

Too quick. It was all happening too quick, from the intensity of that first kiss to Jamie's profession of a decade-long love, to him admitting he'd only offered to take her to L.A. in the hopes that something would happen between them. She couldn't fault him for wanting what she knew they *both* wanted now. She just couldn't quiet the tiny voice in her head that kept asking the same questions. If circumstances hadn't thrown them together like they did today, what would have happened if they'd made it to Adrian and their room with two separate beds? What if they'd made it all the way to L.A.? Would he have told her then?

Sure, Brynn had an epiphany at Cadillac Ranch, but she also thought Jamie was taken. She rationalized *her* excuse for not speaking up before Frank and Dora asked them to kiss. But Jamie didn't seem to have one other than doubt.

Jamie tilted his head back, and she followed his gaze to

the full moon above them.

"Then or now?" he asked, making a feeble attempt at levity. "Fine," he said, when she didn't respond. "I'll start with then. How was I supposed to compete with the guy who seemingly ticked off everything on your list?" he continued. "Football player: check. Band geek: check. Ace student in every AP class offered and even the ones they didn't?" He looked at her then, and she rolled her eyes. "Don't think I wasn't aware he took Mandarin at the community college. Big, fat, fucking check."

Brynn groaned and threw her hands in the air before standing from the bench. And yes, she poked Jamie in the eye when she did it, but whatever.

"I'm sorry!" The apology was a reflex. This was their dance—Brynn wild with exasperation and Jamie with an injury, most of the time not life-threatening. "But you kind of deserved that." He didn't protest, only wiped the involuntary tear away from his watering eye. "It's not a competition, Jamie."

He laughed, a bitter sound, one she hadn't heard from him before.

"Really? Okay, let's go to almost two weeks ago. I had called it off with Liz and was ready to tell you everything before I walked into my office that night." Her stomach lurched again. "So don't tell me it's not a competition. If you had ever looked at me the way you looked at him, you would have seen right through me. You would have known. It took a Goddamned fever to make you delirious enough to see clearly, and even then it was only because I was there and he wasn't." He leaned forward, his elbows on his knees, and when he looked up at her, her heart staggered a beat. She'd been so focused on her own retroactive hurt that she never thought about it from his perspective, what it must be like to love someone from afar and watch her fall for someone else.

"Do you see it? When you look at me now, do you have

any doubt how I feel?"

She shook her head. Of course she had no doubt. But that didn't change what still ate at her, that he would have let fear keep them from what felt undeniably right if she hadn't opened her mouth and turned a fake kiss into something more real than she'd ever felt before.

"But if my 'delirium'…" Okay, maybe the finger quotes were a little much, but this was the part she couldn't get past. "If I hadn't asked you to kiss me, you would have been some stupid martyr and never told me how you felt? You would have done the same thing this week, letting me believe you were with someone else?"

Jamie raked his fingers through his hair. "You would have gone to that party, and everything would have been different. You would have chosen him."

"You don't know that, Jamie. After that night, I chose you, and *you* pushed *me* away. I know you needed a friend more than anything when your parents were splitting, but I could have been both. I could have been your friend, and I could have been more. But you can't use what happened a decade ago to fuel that same fear now. It's not fair—not to you or to me."

He raked his hand through his hair.

"But you never told me that, B. You never told me how *you* felt."

God. He was right. She'd been plenty vocal about her crush on Spencer a decade ago, and the night of the reunion she'd done everything short of skywriting her intentions to finally act on it. Here she was, casting this blame on him, and she'd done the same thing. Hadn't she? She'd lied to herself, willing her feelings for him to bury themselves somewhere deep, and in doing so, she'd lied to him, too.

Jamie stood with a start, something alight in his eyes, but it didn't comfort her. It scared her. She stepped back when he approached because she wasn't about to let him kiss away the anger and the hurt. She wasn't ready for that, but she knew if his lips got close enough she'd be a goner.

. . .

Damn it. How could he not see it? Ten years ago, ten days ago, three days from now—in every scenario Jamie was the same guy, the interruption to the regularly scheduled program. But he was never, not for Brynn at least, the first choice. He wasn't a choice at all. He was her fallback, the stand-in. She was more than ready to give herself to Spencer in every way until a meddling B&B-owning couple demanded that they kiss. She was right to ask the question. If they hadn't kissed ten years ago—if they hadn't been pressured to put on a show for Dora and Frank—would they ever have?

"How do you know it's really me you want if you don't see things through with him?" he asked. "You need to go to L.A."

She groaned. "I can ask you the same thing, Jamie. How can you be sure? You were actually *with* someone else. I was just chasing after a chance at being happy after *you* convinced me the Brynn and Jamie ship had already sailed. But guess what? I've *found* it where I didn't know I could. With *you.*"

He cupped her cheeks in his palms. She pressed into one of them like a reflex, and it gutted him.

"I've always known it was you, Brynn. I was an idiot about it more than once, and yes, I may have been less than honest. But it's because there's always been this other person hanging between us."

He didn't doubt that she was heartbroken ten years ago, but so was he. The only difference was that either way, mono or not, Jamie would have gotten crushed, either by her choosing Spencer or the two of them ultimately crumbling like his parents did. As much as he loved her, he was convinced that saving their friendship was his only choice. Brynn getting sick just let him know what he was missing.

"God, you're an ass," she said. And she was probably right, but that didn't change what had held him back. "I get you pushing me away before because you were scared. But where does that put us for the last decade? If I can trust your feelings even after keeping me at a distance all these years, why can't you trust mine? I don't get it. I got upset about you being dishonest, but I still know I love you." She shook her head. "And now you want me to go to L.A.,—to *him*—despite how I feel. Why do you keep running from this? From us?"

No, Jamie thought. This wasn't running. This was fighting.

"Why didn't you tell me about the text?"

Brynn's eyes grew wide, and she staggered back. Scratch what he said before. This admission of guilt—this is what gutted him.

"What?" she asked.

"The text, Brynn. First we kissed. And then there was the mind-blowing sex—thank you very much for that, by the way. And then Spencer texted you about the room he reserved."

Ugh. Jamie inwardly recoiled at himself because this was a new low, but it was the only way to make her see that he wasn't the only one hiding the truth, which meant she hadn't really chosen. Not yet. As much as he wanted Brynn, he *needed* her to be sure.

"Jamie, you had no right—"

"I know, and as soon as I realized it was your phone I grabbed, instead of mine, I put it down. But I can't unsee what I saw or forget that I asked you what was up in the hallway, and you said nothing about Matthews texting you. You can't storm out of a room because of my lapse in honesty and then not own up to doing the same. Yes, I lied, but not because I wasn't sure how I felt. I broke up with Liz *because* I loved you. I don't think that's why you kept Spencer's text from me."

He had to admit that he'd found reason upon reason to postpone telling Brynn how he felt. He let her believe he was still with Liz this whole time because it all boiled down to the only way the rest of this could play out. He had to take her to Spencer. If Brynn never had the chance to *choose* Spencer, then Jamie could only ever be her default, living in the shadow of what broke the trust between them time and again. He wanted Brynn to love him by choice, not because he was there and someone else wasn't.

"I'm taking you to L.A.," he said, hoping his resolve wouldn't waver. They still had two more days.

"To Beer Fest, with you. I just need to text Spencer —"

He shook his head. "To the book launch."

"So, you'll come with me?" she added, but the fact that the statement came out as a question told him she knew where this was going.

"You need to see this thing through, B. On your own. It's the only way you'll know for sure how you feel, and that I'll know you have zero doubt about choosing me."

He stepped back, ready for a gesture that could second as an act of violence against him, and her hands went wild.

"You're deranged, Jamie! Do you know that? You can't be serious."

"Serious as Gary Oldman in a velvet overcoat."

Brynn's hands fisted at her sides, and she seemed to be stifling a scream.

"You will not use Sirius Black's name in vain to validate your insanity."

He shrugged. Either way it was madness. They'd both violated their trust in each other. If they moved forward from here, he'd never truly know if he was her first choice, and she'd never believe he wouldn't get swallowed up by fear again. If they continued on to the original destination, he was handing her off to another guy, one who could quite possibly sweep her off her feet. But that was saying *Fuck you* to the fear, wasn't it? The only way for her to make a choice was to present her with both options, even if she thought he was nuts. They had to put this behind them—to rebuild their trust and have faith that their love would make things right in the end. They needed to see it through, for both of them.

Jamie braced his hands on her shoulders. Brynn was shivering. She didn't flinch when he closed the remaining space between them, when his lips connected with hers. No, she opened her mouth and welcomed him in. He tasted salt and knew she was crying, but that just made him hold her tighter.

She wrapped her arms around him and buried her face in his chest. "I *love* you, Jamie. And if this is what you need, I'll do it. But you have to know it's not what I *want*."

He kissed the top of her head.

"If we don't follow through with the original plan, I'll always wonder. And you might, too."

He kissed her again, not giving her a chance to protest further. Come the weekend, he might lose her for good. But how much worse would it be six months from now? A year from now? Jamie rationalized that recovery time would be shorter if he didn't let himself fall too deep for too long.

He kissed her wet cheeks, her salty eyes, and then gave her his patented kiss on the forehead. They would be together for two more days, but it already felt like they were saying good-bye.

"I do love you," she said, burying her head in his neck. "You believe that. Don't you?"

He stroked her hair, her back, wishing this could be easier.

He nodded. "And I love you. But this isn't how it was supposed to happen. I should have been honest from the start, but it should also go both ways. The past ten years will always be between us if we don't see this through. I don't want to be the guy who stood in the way if there is someone who could make you happier than I could."

That *was* the truth. She meant enough to him that her happiness came first. He didn't add that it would ruin him, though, if she fell for someone else. That much honesty wouldn't be fair if he was going to see this through.

He backed away. "I think there are some extra pillows and blankets in the closet. I'll take the floor tonight."

"Jamie…"

"I love you, Sleepy Jean."

But he didn't wait to hear her say it again. His determination was wearing thin as it was. He just had to make it through two more nights and two more days on the road. With Holbrook being a regular stop on the trip, Jamie had booked a room ahead at the touristy Wigwam Motel. Two beds. After that, L.A.

Despite the cold outside, Brynn waited until he was in his makeshift bed on the floor to return. He closed his eyes and pretended to sleep, sure she knew it was an act, but neither of them broke character. He heard muffled conversation from the bathroom and assumed she was filling Holly in on the latest turn of events.

When he finally started to drift off, he heard the sound of a door's latch opening and then quietly closing. He sprang upright to see the bed empty. When he looked at his phone to check the time, only ten o'clock, he saw a text waiting.

Brynn: *Dora and Frank had a room to spare. Don't worry. I'll pay for it. I know we have a long drive tomorrow, so I'll meet you at the truck at eight. You need to be well rested for the drive.*

Jamie: *OK.*

He collapsed back on the floor, the pillow not enough to

cushion his head against the force of his frustrated momentum.

"Shit," he said, rolling to his side and massaging his now throbbing skull. Then he settled back into position, prepared for a less-than-restful night's sleep, the bed remaining empty till morning.

. . .

"Please," Jamie said. "I insist."

Dora shook her head. "That room would have sat empty last night. Now at least it was put to good use."

Jamie looked at Brynn waiting by the door.

"I'm not so sure about that," he said. "I'd also like to take care of her room."

"Oh, hush," Dora said. "That's between her and me. As for the two of you, married or not, it's as good a love story as I've ever heard. Y'all just haven't gotten to the happy ending yet."

He sighed. They'd reached an ending, all right. But it was far from happy.

"Thank you. It's too generous."

She pulled something from behind the counter. "Here. You almost forgot this."

In a freezer-size Ziploc bag, Dora handed him what she'd found this morning in the Garden Cottage's trash can—the lucky bouquet.

He had no choice but to take it. He'd insisted on carrying both their bags, so Jamie zipped it into the one empty spot in Brynn's bulging suitcase, the outer front pocket. It would get crushed no matter what. This way it would be crushed and contained.

"Don't waste it," she said.

Frank snuck up from behind and threw an arm over Jamie's shoulder.

"So you're not married, huh?"

"No," Jamie said. "I'm sorry we lied."

"Aw, hell," Frank continued. "Enough with the apologizing. Make it up to us by making things right with that girl."

"Lasso the moon for her," Dora added.

Jamie's eyes widened, but there was no way Dora knew about his plan for this weekend. "I'm not sure I'm the one who's supposed to," he said.

Dora laughed. "Silly boy. The one who *can* lasso the moon is the one who is supposed to lasso the moon."

Jamie's brows pulled together. He wasn't sure where this metaphor was going, so he thanked the couple again, these people who knew him and Brynn for a minute and seemed to have more confidence in their relationship than he'd had in a decade.

"Come see us if you ever pass through Amarillo again," Frank said.

Jamie pulled the brim of his Sox cap down in what he hoped was a gesture akin to tipping his hat.

"Will do," he said and headed to the door. "Wait." He turned back toward the couple. "Please tell me you have a gas station and an ATM nearby. We're out of, well, everything."

Frank smiled. "Hang a left when you head out. One mile up on your right, both in the same place."

Jamie filled the tank and replenished his wallet. He may have hid an extra twenty dollar bill apart from the rest of his cash, but he didn't think Brynn was in the mood to hear that he'd heeded her ludicrous advice. She hadn't said anything before they got in the truck. Now it seemed like the window to break the ice was closing. They grabbed coffee, snacks, and cash inside the shop at the gas station before getting on the road, and once they hit the highway, that proverbial window felt sealed shut.

It was a seven-and-a-half hour ride to Holbrook, Arizona, and for seven and a half hours, neither of them said a word.

Chapter Twenty-Two

As the tires of the truck crackled through the gravel parking lot, Brynn felt the deceleration of the vehicle and roused from one of her many naps.

Never had Brynn Chandler been at a loss for words and certainly not with Jamie Kingston. Yet here they were, travel weary—and for Brynn, heart weary—and silent. An entire day spent together and not a word passed between them. How did they get here? And by here, she didn't mean parked in front of a kitschy teepee where she was about to spend her last night with Jamie before L.A. No, *here* meant sitting next to him in the passenger seat of his truck yet knowing he was a million miles away.

"There're two beds," he said, the first words to leave his lips since Amarillo. "They don't have any other vacancies, or I would have gotten you your own." He motioned with his hand to the structure in front of him. "Is it a teepee or a wigwam? I know it's the Wigwam Motel, but I think that's a teepee."

Brynn let her head fall back against her seat.

"I don't need my own wigwam. Or teepee. Or whatever

it is."

"You needed your own room last night. I just thought…"

While they'd both become quick experts at pretending the person right next to them didn't exist, she supposed they couldn't go on like this for another twenty-four hours.

"Let's not do this, Jamie. Okay? You're the one who wanted to sleep on the floor. I left so you wouldn't have to." She let out a shaky breath. The only place she'd wanted to be last night was in his arms, and it killed her that he couldn't see that.

The truck was in park, but he still gripped the wheel like they were driving seventy-five on the open highway.

"Do what?" he asked, the words spoken through gritted teeth, and Brynn's blood boiled. He was angry? *He* was angry?

"What are you so pissed about?" she asked him, but he still stared out the windshield. "You've made up your mind about how the rest of this trip is going to go. This is what you want, right? Because you sure have a hell of a way of showing it."

He faced her now, those blue eyes piercing her with an intensity she'd never seen from him.

"I want us to trust each other. I want you to know I'm not going to get scared and run, and I want you to be sure I'm not just your backup plus-one anymore, B. The only way for you to know how you really feel about me is for you to know how you feel about him. Physical distance will give us perspective."

She opened her mouth to protest, to tell him that physical distance is what made her think she needed to chase after a fantasy like Spencer in the first place. That closeness — *being* with Jamie — showed her what reality could be. But he'd already turned away. With a flick of his wrist, the key was out of the ignition and his door was open.

"I'm starving," he said. "No food here, but they told me we can order pizza. Pineapple and bacon, if they have it?"

She gave him a weak smile. Jamie was the only one who would eat pineapple and bacon pizza with her, and the fact that he still would—well, that was something.

"Fine," she said, and they exited the small confines of the truck for the equally small confines of their room at the Wigwam Motel.

The rest of the afternoon and evening passed with minimal yet civil conversation. They were in the same room, yet it felt like Jamie had closed a door between them, eliminating any opening for her to state her case.

Turned out the pizza place did not have pineapple, but she still got her bacon. There was a wall-mounted TV in their small, circular room, and it got basic cable, so she considered that a tiny victory. She found a marathon of *Diners, Drive-Ins, and Dives* on The Food Network, and they both tacitly agreed that would be their evening activity.

One of the dives visited on a later episode was the Coyote Bluff Café. Brynn gasped when she recognized the parking lot where she caught the bouquet, and when she looked at Jamie, he pressed his lips into a thin smile, but that was all she got.

For ten years she had what would be called a less than stellar love life. It wasn't as if she full-on pined for Spencer Matthews for a decade. But yes—the reunion dredged up old memories and questions. What if Jamie hadn't kissed her that night? What if she'd never gotten sick? If she'd made it to the end-of-the-year party, would Spencer have been the one? Would he have been the one two weeks ago? And what did that mean for tomorrow?

The funny thing was, Brynn thought she'd already answered that question. She loved Jamie. But he didn't trust her feelings. He loved her, but she didn't trust his ability to outrun his fear. Maybe he was right. They were stuck and needed to figure out a way to believe in each other, so she'd give Jamie what he needed and hope she'd get what she needed in return—*him*.

She had bitten the bullet and texted Spencer back, telling him she wasn't sure if she'd make it by Friday even though she knew she would. Committing to spending the night with him felt all sorts of wrong, and she wanted to tell Jamie this, that even when they made it to L.A. tomorrow she wouldn't stay with Spencer. She'd see this thing through, go to the book launch on Saturday, but that would be it. Her thoughts were interrupted by Jamie, wearing a T-shirt and flannel pants, exiting the tiny space that was otherwise known as the bathroom.

"Keep your limbs inside the vehicle at all times," he said, raising a brow. "It's like playing Operation trying to get through there."

Brynn giggled quietly. The doorway that separated their two beds was barely wider than a human body.

"I'll make sure to keep my spastic gesturing to a minimum."

He smiled, and she felt a tiny weight lift from her chest. Not enough to tell her they were going to be okay, but breathing got a little easier.

"Just be careful, B. Wouldn't want you losing a hand or anything."

"I appreciate your concern," she told him. "I'm just going to let Holly know we'll be in L.A. tomorrow, and then I'll wash up for bed. And about tomorrow, Jamie—"

"Can we continue *not* talking about tomorrow?" he asked. "I know it was my idea, but that doesn't mean I'm excited about it."

She nodded. Fine. They had eight hours in the truck for her to make her final case, to tell him she was spending tomorrow night in L.A. with *him*—and not Spencer.

"Good night, B." He pulled the T-shirt over his head and

climbed into bed, his back to her. She watched the muscle and bone of his shoulder work in tandem as he situated himself for sleep, and all she could think was how much she wanted to be there with him, his arms around her, convincing her they would be okay. It wasn't sex she thought about now, only the comfort of being close to him and the promise that however this trip ended, they'd still be Jamie and Sleepy Jean.

She turned off the TV and texted Holly:

Everything's a mess right now. I'll be in L.A. tomorrow. Headed to book launch Saturday.

Holly's reply came in seconds: *Wanna talk?*

Brynn: *Can't. No privacy in the teepee.*

Holly: *Teepee?*

Brynn: *Teepee.*

Holly: *Call me when you get to L.A.?*

Brynn: *Yeah. Love you.*

Holly: *Love you.*

As much as she wanted to talk to her sister, she knew Holly couldn't make her decisions for her—or Jamie, for that matter. She changed into a T-shirt and shorts right there in the open, and Jamie never turned around. She grabbed her toiletry bag from her suitcase and left her glasses on her pillow so she could wash up for bed.

Arms at her sides, Brynn concentrated on not severing a limb as she stepped toward the narrow doorway. But as luck would have it—or maybe this was finally karma rearing its ugly head—she never had to worry about her limbs. She made it through the doorway and, thinking herself out of the woods, never saw the metal towel rack coming.

She could blame her haste. Or maybe her need to lighten the mood with Jamie. But when she spun to poke her head out of the tiny doorframe to tell him she made it unscathed, her new friend—the metal towel rack, of course—greeted her forehead with a crack.

She was too stunned to cry out, but it didn't matter. Jamie was there in a flash, the face-to-metal contact enough to rouse him from any faux or actual slumber.

"Jesus, Brynn!" He whipped one of the towels off the evil rack and pressed it to her forehead. "You're bleeding. What the hell happened?"

He pulled the towel back to get another look and winced.

"How bad is it?" she asked.

She knew it wasn't good because, holy shit, it hurt. And it wasn't normal for white spots to dance across her vision even when she had her glasses off. She staggered a step, and Jamie caught her before she fell. Yeah, this dizziness wasn't normal, either.

Jamie guided her to the bed and sat her down. He propped pillows against the headboard and leaned her back. Then he pulled off the towel, presumably to inspect the wound again. Brynn couldn't see the injury, so she could only guess.

"I don't think you need stitches, but that's one hell of a goose egg you've got already." He handed her glasses to her, and she managed to get them on. "I'm guessing based on proximity that it's the towel rack's ass I have to kick?"

She nodded and tried to smile, but the movement filled her vision with stars again. "Dizzy," she said. "Am I still bleeding?"

He pulled the towel away, the white towel that now

looked like part of a crime scene, and Brynn gasped.

"I could put you in a taxi to the ER," he said, and a smile crept on to his face.

She thwacked him on the shoulder, and even though her head throbbed, she laughed.

"I couldn't leave Annie's store unattended, you jerk. You know I felt like crap stabbing you and then making you go alone."

His smile broadened. "You finally admit to stabbing me!" He was exultant now. "And I know you hated letting me go on my own, B," he said, and he blotted the wound again. "It's not bleeding too badly, which is a good sign, but you could have a concussion. I'm going to run to the main office and see if I can get you some ice and a bandage. If the dizziness hasn't gone away by the time I get back, we're finding a hospital."

Brynn groaned. "Stupid karma."

He narrowed his eyes at her. "I'll be right back. Don't go to sleep or anything, and keep pressure on the wound." Jamie kissed her on the top of her head as if everything between them was fine. "And stop blaming karma. You're legally blind without your glasses. Plus, I know you've got some twisted vendetta against motel towel racks. You should probably seek professional help."

He was out the door after that, and Brynn resisted the urge to close her eyes, just in case she was concussed. She was grateful they could still come together in a crisis—a small, stupid crisis that would mean her having to explain her injury to anyone who saw her in the next week at least. The valley between them hadn't grown too wide to cross. Not yet, at least.

Minutes later, the door burst open, and Jamie walked in— still shirtless, by the way—with a bag of ice, a box of gauze, and a middle-aged man.

"I didn't think I was that dizzy," Brynn said, "but now I think I'm seeing double. Except the second you is a few years older and maybe more ruggedly handsome."

The man did wear his salt and pepper hair well and had that perma five o'clock shadow look that she liked.

"So she's making jokes," the stranger said, moving to sit on the edge of Brynn's bed. "That's a good sign."

"Not good ones," Jamie mumbled, and then he added, "Brynn, this is Dr. George. He's a pediatrician from San Jose."

Her brows furrowed. "And they had him up at the front desk for you to borrow?"

The man laughed. "I was getting a bag of ice to bring back to my room. My wife hates drinking soda without it."

"I like her already," she said.

"I can't consider this an official medical evaluation because we aren't in the office, no insurance, you get the gist. We will have to consider this an evaluation by a civilian, regardless of my credentials. I can tell you whether or not you have a concussion, which may save you a trip to the ER, but you should follow up with your regular doctor within the week if you're still experiencing symptoms."

Jamie sat on the side of his own bed to face them.

"I checked his ID. He's legit."

Brynn squeezed her eyes shut. "I'm kind of mortified he pulled you away from your family for my ridiculous accident."

Dr. George shook his head. "I offered. Happy to help." He leaned closer to her and spoke softly. "Plus, your friend here was out of his mind with worry. I'm sure you're fine, but I couldn't leave *him* in that state."

She bit her lip and looked at Jamie, knowing he heard every word the doctor said because, duh, they were in a teepee.

"Even Mr. Level-Headed loses his cool sometimes, I guess."

Jamie pressed his lips into a thin smile, but the worry in those blue eyes was evident.

Dr. George pulled a penlight out of a messenger bag he

wore across his body.

"I'm just going to do a quick examination, and then it's up to you two what you do next, okay?"

Brynn nodded and let the doctor get to work.

Fifteen minutes later he confirmed she didn't show any early signs of concussion, but he reminded Brynn that this couldn't be considered a real examination. It was her choice if she wanted to still go to the ER. He helped her clean and bandage her wound and also suggested ibuprofen, which she fished from her bag and took without protest. She held a handful of ice wrapped in a clean towel against the swelling, and she was as good as new. Okay, she was a mess, but she was a patched-up mess, and that was as good as it was going to get.

"Thank you, Dr. George," Jamie said when he was done.

"Get some rest, Brynn," the doctor said to her. "And you..." He turned to Jamie. "You keep an eye on her. If anything worsens by morning, seek further medical attention."

Jamie nodded, his brow knitted in concern.

"I'm fine. Really," Brynn told them.

Jamie shook the man's hand and saw him to the door. He tried to offer him money, but Dr. George waved him off and then headed back to his teepee. Or wigwam. Whatever.

The ice made her cold, and she was too exhausted to hold it, so she dropped it into the glass of water on the table next to her bed and let the towel fall to the floor.

After locking the door, Jamie leaned forward and rested his head against it. She opened her mouth to say something but held her tongue as she watched the tension leave his body on an exhale, only now realizing just how worried he was. So she let him have his moment of release. Soon he turned to face her, and when he did, he walked straight to her bed and climbed in, positioning himself so he spooned her from behind.

She swallowed back the threat of a sob even though she

could really use her own release. Instead she relaxed into his chest, felt the heat of his skin against the cotton of her T-shirt warming her body's chill.

"I'm keeping an eye on you, okay?" he asked, though it was more insistence than it was a question.

"Okay," she said without protest.

His hand rested tentatively on her hip, and she placed her palm over it, pulling it to drape across her stomach. She squeezed his hand, and Jamie responded by holding her just a little tighter. Neither of them said another word, but Brynn couldn't let go of the fear that despite his need to protect her, she and Jamie seemed to be moving further and further from the way they were. They were lucky to find their way back to friendship after college. But they were too far across the line now. Friendship was no longer an option.

She held it together as long as she could—Amarillo, the silent car ride, the unanticipated towel rack attack, and the whole decade preceding all of it. When Jamie's breathing finally evened out and she thought he must be sleeping, that's when she finally let the tears flow.

Chapter Twenty-Three

It was a shitty thing to do, but Jamie didn't have any other option. If he hadn't slid out of bed before she woke, he would have caved completely and called off the rest of the trip. They could hole up in their teepee instead, pretending nothing else existed outside of him pressed up against her in that bed. But there was a world outside of Holbrook, Arizona. There was Spencer Matthews in L.A. And he was going to follow through on his offer and bring the woman he loved to another guy.

Besides, his shoulder ached and his hand was asleep, but really none of that mattered when the cause of it was Brynn in his arms.

If he waited for her to stir, risked her facing him with what he knew would be swollen eyes from the quiet sobs he pretended not to hear last night, he would have kissed her like he'd wanted to since he crawled into her bed, and where would they be then? Nothing had happened to rebuild their trust in each other, and he knew it couldn't be done with just a kiss.

He went over last night's events in his head as he quietly dressed and packed his things, Brynn's steady breathing assurance that she was okay after her injury. Jamie, however, was far from it.

He closed his eyes, and the scene played out again before him—Brynn frozen in place as blood trickled from the gash in her forehead. His stomach had dropped, as if he sat in an airplane that had just lost a few thousand feet of altitude. But the adrenaline had kicked in enough for him to guide her to the bed, help her keep pressure on the wound, and ease her mind while his quietly raced.

His lids flew open, the vision of Brynn asleep and okay the only thing that slowed his frenzied breaths. He listened to her soft exhalations, letting them lull his own into sync with her rhythm. He didn't have to pretend everything was fine anymore in order to protect her. She would be okay, but things between them were far from fine.

He'd only ever wanted Brynn to want him back, and when that finally became a reality when they were seventeen, all he could think about was how much it would suck to lose her. Yes, his parents' split rocked his world. He wouldn't deny that. But what rocked it even more was the thought of something like that happening to him and Brynn.

Then there was the other guy. How could she go from being so convinced Spencer was *the* guy to being sure she wanted *him*? It was easy back then to blame the divorce for his reluctance to change their status from friendship to something more, but he could never shake the feeling of being Brynn's consolation prize. And here they were again in the same position, but this time Brynn knew how he felt— how he had felt for ten years. Yet he had deceived her about his intentions with this trip. And she had kept secret Spencer's request for her to spend the night.

The way he saw it, any hesitation to be honest with each

other was hesitation *about* each other, and Jamie saw only one way to fix that.

"Be right back," he whispered and kissed her lightly on the cheek.

"Mkay," she said dreamily, then rolled to her other side.

Remembering a McDonald's a mile or so down the road, he quickly dressed and grabbed his bag to sneak out and bring back coffee, a peace offering, he hoped. But when he put the key in the ignition and attempted to start the engine, he got nothing. Not a chug, not one turnover.

Mr. Level-Headed was about to lose his cool now because he *had* to get to L.A. Today. He hadn't told Brynn about the business portion of his trip, even though she'd been the inspiration for it. He was so bent on putting L.A. out of his mind until they actually got there that he'd ignored the part of this weekend he was actually looking forward to, the unveiling of his newest brew, the one that was always for her. After Amarillo he decided telling her would only make him look and feel like more of an ass than he already did. Still, even if she didn't know it, he had her to thank for convincing him the trip would do him good. When he'd found out they had an extra tent after another brewer dropped out, well, he just figured it was a sign.

That's right. A sign. And the one he was getting right now was far from promising.

He tried the truck again. Nothing. Shit. So much for the tune-up he got before they left, not to mention the flat tire that was supposed to mean they'd gotten the car trouble portion of the trip out of the way.

He popped his head back in the wigwam. Brynn was still asleep. Then he went to the front office to find out about a mechanic.

"Closest one doesn't open for another hour, but I can give you a jumpstart and see if that does the trick."

Jamie nodded emphatically. "God, yes. Please," he said to the man at the front desk. At least if it was the battery it was easily replaced. It was just a matter of someone getting here with one as soon as humanly possible.

Phil, the front desk guy, pulled his car around to Jamie's wigwam and hooked up the jumper cables. When it was time for Jamie to start 'er up, Phil gave him the thumbs-up and— nothing. Nada. Not even a sputter.

Shit.

"Still could be the battery. Or maybe your starter. Mickey'll be in the shop soon, and I'll give him a call. He'll get one of his guys to tow you over there. They're real good, should have you on your way by lunchtime the latest if it's nothing major."

Phil headed back to the office, and Jamie told the man he'd be there soon to figure out the whole mechanic situation with Mickey. He crossed his fingers that Mickey didn't have a busy morning, because he was banking on being his first customer of the day.

Lunchtime would put Jamie half a day off course. He'd pretended like this week was a leisurely tour because they were making perfect time. They were poised to get into town with hours to spare. But now, if he didn't check in by seven o'clock this evening, he would lose his spot in the new brewers tents, and it would go to someone else on the waiting list.

He called Jeremy, who answered on the first ring.

"What's up, boss?" He was awake and alert, which hopefully meant Jeremy had made his flight last night without incident.

"Hey, Jer. Tell me you're at the hotel already."

"Uh-oh," he said, and Jamie's heart sank. If Jeremy hadn't made his flight, he was fucked.

"What do you mean, uh-oh? I got you a first-class ticket, man. Tell me you didn't miss the damn flight!"

"Whoa, whoa, whoa, dude. No reason to Hulk out. I made my flight. I'm just not exactly in *my* hotel. See, I met this girl on the plane, and she was staying…"

Jamie blew out a breath and then cut him off. "Okay, okay. I don't need details. You're in L.A., yes?"

"Yes. And you will be soon, right?"

That was the plan, but Jamie needed a contingency.

"I know I said I didn't need you to work until tomorrow, but I'm going to miss check-in, and I need you to do it for me, or we're nothing but spectators instead of participants."

"No problem," Jeremy said. "Do I just need to sign your name or something?"

Not only would Jamie need to get this car situation taken care of—and fast—but he'd also need to forward Jeremy his registration documents and hope the guy would be able to oversee the tent setup and sign for the product delivery this afternoon, all things Jamie had planned on doing by getting an early start today.

"It's a little more complicated than that," Jamie said. "But, Jer, if you can do what I need you to do today, your Christmas bonus is going to be huge."

Jeremy laughed. "Kingston, you know I'm your guy. But I'm holding you to that bonus thing now that you said it out loud."

"Deal," Jamie said, and he spent the next half hour prepping Jeremy for today's duties.

When he made it back to Phil, the man told him Mickey already had a tow truck on the way. He breathed a sigh of relief. At least things were moving in the right direction. But there was one more thing he had to take care of.

"Phil, is there a bus or a train or something nearby that goes to L.A.?"

Phil glanced at the large analog clock on the wall behind Jamie's head.

"Real nice coach bus service runs from Holbrook to L.A. every day at nine. Leaves right from that parking lot across the street." Phil pointed out the Wigwam Motel's front office window. "I can call and see if they still have tickets. Add it to your tab and print it right here?"

Jamie nodded. "The ticketholder's name will be Brynn Chandler. You're a lifesaver, Phil."

He might be stuck in Holbrook for the day, but he'd still get Brynn to her destination on time. He couldn't be her choice by default. Not again.

Jamie was out the door and back to his wigwam in seconds, bursting into their room just before remembering that he'd left Brynn asleep less than an hour ago.

She was awake and dressed in the Cubs T-shirt and jeans, but Jamie didn't have the time or energy to give her shit about wearing the shirt. At least this time there was a bra underneath it. Not that he was thinking about her bra. Well, now he was. Dammit. He had to focus. When he did he saw that Brynn's eyes weren't puffy and red from last night's tears. Her brown eyes spat lasers at him through her glasses, despite how goofy her angry face looked with the addition of the bandage on the right half of her forehead, and he guessed he was in for a world of hurt.

"Where the hell were you, Jamie?"

Maybe he should have left a note.

· · ·

First she'd opened the door to make sure his truck was still there. It was one thing to wake up with Jamie no longer in bed with her. But then to find the room entirely empty save for her and her suitcase? She'd thought he'd actually bailed. Why were things so royally messed up between them now?

Her heart had settled back into her chest when she threw

open the door and found his truck still parked, but then she texted him and got no response. She texted again—still nothing. In a ten-minute time span she went from hurt to furious to downright terrified, and here he was all awake and dressed and not looking at all like he'd been mugged by some wigwam-trolling hooligan.

"I texted you," she said when he didn't answer her question. "Jamie, I thought you left me, and then I thought something happened to you."

He was still standing in the open doorway, handle in his hand. With the other he pulled his phone from his pocket and drew in a hissed breath when he saw the text notifications.

"B, I'm sorry. It's been a hell of a morning. I was going to get coffee, but the truck wouldn't start. Battery's dead, tow truck is on the way, and I had to make a call, which is probably why I missed your texts. I'm sorry. I should have left a note, but right now we have to get you all packed and on the bus."

She opened her mouth to speak and then closed it again, letting the entirety of Jamie's verbal vomit register. It took a second for her brain to catch up to the velocity at which his words came at her, and the last bit finally registered.

"Bus? We're taking a bus? I thought you said the tow truck was on the way."

He shook his head. "I'm not taking the bus."

She cocked her head to the side, brows furrowed. Then it clicked, and she was suddenly nauseous.

"You're putting *me* on a bus?"

She thought her little towel rack incident last night—and Jamie taking care of her—meant they'd made some sort of progress, or at least were in a good enough place that they could make the last leg of the journey without enduring eight hours of silence. But now he wanted to just get rid of her.

"Look, Brynn…" He closed the door behind them and sat on the chair across from the beds. "I don't know what the car situation is. I'm crossing my fingers I'll be out of here by noon, but that means not making it to L.A. before eight tonight. I don't have time to explain, but I have some things I need to do when I get there, and I know you have...*things*...to do as well. The other option is both of us possibly not making it until tomorrow, which means you'd miss the launch altogether, and we both know that can't happen. This is the only way to make sure you get where you need to go—where I promised to take you." He let out a long breath. "It's going to be a rushed good-bye either way, and I just thought this would be easier."

Brynn threw her hands in the air. She wasn't sure if it was tears clouding her vision or just outright fury. "For *you*," she said. "This will be easier for *you*, Jamie. But you didn't think to ask what I want. You didn't think to ask if I wanted to play along with your whole *Brynn needs to make her choice* scenario, either. You just decided for me because it's what *you* want or need or whatever. You need proof about how I feel, right? Well, guess what, James? All you've been proving to me is that you're just as good at pushing me away now as you were a decade ago."

He stood and took a step toward her, but she shook her head, and he stopped.

"Don't. Just don't. You win, okay? Where's the bus?"

He sighed, shoulders sagging.

"Across the street. It leaves in twenty minutes."

She turned to where her suitcase sat on her bed, packed but not yet zipped. She slammed it closed, struggling to get the zipper around the diameter of the stuffed bag, but she didn't want his help, and she certainly didn't want another eight hours in a vehicle with him now.

"You're unbelievable," she said, her back still to him as she forced the zipper the rest of the way. "So worried about your own damn heart you don't think about what you're doing to others." She turned to face him. "And just so we're clear, by others I mean me. *My* heart, Jamie." She touched her fingers lightly to the square of gauze on her forehead, but she knew the searing pain behind her eyes would have been there whether she'd bumped her head or not.

"Are you okay?" he asked, and his tone told her he knew it was a loaded question.

"If you're asking if my symptoms have worsened, no. They haven't. But thanks for taking that into consideration before shipping me off to Los Angeles."

His hand raked through his hair, and she could see he was in agony. Though she felt justified in her reaction now, she still felt the poison with each word she spat at him, hating herself a little as she did. He was obviously stressed about the car situation, but that didn't give him the right to make this kind of decision for her.

"I'm sorry," he said. "But I didn't want you to be stuck here. I didn't want to be the one who stood in your way *again*."

Ooooh. That's right. She had shown Jamie her angry side before—her drunk, angry side when he barged in on her and Spencer at the reunion. That wasn't Brynn, though. *This* wasn't Brynn. It was a new version she didn't like, one that Jamie somehow brought out in her.

She let out a breath and with it a bit of the anger. They could do this all day, but apparently there wasn't enough time.

"I have a bus to catch," she said softly.

"Can I at least walk you over there?"

As spent as she was, Brynn didn't want to say good-bye just yet. Not like this.

"Okay," she said, and without another word, Jamie hoisted her suitcase from the bed and carried it to the door.

After stopping in the office for the ticket, they were across the street with minutes to spare, and Brynn didn't want to leave angry.

"You were going to get coffee?" she asked, and Jamie

shoved his hands in his front pockets and nodded.

"Figured it was warm enough for that frozen chocolate chip drink you love."

Come on. He was killing her now.

"You were going to get me a chocolate chip frappe?"

"Kinda glad now that I didn't have to say chocolate chip frappe."

"Jamie."

"Brynn."

He smiled, and her anger softened to a dull ache that tugged at her heart a little too much.

"Phil said the next pickup is right next to a gas station." He reached for his wallet, but she grabbed his arm.

"I've got money, Jamie. I already owe you for the glasses, the ticket. I think I can manage some snacks at a gas station."

The bus pulled up, and Jamie let his wallet fall back into his pocket.

"You don't owe me anything, B."

He gave her a weak smile.

Yeah, she did. She owed him honesty and trust and a love he could count on. But he owed her the same. Neither of them had made good choices these past two weeks—hell, these past ten years. No matter what happened when she saw Spencer, this small separation would be good for her and Jamie, some distance to think. It was pretty impossible to reconcile your feelings for someone when he was always a seat or a bed away.

"I guess it wasn't smooth sailing after the flat, huh?" she asked.

He laughed quietly. "Not even close."

"I'll text you when I get there."

He nodded. "I'm heading back on the road Monday. Passenger seat's yours if you want it. And if you don't, it's okay, Brynn."

Her eyes burned. "Is it really, Jamie? If that's how this all plays out, is it really okay? Are *we* okay?"

He shook his head. Ahhh, there's the honesty.

"Probably not," he said. "But I can't stand in the way of your happiness. That's never what I wanted from this. I love you too much." He laughed again, but this time he did it without a smile. "I lied to myself—and to you—for a long time. But every day for eleven years, even when I wouldn't admit it, I've loved you. It never lasted with anyone else because you've *always* had my heart."

She reached for his cheek, and he didn't pull away. She swiped a thumb underneath his eye, spreading wetness across his skin.

"*Jamie.*" Her voice broke on the second syllable of his name. "Is this really the only way you'll believe that you have mine?" Because every second they stood here like this, she felt the crack widen—a fault line traveling down the center of her heart, the one that belonged to him.

He nodded, pressing a kiss into her palm, and her vision blurred with tears. *Shit.*

"I love you, Jamie Kingston. And I'm going to prove it."

She stood on her toes and kissed him, grateful that he didn't resist. She slipped her tongue between his lips, and he answered by doing the same. She didn't care that they had an audience or that this kiss was the only thing keeping her from dissolving into a sobbing mess. All that mattered was his touch, that they connected before the road stretched out between them.

He pulled away first, his eyes dark with desire and pain.

The bus driver was loading the passengers' luggage now. He'd already tried to throw hers below, but Brynn insisted on keeping her bag with her since the bus wasn't too crowded. She wasn't a fan of letting her stuff out of her sight while on a strange journey, and the bus driver didn't argue with her. After he loaded the last few passengers' bags, she'd have to board the bus.

She wasn't sure what else to do, and when Jamie pulled her back into a hug, she breathed him in—their last connection before she said good-bye.

"We'll find our way," he said, but his tone didn't match his words.

Friends. More than friends. Whatever it was, Brynn had to believe he was right. Because the alternative was unthinkable.

Chapter Twenty-Four

Jamie *was* an idiot. He didn't need Annie to tell him that again, but as he sat in the small waiting area of the auto body shop with a woman who was knitting something far too warm for autumn in Holbrook, that's exactly what she was doing. At least he considered himself an idiot with purpose. That was a thing, right?

    Annie: *How could you put her on a bus?*

    Jamie: *I bought the ticket and walked her to the bus stop.*

He was glad he and Annie weren't the type who actually spoke on the phone because he could picture her ready to explode at him right now. When she didn't respond immediately, he worried his attempt at levity—for *his* fucked-up situation by the way, not hers—had royally backfired. When his phone finally vibrated again, he was ready to apologize for the stupid joke, but then he realized the vibration was not a text notification. The phone was ringing.

Jamie guessed their friendship was about to reach another level. He stepped outside to avoid any stares from knitting lady and answered the phone.

"Hey, Annie."

"James..." She didn't sound pissed, but she also didn't sound like she was calling to comfort his wounded heart. Maybe he should remind her that *he* was the one with the potential to get obliterated here, that Brynn would probably get to L.A. and realize that Spencer Matthews actually *is* Mr. Right and Jamie, for the second time, was just Mr. Right Here. But Annie didn't give him a chance to protest.

"Have you ever stopped to think," she started, "that you might be forcing her to choose him? You push her far enough away, she's going to eventually keep moving in that direction on her own."

He cleared his throat. Either the Arizona desert was making it dry, or he was swallowing back the tiniest inkling that maybe she could be right. Because she wasn't right. Right?

"That's actually the complete opposite of what I'm doing. I'm letting her be sure of what she wants—of *who* she wants. I'm also showing her that I can say *fuck you* to my own fear if it means she gets what she wants in the end. I don't want her to be with me and then weeks, months, or even years later still wonder what would have happened if she'd gone to that book launch. I can't live in the possibility of that doubt. I've already been doing it for ten years."

Annie sighed. Then she sighed again, and Jamie groaned.

"Just say whatever it is you want to say, Annie. It can't get much worse than it already is."

He paced while she hesitated.

"Okay," she started, and something in her tone calmed his frenetic energy. "Jamie, I know about that summer after graduation."

Huh. So maybe this could get worse. She waited a beat, probably to give him the chance to play dumb, but he knew better. Annie knew. Of course she knew.

"I figured you might," he said.

"Ha!" she yelled, and he had to pull the phone from his ear. "Lucky guess, actually! I thought something was up, but I was never able to put my finger on it until now. Damn that girl can keep a secret when it comes to you. Okay, tell me everything."

"Christ," he hissed and ran his fingers through his hair.

"Spill it, Kingston. Your future with this girl depends on it, and I may be your only hope."

He shook his head. "Thanks a lot, Obi Wan. I appreciate the manipulation." But Annie was right. She might be his only shot at cleaning up the mess that was him and his best friend.

"You know about the mono the night of the party, right? *The* party, where something was finally going to happen between the love of my life and the guy she drooled over for the entire year."

Annie took in a sharp breath. "Love of your life. God, tell me you told her that."

He shook his head and realized she couldn't see him. Whatever—he didn't want to confirm what she already knew. Maybe he finally told Brynn he loved her, but he hadn't quite put it like that—the finality of it, that there was no one before her and certainly would be no one after, at least not a woman he'd love like her. No matter who her first choice was, Brynn would always be his.

"So she missed the party," he continued. "And I took her to urgent care because her parents were downtown."

"Yeah, I got that part," Annie said. "Tell me the part I missed."

He felt like he was seventeen again, reliving that night. He'd played it over and over in his head countless times throughout the years, but he'd never spoken of it out loud.

That wasn't his thing—talking about stuff. Unless it was with Brynn. But this night was the one part of his life he couldn't hash out with his best friend because after he told her they were better keeping things as they were, Brynn made him promise not to bring it up again.

"I stayed with her, and nothing really happened. She fell asleep on the couch watching *SNL*. Her fever broke, and when she woke up and saw that I hadn't left her, she told me she was supposed to get kissed that night."

He could swear Annie had stopped breathing.

"You still there?" he asked.

"Did you kiss her?"

He nodded, again remembering she couldn't see him, so he offered verbal confirmation.

"She asked me to. Of course I kissed her. I was in love with her, enough that I freaked out as soon as it was done. All I kept thinking was if I hadn't been there, it would have been him."

"And then your parents split."

Wow. She was good.

"Yep. And all I kept telling myself was how that would be me and Brynn someday, how even if we had this fantastic summer, she would have always seen me as her consolation prize, and eventually she would have resented me. And I would have lost her completely."

This was the part he hated reliving, the short-lived excitement at the possibility of them followed by what he saw as their eventual reality.

"She would always be in my life if we stayed friends. That's what I told myself then, and I guess to an extent I was right. We've been friends ever since."

"But you were in love with her. You *are* in love with her. Feeling that way and keeping it from Brynn—that doesn't make for the best friendship."

No, it didn't. He hadn't just violated her trust for the past two weeks. It had been the whole decade. And any other woman he'd dated between then and now—Liz included—he'd violated their trust, too. He didn't need to cheat to be unfaithful to any of his girlfriends because, if he really admitted it, he had always been unfaithful with his heart. He knew that now.

"Did you ever once think that maybe Brynn has been living with her own brand of doubt these past ten years?"

He squinted in the midmorning sun and swore under his breath for leaving his Sox hat on the passenger seat of the truck.

"I don't follow." He was, however, following the time ticking away as he waited for Mickey to install a new battery and starter in the truck. Every minute he was stuck in Holbrook put another mile between him and Brynn.

"What if that kiss," Annie went on, "was Brynn's realization that Spencer never was the guy, that it was *you* and she just didn't know it yet?"

He shook his head. "I was in the right place at the right time. You didn't see her that night. She was ready to go to that party even though she was burning up with a fever and couldn't swallow her own saliva without crying."

Annie laughed, and Jamie's jaw clenched. He was thrilled she was enjoying this.

"But she didn't go. And maybe she wasn't supposed to." Great. Now Annie believed in signs? "You can't be *that* blind," she continued. "Can you? It's not like you even initiated the kiss. *She* did. Plus, weren't *you* the one who called things off before they were ever on?"

"I didn't know how else *not* to mess things up between us."

The logic sounded warped when he said it out loud, but it made sense to him then. He'd wanted Brynn. He wasn't denying that. But he needed her to be more for him that summer than he could have been for her. He needed his friend and to know he'd never lose her.

"Honey, you guys messed things up the second you sucked the ChapStick off her lips," she said. "But God, Jamie. It all makes sense, now. How often do you think Brynn came to me upset about missing that party? Do you want to know how much she pined for Spencer Matthews after that night? And don't bother answering, because it's a rhetorical question, and I'm going to tell you whether you want the answer or not."

Jamie was leaning pretty far toward *not*, but he kept his mouth shut since Annie was obviously on a roll. He squeezed his eyes closed to shield himself against the blow. He held his breath. If he wasn't holding the phone in his hand, he would have plugged his ears and yelled *Lalalalalala* like a child throwing a tantrum, because the one thing he'd never asked Brynn after that night was the one thing he knew he couldn't bear to hear.

"Not one bit," she said.

Jamie opened his eyes, but he still held his breath until the word left his mouth.

"What?"

"Not one time that whole summer did Brynn mention *not* kissing Spencer. Not one time did she mention that boy. At all."

Mickey poked his head out of the shop, Jamie's keys in his hand. It was ten thirty, and the car was ready to go. Jamie held up a finger, letting the man know he'd be right there.

"I don't know what you're trying to tell me, Annie."

She groaned. "It was *you*, you idiot." Again with the idiot? "It had to be you. A whole year she goes on and on about finally getting Spencer to notice her, and then poof! She misses her big night and never mentions him again? She doesn't tell me about this epic kiss you guys must have had, one that seemed to have wiped Spencer Matthews off the map. Instead she spends her summer with the same guy she always hangs with—you. Even after you kissed her and rejected her. And now you're doing it again. A girl can only take so much before she says 'fuck it' to the hand she's dealt and travels across the country for a new deck."

Jamie's head was spinning.

"Rejected her? What the hell? I was in love with her. I've always been in love with her. I thought she liked…all she talked about was…a whole year, Annie. For a whole year she never saw me like I saw her. And then…I couldn't risk it. I couldn't be her second choice. Just like now. Fuck." He finally understood exactly what he was doing. "I'm not giving her a choice, am I? I'm *making* her choose him."

He was inside the shop now, handing Mickey his credit card and not even looking at the invoice. Whatever it cost, he was paying the sum and getting the hell out of Holbrook. Knitting lady was still there, eyeing him over her needles. He didn't care. He just needed to leave.

"If it helps, I think she's an idiot, too," Annie said. "And then this reunion thing—you both spent a decade convincing yourselves you were better off as friends, and part of that must have been Brynn convincing herself that maybe she *was* supposed to kiss Spencer that night. If it was wrong to kiss you, then it must have been right to kiss him. But enough is enough. The two of you are finally driving me to insanity. I'm done. Ten years is my statute of limitations on aiding and abetting both of your scared stupidity."

Brynn had said in Amarillo that he'd broken her heart that summer, that she would have chosen him then, but he rationalized it was the heightened emotion of their newlywed kiss—and the heightened everything that happened afterward. She couldn't have fallen in love with him from one kiss when they were seventeen.

Then again, he fell in love with her without their lips ever touching. Kissing her that night was everything, but that's not what made him fall in love or what kept him in love with her for ten years, even if he wouldn't admit it. It was all the other stuff that made Brynn *Brynn*—her ridiculous love of the Monkees; her hair in that crazy bun she'd only wear in front of Holly or him; the way she felt everything so deeply it radiated into her movement, sometimes so much that she stabbed a guy with a letter opener or poked him in the eye. It was her fear of heights and her spur-of-the-moment determination to face it. *She* was everything that made him fall in love. But she was also the nail in the coffin of his fear. Loving her was terrifying. The thought of losing her damn near paralyzed him. Now he let fear take the wheel again, steering Brynn back to a guy who'd be happy to swoop in and clean up the mess that Jamie kept making.

"I'm a fucking idiot," he said, and Mickey the mechanic and knitting lady both uttered a "What?" in unison. But Jamie waved them off and signed the credit card receipt.

"That's what I've been trying to tell you," Annie said, her words dripping with exhaustion.

"I gotta go. And I need to do this right. Don't call her. Or Holly. It needs to be me and only me." Maybe she was right about how Brynn felt. Maybe she wasn't. Either way, Jamie knew how *he* felt. Brynn was his best friend, and he never wanted to lose that. But he also wanted more. He *needed* more, and he could either let his fear keep pushing her away or he could get the hell out of Holbrook and show Brynn that he's the right guy, one she can trust, but who's just had some shit timing.

"My lips are sealed, James. Go get her."

Jamie trusted Jeremy to take care of things in L.A. today. Sure, if anything went wrong, he'd lose his spot at the fest. But he would survive that.

He couldn't survive losing Brynn.

Chapter Twenty-Five

Turkey jerky and Twizzlers wasn't exactly the breakfast of champions—or lunch, for that matter—but it was slim pickings at the gas station. Brynn lucked out with a row of seats to herself, the Holbrook to Los Angeles shuttle apparently not a popular route for a Friday. This meant if she fell asleep, the only shoulder she'd drool on would be that of her suitcase perched on the seat next to her.

She'd tried texting Holly to tell her how this morning had panned out, but either the bus or whatever new town they'd entered or the combination of the two was messing with her cell service, and three texting attempts had failed. It was probably for the best since her head was beginning to ache. She was confident it was no worse than last night immediately following the injury, but she could use an ibuprofen or three right about now.

She rummaged through her purse, which might as well have been that magic satchel Mary Poppins carried, because she produced everything from emergency tampons to a romance novel she was reading but couldn't find the small tube of pain relief pills. It was entirely possible that in her packing haste she'd put it somewhere else. Good thing she didn't let the driver take her bag, because the pills must be buried somewhere in it.

She let the towel rack off the hook and blamed Jamie for the headache. Fine. Maybe she blamed herself a little, too. She could have fought him on this, on the whole sending her off to L.A. thing. But the truth was, as much as she was sure she loved him, she didn't know how to convince him. Or trust him not to lie again. This seemed to be their thing. They were friends. They crossed the line. Jamie pushed her away, and she let him.

She blew out a long breath. The whole situation exhausted her and made her head pound more. Brynn unzipped the large front pocket of her suitcase to rummage for the pills, but when she opened the compartment, a bulging plastic bag popped out. She took in a hitching breath.

The lucky bouquet.

"Dammit, Jamie!"

The woman across the aisle glanced her way, eyebrows raised. She hadn't meant to say it out loud, but if he couldn't hear her, then the other seven passengers headed to Los Angeles should.

Just holding the stupid thing brought the whole day in Amarillo back to her. No, it brought the whole trip back and the reunion and the summer they were seventeen. Jamie skipped out on the biggest party of the year to risk his health and stay with her when she was burning up with fever and tested positive for mono. Ten years later he'd walked in on her with the one guy he thought she'd always put on a pedestal—and maybe she had—and instead of telling her how he felt had let her go off on him in an angry-drunk rampage. Not her finest moment. Then he offered to make it up to her by bringing her exactly where she thought she wanted to go:

L.A. Maybe she could understand how professing his love to her after all of that may have seemed less than optimal.

But it wasn't the texts from Spencer or the anticipation of finally finding out if something was there that flooded her thoughts now. It was Jamie showing up at her apartment in his hoodie and baseball cap. It was the flat tire, riding to the top of the St. Louis Arch (without hurling, thank you very much), going blind in Galena, and naming that beer on her first sip. She thought of sneaking a peek at him as he leaned out of the shower and the places her mind went after that delicious sight. And then when he almost fell off the top of that Cadillac…she knew.

Oh.

She was so worked up over Jamie's lapse in judgment that she'd sort of, kind of, maybe neglected to tell him that her big revelation hadn't been the kiss. Or the phenomenal sex. Or even what happened again after the shower. Her first revelation was when they were seventeen. But Jamie needed a friend that summer, and as much as it hurt to realize too late how she felt about him, she promised herself she'd be that friend.

This time around, she let him freak out again, but he wasn't alone. She allowed her own fear to get in the way, too, and together they'd let doubt push them further and further apart when, after ten freaking years, they'd finally found their way to each other. It took a little bit of tequila to fully kick in, but Brynn realized she loved him while he nearly killed himself spraying graffiti on an upside-down car in the desert. She didn't need to see Spencer to know he wasn't the one, so what the hell was she doing taking a bus to him now?

"I'm an idiot," she grumbled. Across the aisle, the lady shot her a look again, and Brynn threw up her hands, knocking her pinky on the frame of the window. "Ow. Shit!" She cradled her hand against her chest and then laughed. If Jamie had been there, she most likely would have just clocked him in the face. The thing was, she wasn't clumsy by nature. She'd never accidentally punched, poked, or stabbed any other person in her life. Just Jamie, because he was the only one who got her fired up emotionally—usually out of exasperation, but it seemed like that was changing. Good or bad, he pulled that extra dose of passion out of her and made her feel really and truly alive.

It amazed her that she'd let ten years go by without admitting to herself he was the one person with the power to do it. And it infuriated her that he didn't know, couldn't tell that there was no competition. *Spencer* was the stand-in. At least the idea of him was.

"Is it your bouquet?"

Brynn turned toward the voice, the same woman who had been looking at her before. She was older, with a long salt-and-pepper braid that draped over her right shoulder. Her green eyes crinkled at the corners as she smiled.

"What?" Brynn asked.

"The bouquet? I don't mean to pry, but if it's yours, I was going to ask where the groom was."

Brynn looked down to where she unwittingly clutched the bouquet to her chest. Her lucky bouquet.

Her heart swelled as she thought of *the groom.*

"He's stuck in Holbrook," she said, not correcting the woman. "We're meeting in L.A."

"Rough honeymoon?" the woman asked with a wink, and Brynn remembered the bandage on her forehead and the headache that seemed to throb less the more she thought about making her way back to Jamie in Los Angeles.

Her fingers brushed over the gauze. "You could say that. Rough courtship, actually." She laughed, and the woman's smile broadened.

"How long were you together before the wedding?"

Brynn shifted her body so she was facing the woman now, lucky bouquet still pressed firmly to her heart.

"Ten years." And as she said it, Brynn knew it was true. Maybe they went about this whole thing in the most messed-up way possible, but no matter which way you looked at it, her heart had somehow been his. "Holy shit. I've loved him for ten years." She let go of the bouquet to fish her phone out of her bag. "I need to tell him."

The woman's brows pulled together. "He doesn't know?"

"No! I mean, the bouquet's mine, but we're not married. I caught it. At the wedding we crashed. And then he kissed me because Frank and Dora told us to so we could get the free room. I thought we were putting on a show, but it was real. And then he told me he loved me and he—let's just say he did some things, amazing things. I think he knows I love him, but he doesn't know I've loved him the whole time. *I* didn't really know it until now. I need to tell him I was an idiot for not fighting for him then or today when he put me on this bus and, *oh my God*, why isn't there cell phone service here?"

She stopped to catch her breath. She expected braid lady to pull the emergency stop cord and have her removed from the vehicle, but instead the woman looked at her and sighed, a soft smile on her face.

"Messy courtship indeed."

Brynn laughed, but tears sprang to her eyes as she did.

"Oh, sweetheart. It's okay. The dead zone only lasts about an hour, until we're out of Coconino County. Relax for a little bit, and then you can call your guy."

Brynn nodded and took in a slow breath. Then out. She repeated the calming exercise, and it seemed to be working. She needed the rest of the hour to go by as quickly as possible. Then she'd call Jamie. She'd tell him they were both idiots, and that would be that.

"Thank you," she told the woman. "I think I'm going to

close my eyes for a few minutes."

She leaned her head against the window and clutched the plastic-bagged bouquet like a teddy bear.

Just a few minutes was all she needed to collect her thoughts. Her eyes fell shut, and she didn't bother to set an alarm on her phone. She was too excited to talk to Jamie. Her body would know to wake her when the cell service returned.

Only it wasn't her body that woke her. It was the pothole on the 101. In L.A.

Brynn had cell service all right, and while she cursed herself for sleeping through her adrenaline rush to call Jamie, the one text notification on her phone deflated her completely.

Spencer: *Assuming you aren't making it tonight, but if you do, we'll be in the Tower Bar from eight until we close the place down. Hope I don't seem too eager. Just looking forward to seeing you again.*

She didn't know what she expected when she looked at her phone, not until she saw what *wasn't* there. She had an excuse for not contacting him—exhaustion plus the hypnotic lull of a moving vehicle. Brynn should have known better. But how could he not have checked in? Why didn't he have the same sort of revelation? She wasn't sure what she expected, but for her to hear nothing the whole day after he shipped her off and out of his sight... Maybe this was Jamie's final push, his way of telling her no matter what happens in L.A., he can't handle what happened in Amarillo.

One final stare at her screen solidified her plan. She had nowhere to stay but knew the name of one hotel. As luck would have it, the Sunset Tower Hotel—the one Spencer had invited her to—was less than ten miles from Center Studios, the location for tomorrow's beer fest. If she needed Jamie for a ride home, he wouldn't be too far away. Though she couldn't imagine another few days in the car with him now. She also couldn't afford to get home any other way. How had one unintentional nap completely changed her perspective?

It wasn't the nap, and she knew it. Something had made her believe—no, expect—that Jamie would come after her, that he would realize how ridiculous he was being asking her to make a choice she knew in her heart was already made. But Jamie wasn't the one looking forward to seeing her tonight, and that realization threatened to knock her on her tired and virtually numb ass.

A girl of her word, Brynn kept her promise and texted Jamie:

> *Made it here safely. Have fun tomorrow. Let's talk about travel-home arrangements when you get to town.*

She waited. And hoped. And waited some more. *Come on, Jamie*, she thought. *Reply. Make contact.* If they could just connect, somehow bridge the distance of this canyon growing between them, they could figure out the rest.

Brynn watched the other passengers exit the bus. Braid lady stood and hoisted a bag over her shoulder, then looked down to where Brynn still sat in her chair, staring at her phone.

"Maybe he's in a dead zone," the woman said and gave her shoulder a reassuring squeeze.

Brynn tried to smile. She wanted to play along, but she was so tired of pretending.

"I don't think so," she said. "But thank you anyway."

The woman's smile, however, didn't falter, and the sight of her as she looked back at Brynn one last time before exiting the bus gave her a final glimmer of hope.

One Mississippi. Two Mississippi. Three Mississippi.

She counted to a hundred and would have kept going if the driver didn't insist she get off the bus.

Nothing.

How, after everything she'd said, could he push her over the edge? Did Jamie *want* her to choose Spencer just to prove himself right? Because nothing had changed, not for Brynn, at least. She'd made her choice.

Even if Jamie didn't chase her down, if he let fear win, Brynn was done lying to herself and to everyone else about how she felt. She owed someone the truth, and right now there was only one person here who would listen.

She tapped on her most recent text and typed a quick reply:

Hey, Spencer. I'll see you at eight.

Chapter Twenty-Six

Jamie knew the first thing he would purchase when he got to L.A. A Bluetooth headset. He couldn't stand the people who walked around the city looking like they were talking to themselves, but now that cities and states across the nation were making hands-free phone usage laws—and seeing as how he could have spent the entire drive convincing Brynn that he was wrong for pushing her away and that everything about them was right—he could use a freaking hands-free headset.

He tried calling her before he left Holbrook, but it went right to her voicemail. He didn't exactly want his big Eureka moment to be a recording. Jamie thought about stopping more than once along the way to try calling her again, but that would only get him to L.A. later, which didn't bode well for him professionally *or* personally.

Now here he was, eight p.m. already, and checking in at his hotel. Jeremy had texted that everything went well and they were all set for tomorrow. Brynn had texted, too, only to let him know she made it safely, and he was at the very least relieved to hear that. Now he just had to find her.

"How long will you be staying with us?" the woman behind the counter asked him.

Jamie peeled his eyes from his phone. "Just through the weekend. I head back to Chicago on Monday."

She handed him a pamphlet with a folder that held his room key, but all he could focus on was whether or not he'd be leaving here Monday alone.

"Checkout is at noon," she told him, and he nodded his understanding. She smiled warmly, but he could barely muster the same in response. He just wanted to get upstairs, throw his crap in his room, and find Brynn.

He glanced to his left, at the swanky bar in the equally swanky hotel he had hoped he wouldn't be staying in alone. Jamie had promised himself that by the end of the trip he'd tell Brynn how he felt, and if things went well, maybe he'd get to spend the night with her in a place like this. He did the first part — the telling — but then he fucked it all up.

His eyes landed on a group of people standing near the bar's entrance, only about twenty feet away. Specifically, they landed on the back of a woman who wore her hair in a braid that fell over her shoulder, exposing the bare back of her black halter dress. She was deep in conversation with a man in a suit, and Jamie laughed quietly to himself as he noted his own attire — a T-shirt and a pair of jeans that were getting ready to walk themselves to the hotel room's laundry bag.

Something tugged his eyes up once more, and his gaze locked on the woman's back. A momentary pang of guilt rose inside him as he saw his attraction to this stranger as some sort of betrayal to Brynn. But then it clicked. The guy in the suit — the tailored suit that only a dude from L.A. could pull off — Jamie recognized them both now. And the man staring back at him recognized Jamie, too.

Jamie's jaw ticked as he woke up his phone and pulled

up *Sleepy Jean* from his contact list. The guilt vanished as he pressed send and waited.

The woman in the halter dress reached in her purse and pulled out her phone. She hesitated—fucking hesitated—before answering, and that small reaction was enough to crack Jamie's heart wide open.

"Jamie."

But it wasn't his name he heard, not at first. It was Spencer's low hum of a voice, caught in the few seconds of delay from Brynn answering the call and actually speaking.

"...knows you're staying with me, right?"

He remembered Spencer's text, the one he shouldn't have read. He'd booked a room for them. And then Jamie put her on a bus. He let out a long breath, but he couldn't form a single word in response. Spencer's eyes found Jamie's, and he tapped Brynn on the shoulder and pointed behind her. She turned.

Nope. Jamie was wrong. *This* cracked his heart wide open. Even in that awful Cubs T-shirt, pajama pants, her glasses, and a bun on top of her head, Jamie thought Brynn was the most beautiful woman he'd ever seen. But tonight she was magnificent, and the only thought in his mind was that she dressed this way for another man, one she was staying with tonight.

She took a step toward him, but Jamie held up his hand.

"It's okay, B," he said, his voice hoarse but at least able to articulate a few words. "I wanted you to be happy, either way. This was what I wanted, right? For you to figure this out. A heads-up you were staying with him would have been nice, but what's done is done, isn't it?"

We're done, he thought and started backing away, but he couldn't take his eyes off her. Not yet. Because as soon as he looked away, broke that last semblance of connection, they really would be done.

"Jamie…" Her voice pleaded with him. She moved in his direction again, but something in his gaze must have stopped her because she only made it a couple of feet. "We should talk about this."

Spencer guided the two other people in their group farther into the bar.

"You'll miss your party," he said. "Or whatever it is." He scrubbed a hand over his jaw and felt that his stubble was getting close to being a beard. Had he really not shaved all week?

"It's just dinner," she said quietly. "I only came here to tell Spencer… Shit. Can we talk after, maybe? I just think—"

"It's been a long day," he said, fighting to keep his voice even. "I should really just crash."

Now she crossed her arms and narrowed her eyes, giving him *the look*. It was the same look his mom used on him and his brothers, the one that said, *I have fucking had enough*. Not that he could ever picture his mom saying *fuck*, but in his head, he'd known she'd meant it. Brynn had had enough, and so had he.

"I can't do this anymore, Brynn. He wins, okay?"

He lingered for another few seconds, long enough to think twice about begging her to reconsider, but he tucked the thought away. He wouldn't ruin this night for her no matter how much it had been obliterated for him. Because, broken heart or not, he still wanted happiness for her.

"Good night, Brynn."

She stood there, mouth open and poised to respond, but said nothing. So he disappeared around the corner where he found an elevator about to close and squeezed in just in time.

Just in time to run, he thought. He was getting damn good at this, and he hated himself for it.

Jamie did have work to do, but it would have to wait until morning. He had only one plan for this evening, and it involved a quick phone call to the concierge.

"Sure, Mr. Kingston. We can charge the bottle to your room."

Ten minutes later there was a knock at the door. The room-service attendant was a guy not much younger than him, and he smiled wryly as he handed Jamie the pint of Jack. Just enough to get him through the night without making him useless in the morning.

"Here," Jamie said, handing the kid a tip. "You can keep the glass."

Jamie closed the door and seconds later collapsed into the chair by the window that looked out over the pool. He unscrewed the bottle and held it up as if to toast himself.

"Well, Jack, I guess we meet again."

At least he wouldn't spend the night completely alone.

• • •

"Staying with you?" Brynn whirled to face Spencer, the boy— now the man—she'd fantasized about, put on a pedestal for *ten years*, and here she was, yelling at him.

The confidence in his blue eyes wavered for only a second, but Brynn saw the way her anger could slice at someone, especially one who didn't deserve to be on the receiving end of it. That was Spencer now, and it had been Jamie two weeks ago.

"Shit," she said. "Shit. Spencer, I'm sorry."

Her eyes stung, and her head pounded. She reached for the flesh-colored bandage that replaced the square of gauze she'd worn all day. Spencer hadn't asked her about it, and she was glad of it. Just seeing Jamie, though, and the weariness in his eyes, made everything in her pulse. Pain, love, passion, complete and utter fury—he ignited it all, her heart racing as she realized she'd just let him walk away from her.

And then this man whom she barely knew, who was the boy on the pedestal, smiled at her.

"You're not staying for dinner."

Brynn shook her head.

He chuckled softly. "And it's safe to say I was a bit presumptuous about you staying in my room. *I'm* sorry, Brynn. I shouldn't have said what I said."

She had to hand it to herself. She really could pick them. Spencer was Mr. Perfect in high school, and here he was, living up to that label once more. She could tick off the list like Jamie thought she would. Spencer was gorgeous, successful, understanding, and he wrote books. Books! On paper, yes, he fit the profile—ten years ago and today. The only difference was that Brynn wasn't blind anymore.

He wasn't perfect for her.

"I'm sorry," she said again, even though her whole point in coming to dinner was to say exactly that.

He shook his head. "Don't be. I admit I am disappointed but not surprised."

"You're not?" she asked.

He walked her into the lobby.

"I had the biggest crush on you in high school," Spencer said. "But I always figured you and Kingston were a thing."

She sputtered. "You had a…I'm sorry did you…a crush on *me*?"

He smiled. "Don't sound so surprised. It's not like I was the only one." He nodded toward the upper floors of the hotel.

Brynn crossed her arms. "Yeah, well, he's got a funny way of showing it."

Now Spencer was laughing. "Hey, remember how the boys used to show they liked the girls in grade school?"

"What, like hair pulling and hitting?"

He shrugged. "I think we've come a long way since then. Not like we don't still have a ways to go. Took me until the reunion to make my move. I imagine it gets more complicated when you have a history."

Brynn grabbed his hand and squeezed. "God, you really are the whole package, aren't you? And I suppose because you are this amazing guy you don't think I'm a horrible person for the way I behaved at the reunion and for coming here now just to tell you I'm in love with the guy who brought me here. I guess I have a funny way of showing how I feel, too."

Spencer squeezed her hand back. "No. I don't think you're a horrible person. You just finally saw what the rest of us did ten years ago."

She really wanted to punch Jamie or pull his hair or something, not just because she loved him but because they'd wasted ten years pretending.

"Good night, Brynn," Spencer said. "It was good to see you."

"Good night," she said. "Good luck with the book."

And that was that. She had traveled over two thousand miles to chase the guy who was sitting next to her the whole time. And now, because he was stubborn and scared and selfless and, well, perfect for her in every way, she had to chase him some more.

As Spencer turned back toward the bar, Brynn pulled out her phone. Jamie let the call go to voicemail. She groaned and tried again. Five rings and still no answer.

"Shit!" she said, not caring about the volume or level of distress in her voice *or* that she seemed to have no other word to convey anything she felt this evening.

She hurried up to the desk where the hotel attendant had been eyeing her, Jamie, and Spencer through the whole exchange.

She smiled, but it came off as more of a sneer.

"I'm not at liberty to give out other patrons' room numbers," the woman said before Brynn could ask. "And based on what I just witnessed, I don't think that gorgeous, rugged man I sent upstairs wants anything to do with you."

Gorgeous, rugged man? Not that Brynn was arguing, but that was *her* gorgeous, rugged man this woman was talking about.

"Please..." She focused on the woman's name tag. "Victoria, this is an emergency."

"Uh-huh." She smirked. "Emergency. Yeah, still not giving you his room number."

Brynn took a cleansing breath. *Kill her with kindness*, she thought.

"Look, Victoria. Can we talk, woman to woman? That is my best friend who just walked away from me, thinking the worst about me. But he's wrong. And I'm in love with him, and if you could just tell me where his room is, I can make everything right. Haven't you ever been in love?" she asked hopefully. Then she leaned over the counter and whispered, "I know it's bending the rules, but it's for a good cause, right?"

Victoria pressed her lips together, glanced at her computer monitor, and then back at Brynn.

"Yes. I've been in love before. And would you like to know what that got me?"

Uh-oh, Brynn thought. *Abort mission. Abort. Abort!* But it was too late.

"It got me double the rent after I found the *love of my life* in our bed with the cable guy."

Brynn wrinkled her brows.

"Now you want to ask me if the love of my life was a guy or a girl, right?"

She chewed her bottom lip. "I kinda do," she said. Maybe she and Victoria were bonding, and this did sound like a great story.

Victoria crossed her arms. "My sexual orientation is none of your business, and the same goes for your *friend's* room number. Is there anything else I can help you with tonight?"

Brynn groaned. She wanted to sneer at the woman, give her one of her most practiced disdainful looks, but she didn't want to risk — what was the equivalent of a waiter spitting in your food? — dirty towels or a bedspread that should never be seen under a black light? Besides, she *was* just doing her job. What if one of Brynn's hypothetical muggers not only found her hidden money in her wallet but also followed her back to her hotel to mug her *again*? Would she want the front desk attendant to divulge her whereabouts? No. Of course not.

But Brynn wasn't here to mug Jamie. In the past few months she'd already stabbed him and clocked him in the face. This week she'd certainly helped deplete his funds. It was as if she'd been mugging him all along. Maybe that was just her way — like punching the boy you like on the playground at recess. She was here to *be* with Jamie. To fight for him, even if he had finally lost all his fight.

She considered walking each floor, dialing Jamie's cell phone, and hoping she could hear his ringtone through the door. But Jamie was a man of simplicity, which meant he always left his phone on vibrate. In a one-room home for the next few days, Brynn knew he couldn't miss the phone's ring. But she would. Nope, stalking the floors wouldn't work.

She tried Jamie's cell one more time, willed him to pick up, but this time it went to voicemail after one ring. That meant he saw it was her and actively canceled the call. He wasn't going to make this easy.

"Jamie," she said. "Please. We need to talk, but not like this. I need to see you. Call me back. Or...or come to my room. Room 460. Just talk to me, okay?"

She wouldn't admit defeat. Not yet. Brynn rode the elevator to the fourth floor and found her way back to room 460. If Jamie wasn't going to listen to her, she would find a way to make him hear.

Chapter Twenty-Seven

One swig was all he allowed himself before getting in the shower to rinse away the day—this week—all of it. Jamie knew that if he finished that pint (and he planned to finish that pint) first, he ran the risk of passing out before the whole showering thing, and that didn't bode well for having to wake up early to get to the fest for setup. He just needed enough to dull the edges, but even now, as he braced his arm against the tiled shower wall and let the hot water pelt his skin, he still felt raw.

In a way he always expected the week to end up like this, but Amarillo and Annie let him cling to that shred of hope. He blamed himself, not Brynn. He pushed her away when he finally got what he wanted, too scared to believe he could keep it.

All the shower managed to do was make him wish Brynn was there with him. Fuck, she almost was. She was in the same building. It was just the whole *with* situation that wasn't what it should have been. He sent her here to see Spencer and then lost his mind when she did what he'd asked her to do.

Not until he was sure he'd most likely depleted the hotel's hot water reservoir did he finally turn off the shower. He plopped back down in his chair, towel wrapped around his waist, and unscrewed the bottle again. Tipping it back against his lips, he let the spicy heat of the liquid pour down his throat and warm his insides. The edges of the day's activities were getting duller by the minute. Since he really had nothing else to lose other than his body's ability to metabolize his intake at a speed fast enough *not* to give him a hangover, he let his next sip be the one that drained the bottle. Jamie hissed a breath through his teeth. For a guy who slow sips a pint in an effort to savor a brewer's craftsmanship, a pint of Jack in one sitting was stronger than expected, to say the least.

He stood when, honestly, he should have sat for several more minutes, or at least until he got used to his slowly blurring vision.

He laughed. This must have been what it was like to be Brynn in Tulsa, but at least her vision cleared the farther away things got. For Jamie it only cleared if he pressed his eyes shut.

Yes. That's what the back of an eyelid should look like.

He decided brushing his teeth would make things clearer because—because—shit, he didn't know what came after because. But he remembered his errand when he got to the bathroom, so he took to brushing his teeth.

Somewhere between the bathroom and the bed, Jamie's towel fell off, so he climbed naked into the sheets after grabbing his phone.

When the hell had that voicemail notification popped up?

He swiped the lock on his screen, grateful he didn't have a lock code, and opened his voicemail. Even though the alcohol had made the day's events sufficiently fuzzy, his gut still twisted when he heard Brynn's voice—recognized its plea.

She gave him her room number, which was all well and good, but he wasn't going to barge in on her and Spencer.

Again.

Jamie wasn't a drunk texter, but coherent speech felt beyond his capacity at the moment. Plus he was both drunk and naked this evening, a new combination, which he thought called for a new experience. Drunk texting.

Only because Brynn's number was the last to send him a message did he choose the right one. Otherwise, the message could have gone to his brother Ben as he would have looked for Brynn in the *B*s rather than under *S* for Sleepy Jean because, dammit, he was drunk, which is why, thankfully, he did *not* text his brother.

Jamie: *Dr. Unk*

He tried three times to get rid of the period, but damn Autocorrect won this round. He hit send without typing anything else, figuring he shouldn't be drunk texting her, but that was the thing about drunk texting. You did it even though you shouldn't. Because of the whole drunk part of the scenario. Somewhere in his cloudy brain he rationalized that letting her know he *was* drunk would also explain to her *why* he was drunk, that it would somehow say all the things he should have said before Amarillo and not waited for complete strangers to light the fuse that he'd been trying to douse for years.

He closed his eyes and laid the phone on his bare chest. The vibration came seconds later, which was a good thing because a few seconds more and he probably would be asleep.

He sat up and rallied, rubbed his eyes, and then read.

Sleepy Jean: *Dr. Unk?*

Crap. She hadn't cracked his code. He was about to reattempt the word sans extra space and autocorrect assholery when she texted again.

Sleepy Jean: *You're drunk? I just left you thirty minutes ago.*

Even in his state, Jamie had to laugh at the irony of this.

Jamie: *You left me twelve hours ago, B. As you should have.*

His texting fingers were working better, not that it mattered at this point.

Sleepy Jean: *What room are you in?*

He could tell her. He could explain that her name was actually on the reservation, but what good would that do now? And how many points would he earn by letting her see him like this? Even he didn't want to look himself in the eye.

He lay back down, closing his eyes just for a minute. He'd think this through, weigh the pros and cons, and if he didn't find enough reasons *not* to tell her his room number, then he would.

But a pint of Jack on an empty stomach meant two things. One: Jamie passed out for an hour. And two: for the first time in at least five years, he hurled.

It only took seconds for his stomach to empty itself of its sole contents, the whiskey. Fairly sober and head pounding, he cleaned himself up and dressed in a T-shirt and flannel pants before glancing at the phone he'd unwittingly tossed to the floor on his flight to the porcelain god.

Sleepy Jean: *What room are you in?*

The text was time stamped over an hour ago, and he'd never responded. And Brynn, well, it looked like she'd given up. He figured she'd reached her statute of limitations for giving him another chance, and how could he blame her?

He set his alarm and crawled into bed. He'd looked forward to tomorrow for two weeks. And when Brynn agreed to go with him on this trip, he allowed himself to hope. Now all he wanted was to get through the next day and get his ass on the road back to Chicago.

. . .

Brynn headed down to the lobby and grimaced when she saw Victoria behind the front desk again. Did the woman not sleep?

Serenity now, she thought to herself. She approached the desk and cleared her throat, forcing Victoria to look up from whatever it was she was doing—probably intentionally ignoring the woman who wronged the *gorgeous, rugged man* the night before.

"My travel plans have changed, and I'm going to need to check out a day early."

Brynn slid her hotel room key across the counter to Victoria, who pursed her lips as she stared at it.

"There is a fifty dollar surcharge for canceling less than twenty-four hours in advance."

Brynn let out a long breath. "Then charge me," she said.

Victoria said nothing else as her fingertips started clicking and clacking the keyboard, but then the woman's eyes widened.

"What?" Brynn asked. "Is it a hundred dollar surcharge? I don't care, okay? Just check me out and find someone to call me a cab to the airport. I'll spend the rest of my savings on a same-day flight to Chicago."

Victoria's whole countenance changed. "Miss, I...uh... I'm terribly sorry. It seems there has been a mistake. When I typed in your name, *two* reservations showed up."

Great. Now this woman wanted to charge her for two

rooms?

"I don't know what kind of racket you're running here, lady…" She could pull off *racket*, right? "…but I am not paying for two rooms."

Victoria shook her head, and her cheeks flushed. Brynn realized the woman was panicked.

"When you asked for his room number last night, I should have checked his reservation, just to be sure. But he was…he had that tortured-lover look going for him. Plus the almost beard and the baseball hat—so Midwestern…"

Brynn's breathing grew shallow as she started to put the pieces together, but she needed Victoria to confirm it.

"Can you get over your fantasy for a second and say what you're trying to tell me?" Brynn's voice shocked even her—strong and demanding, because, dammit, this was *her* tortured lover with the beard and baseball hat.

"Your name is on his reservation," Victoria finally blurted.

Brynn swallowed and cleared her throat again, this time not to get Victoria's attention but to make sure she had voice enough to speak. When Jamie hadn't texted her back last night, she'd assumed that was his final response to whatever it was they were still negotiating. But maybe he was drunker than she thought. Maybe he'd just forgotten. Maybe…she wanted to scream. Because maybe it was time for them to stop being fools and make this right.

"Did he add me to the reservation on arrival?"

Victoria shook her head. "This reservation was made two weeks ago, in both your names."

Brynn's throat went dry, and she choked back what could have been a laugh or a sob.

James T. Kirk, you always intended on us ending up here together!

She scurried around to the side of the desk and wheeled her suitcase behind it. Victoria flinched, and Brynn rolled her eyes.

"Do I look like the violent type?" she asked, and Victoria shook her head. "Have you seen Mr. Kingston this morning?" Now Victoria nodded. "Then I need you to watch this, and I need you to call me a cab to Center Studios. That's where this beer festival thing is, correct?" Another nod.

In less than five minutes, Brynn was in a taxi on her way to find the man who was too stubborn and scared to admit what this trip had been all about, to prove to him that *she'd* been too stubborn to see what was right in front of her, and to convince him that they'd spent enough time apart already.

She looked down at what Jamie considered her godforsaken Cubs T-shirt. She'd planned on spending the day on a plane not trying to win out over Jamie's fear. And though she'd showered and put on clean undergarments, she was pretty much out of clothes that hadn't already been worn. Well, if he loved her, he'd take her in spite of the shirt. Now she just had to find him.

Chapter Twenty-Eight

Jeremy opened another bottle of the new brew to fill the sampler cups.

"We're getting good traffic," he said, and Jamie grunted a response he hoped came off as an affirmative.

"My sister keeps texting me saying that you and Brynn aren't returning her texts. Can you just answer her so I can stop being the middle man?"

Jamie grunted again, this time a negative.

Jeremy continued pouring and passing out samples while Jamie occasionally greeted a patron who wanted to meet the brewer. He was happy for the band playing across the way, though he thought about requesting something other than Van Halen's "Why Can't This Be Love." Instead he gritted his teeth. He could make it through the next three minutes. For the most part the music helped drown out his thoughts enough to keep working. If he stopped moving, stopped listening, he'd have a hard time keeping himself from just hopping in the truck and saying *Fuck it.*

"So you're going with the stoic lumberjack thing, then?"

Jeremy asked, a smirk plastered on his face as he gave Jamie's plaid and denim look a once-over. Jamie still didn't feel like talking. "Where is Brynn, anyway?" Jeremy asked. "Between the texts from my sister and the fact that Brynn's not here for the big unveiling, I take it the trip didn't quite work out as planned?"

"I'm going for a walk," Jamie said, rolling up the sleeves of his button-down. He scrubbed a hand across his jaw. Yep. It was definitely a beard now. He adjusted his Sox hat and felt the hair tickling the tops of his ears, brushing the collar of his shirt. And just as he was about to set off for a little solitude in a sea of strangers, he heard his name.

Not from someone nearby, yet not a voice shouting across the expanse of the studio field. Nope. *I'm looking for Jamie Kingston* blared through the lot's speakers, the ones being used by the cover band who just finished their song. And dammit if he didn't know that voice.

The stage was in his line of sight, and as he got closer, he saw first—Jesus, he saw the Cubs shirt, but he didn't care. He laughed, something he thought he wouldn't do today or any day soon.

"Jamie. I know you're out there. At least, I hope you are or else Chainsaw and the boys are going to really regret playing this next song if it's totally in vain. Did you know the singer's name is Chainsaw? Great name, dude." She'd turned her face from the mic to acknowledge the long-haired, leather-pants-wearing band member who must have been Chainsaw.

"Anyway," she continued, "I need to tell you something, and I was hoping if I did it with enough witnesses, you'd finally believe me."

Jamie pushed his way through the crowd, as close to the stage as he could get. The ground was wet up front, muddied by spilled beer from patrons who were already drunk by eleven a.m.

She saw him then, and she chewed her top lip before breaking into a smile.

"What the hell are you doing?" he yelled up to her.

She looked at the band poised to play, then back at him.

"Your laugh," she started. "I love the deep rasp of your laugh and the way I can't help but smile when I hear it."

He lifted his hat and ran a hand through his hair before adjusting it again. Then he crossed his arms. Since when did he get so fidgety?

"And that!" She pointed at him. "That hat, how it's a part of you, a reminder of your loyalty, no matter how good or bad the Sox are doing."

"Hey!" he called to her, the crowd circling around him to listen to their show. "We're in the playoffs. We could make it to the Series!"

Her smile broadened, and he itched to move closer, then crawl up on that stage and grab her. She was here for him. She had to be. After last night—after the past few days—he let hope wriggle its way in.

"The way you stay so even-tempered to balance my..." She threw her hands in the air in a wild gesticulation, and he laughed. "But with the things that matter—your work... and the people you love—you fill with passion, one that's so contagious people can't help but love what you love."

Her voice broke on that last word, and Jamie's heart hammered in his chest.

"*That's* my checklist, Jamie. It was never a contest, because it was always you. It only took me one night to fall for you, but it wasn't in Amarillo."

His brows furrowed, and she beamed at him. That beautiful smile was for him.

"It was on my couch, ten years ago. You win, Jamie. Every time."

She stepped away from the mic and allowed Chainsaw

to take his rightful place. And then the band that had been covering nothing but eighties and nineties hair-band songs since the fest had begun erupted with the opening guitar solo to "I'm a Believer" by the Monkees.

Brynn inched toward the edge of the stage and sat, poised to hop down, but he could tell the stage was higher than she'd anticipated. Jamie shook his head and laughed, reaching for her, and as soon as he held her, felt the warmth of her skin against his as her arms draped around his neck, he misstepped, his foot hitting a patch of particularly slippery, beer-soaked grass, and the two of them went down *not* in a blaze of glory but in a puddle of mud and beer.

The crowd around them gasped, the band kept playing, and Jamie lay flat on his back, the woman he loved on top of him, and the wind, quite literally, knocked out of his lungs.

Brynn's eyes were wide.

"Are you okay?" She lifted her body weight from his chest, and he gasped in a breath. When his lungs were filled enough for him to utter a sound, he laughed, then pulled her to him and kissed her with everything he had. They were both laughing—kissing and laughing and lying soaked on the ground while the band played on and the crowd applauded for the couple who'd been too crazy about each other to get things right for ten long years.

"Loving you is going to kill me, isn't it?" he asked, and she tilted her head up and smiled.

"But you do still love me, right?"

It wasn't really a question. Her voice held an air of triumph.

"Even in that shirt," he said, "which we are tossing as soon as we get back to the hotel."

She peeled herself from him and stood, pulling him up with her. Then he saw the Cubs shirt, wet with beer and plastered to her curves.

"Okay, you can keep it," he said. "If you promise only to wear it wet."

She raised a brow.

"You're impossible," she said.

"Impossible not to be madly in love with me?"

She laughed.

"I want you to catch me, Jamie. I'm sorry it took me so long to tell you."

"And I want you to catch me right back," he said, taking off his Sox cap and placing it on her head. "Much better. Wait. How'd you get that band to let you take over their set?"

She shrugged. "They're a hair-band cover band. They love a good love story as much as the next person, and I begged them to let me fight for my happy ending."

He leaned his forehead against hers, as if touching her could reassure him that this was all real.

"Because I'm your happy ending?"

She smoothed her hands over the scruff on his jaw and smiled, the look sweet and soft.

"You are," she said, and pressed her lips to his again.

. . .

Jeremy waggled his brows at them as they strolled up to the tent.

"Hey, Jer," Brynn said.

"Nicely played, Chandler. And by the way, my sister is expecting a call from you," he told her, and she laughed. "And no offense, but you two look disgusting."

"Can't argue with you there," she said. "And I can't believe you two didn't tell me you actually had a tent here. I thought this trip was like a vacation or something." She looked at Jamie, and he grinned sheepishly.

He stepped behind the makeshift bar of the Kingston Ale

House tent, and when Brynn tried to follow him, he held up his hand to stop her.

"You're not serious, are you?" she asked, but Jamie's expression was impassive. What was he doing?

"We need to run back to the hotel and shower, but first, Miss Chandler, I'm going to need your glasses," he said.

Brynn crossed her arms and gave him a pointed look, but she couldn't help that the corners of her mouth turned up. Whatever was going on, whatever else he'd kept from her, it felt more like a surprise than any kind of lie, so she played along.

She leaned over the bar.

"Why don't you take them, then?" she said.

He did, but not before stealing another kiss, and Jeremy groaned.

"Okay, like I'm all happy you two finally got your heads out of your asses, but if I have to watch this all day…"

Jamie laughed. "Dude, I'm paying you to be here."

"You're paying me to sell your new brew."

"New brew?" Brynn asked. With her glasses in Jamie's hands she was reliant on just her senses now, and her sense of smell was begging for anything other than what was emanating from her clothing at the moment.

"You ready for a taste test?" Jamie asked as the band went back to its set list, covering "Talk Dirty to Me" in the background. She could think of someone she wanted to talk dirty to her. That was for sure.

Focus, Brynn, she told herself. *Not in front of your best girlfriend's little brother.*

"Hell yeah!" she said. It was nearing noon, and she was ready to get her brew on.

Despite her better judgment, she took in a deep breath through her nose.

"You just cut an orange," she said, the scent of citrus

permeating the air around her and drowning out the less satisfactory odor of her shirt and jeans.

"Ooh, she's good," Jeremy said. "But is she good enough?"

Brynn huffed out a breath. "What kind of conspiracy are you two planning?"

Jamie grabbed her hands, kissed each palm, then placed them around a cold plastic cup.

"Think you can name it in one sip?" he asked.

Her teeth grazed her bottom lip as she smiled.

"You have taught the young Padawan well," Jeremy said. "It is time to see if she is a Jedi."

Brynn snorted.

"That's my girl," Jamie said.

She regained composure and brought the cup to her lips, recalling the last time she did this and how Jamie must have felt watching her. So she decided on an encore performance and closed her eyes, dipping her tongue into the creamy foam at the top of the cup.

"For fuck's sake." This came from Jeremy. "I can handle the flirting, but come on, guys."

"You really are going to be the end of me, aren't you, Brynn Chandler?"

She could hear Jamie's smile.

"I sure hope so," she said, and then she sipped.

She couldn't see him clearly, but her eyes widened just the same.

"It's a Belgian white," she said, but her voice cracked as she started to make sense of this so-called conspiracy. "Jamie, I need my glasses."

And in a perfect instant replay, he gave her one soft, slow kiss. Then he gave her back her sight.

He handed her the empty display bottle, one Jeremy must have had hidden when they arrived. She read the label and choked back a laugh. Or maybe it was a sob. Either way it was a giddy, ridiculous kind of happy.

CHANDLER'S WITBIER read the label, and the logo was a starry sky with a full moon.

Her breath hitched. She looked at him, then the bottle. Then him again. "You lassoed the moon for me," she said.

"Hey." He cupped her cheek in his hand, his thumb swiping at a tear she didn't realize was there. "It took a while to get it right, and I didn't want to tell you until I did." He laughed then. "In Amarillo, Dora said... I thought she knew."

"It's my name...on the bottle. Jamie, I don't even know what to say."

"How about...lucky freaking bouquet?"

She ignored his earlier direction and joined him behind the bar just as Jeremy decided to go and check on *something*, though he couldn't say what that something was. She fisted her hands in Jamie's wet shirt and tugged him to her.

"I almost let you get away," she said, realizing that they almost didn't make it here together.

"Nah," he said, pulling the bill of his hat over her eyes. "I would have chased you down eventually. Maybe in another ten years."

She stepped back in a flurry of movement, her hands splayed against his chest, and Jamie winced.

"What?" she asked.

"Nothing," he said, opening one eye to peek at her, then the other. "Just bracing myself for a stabbing or some other random act of violence."

She wanted to argue with him, but he was right, just one step ahead of her this time.

"You really would have waited that long?" she asked.

"I guess we'll never know," he said. "Doesn't matter now, because I'm not letting you go."

That satisfied her enough to let him pull her into a kiss, and it felt like another first. In high school their kiss was a revelation, awakening feelings she never admitted were there. In Amarillo, it was a confirmation that what they'd both kept at bay for so long had been real. But this—this kiss was a promise, one that told her she wouldn't have to travel across the country to find happiness again. It was always there, right next to her, waiting to be discovered.

Jamie held her tight, pulling her closer with each sweep of his tongue, each brush of his lips against hers. And when she closed her eyes, she finally saw what she'd been blind to for years.

"Fireworks," she told him as she kissed him back.

"Yeah," Jamie said. "I know what you mean."

Chapter Twenty-Nine

Brynn's breath hitched, and she bit her bottom lip as she watched him.

Jamie was so intent on getting out of his now stiffening shirt and jeans, he wasn't prepared for his dick to stand at attention at the sight of her reaction to him. Scratch that. Apparently his dick worked independently of his brain because he was ready to salute, and she wasn't even undressed yet.

Her teeth still tugged on that lip, and she pulled her shirt over her head. It was Jamie's turn to gasp as his eyes fell on her breasts, nipples taut and hard behind the fabric of her bra. He reached for the clasp, and she shook her head.

"We need to talk first," she said.

He didn't disagree. Even though they'd had their reconnection at the fest, they really hadn't spoken about last night or Amarillo or the past ten years. But he was hard as a rock, and those breasts needed his hands on them. He could see she was fighting instinct, trying to stay restrained, and it only made him want her more.

This woman had been put on this earth to torture him. He

couldn't think of another explanation.

In a flash, her jeans pooled at her ankles, and all that was left was a black lace thong. Brynn wore a thong? Well, after the little shimmy she did to get out of it, he would have to say no. At least, she wasn't wearing one now.

Holy shit, she was going to drive him insane.

"Get in," she said, poking a finger into his chest. Jamie's eyes widened, but he obeyed, stepping into the shower, the water already running. The plan was to head to the hotel in between the two legs of the fest, shower, and return to the beer tent before round two began. They had two hours, and apparently Brynn had an agenda.

He backed against the tiled wall, and she followed him in, beads of water collecting on her nose, her shoulders, her breasts. Her hair clung to the sides of her face, her neck, and yep. This was what insanity felt like—complete and total madness. The water made the cut on her forehead more visible, and her glasses, still on, were starting to fog, but it didn't matter. Before him was the most beautiful woman he'd ever seen, one he'd loved since he understood the meaning of the word, and the one, until a couple of hours ago, he thought he'd lost. He ached to touch her, agonized as he stood there staring. But this was not his move to make. He understood that much. So he'd wait her out, even if it killed him.

She started by washing her hair. She stood there, naked in front of him, and *washed her hair*. Jamie swallowed hard as he watched her, admiring the sight in front of him. When she was done, she pressed the shampoo bottle into his chest but said nothing. So he did the same, washing away the remnants of their time at the fest as well as the pain of waking this morning and thinking Brynn was out of his life for good. As he closed his eyes to rinse, he imagined it was her hands on him rather than his own, but she was winning this war of restraint, one that had him aching for her touch.

"You were never with Spencer?" he asked, needing to break the silence. If he couldn't touch her yet, he'd at least get her talking. He started by stating what was now the obvious. Other than *You're naked and in my shower and I might explode if I don't kiss you*, this was all that came to mind.

She pushed his shoulders with more force than he expected, and he slid into the shower wall, bracing himself with both arms so he didn't fall.

"Jesus, Brynn. A little shower safety maybe?"

Her hand flew to her mouth. "Sorry! Ugh. I suck at authoritative seductress."

He pulled her hand away, wrapped his fingers around her wrist, and tugged her to him.

He breathed her in, still able to distinguish her scent from the rising steam surrounding them, grateful it was no longer masked by the spilled beer.

"Are you seducing me?" he asked, finally cracking a smile. "Because I thought I was in some sort of trouble."

She gave in and wrapped her arms around him, her breasts firm against his chest. His erection pressed against her stomach, and they both exchanged something between a sigh and a moan.

"Maybe," she said. "But I was supposed to yell at you first."

"I deserve it, I guess. But I'm not sure I get it," he said, his voiced laced with equal amounts pain and desire. "I heard him say you were staying with him. You looked like you were with him, and that dress..." He didn't want to think about how she looked in that dress, the one he thought she'd worn for another man.

She released her grip on him, not backing away completely but enough so their eyes could meet. She rested her arms on his chest.

Brynn groaned. "You know you infuriate me, right?"

"Part of my charm?"

She shook her head. "Not yet. No being cute until you're done listening. Got it?"

He nodded. She had the authoritative thing down.

"You put me on a bus, Jamie."

She might as well have punched him in the gut. Because that's how the sentence sounded, full of hurt.

"I know. I thought I was doing the right thing. I thought I was doing what you needed."

She shook her head slowly.

"And you didn't call me."

He hadn't, but she needed to know he tried.

"I did. I called you right before I left Holbrook, but it went right to your voicemail. I didn't want to tell you everything in a message—that I'd messed up, that I loved you and didn't want to push you away anymore. I had no right to ask you to prove how you felt. I was just—"

"Scared." Brynn finished his sentence. She was always good at that.

He laughed. "That's putting it mildly. I'm terrified, Brynn. For ten years I've been so scared of losing you. But I realize now that if I keep running from how I feel, then I've already lost. That's why I didn't stop on the road to call again. I needed to get here. I needed to find you and tell you that I was wrong—about so many things. I needed to run *to* you this time, even if I didn't find what I wanted when I got there. But I fucked up again when I saw you with him."

She threw up those wild hands, and he grabbed her wrists, dodging another injury yet again. He was getting good at this. Maybe she wouldn't kill him after all.

Then Brynn turned off the water. The lingering steam, along with the closeness of their bodies, kept him warm, but the room was silent now except for their breathing.

"I need you to hear me, Jamie. To *really* hear me. Do

you honestly think I could have been with you like that in Amarillo if there was a chance I felt anything for someone else? I meant what I said on that stage today, and now that I know how you felt ten years ago, I get it—what it must have been like to watch me crush on someone else for the whole year. I was seventeen, Jamie. I didn't know, not until that kiss. And then that was it. Everything finally made sense—I already loved you. I was just too much of an idiot to see it."

He lifted a plastered curl from her forehead and tucked it behind her ear. He pressed his lips to the wound on her skin, because damn it if he wasn't going to find a way to kiss her now.

"I finally had you and pushed you away."

"You were going through a lot," she said. "I understood. But to hear you say, in front of all those strangers in Amarillo, that you'd been in love with me since then? To find out you lied about Liz?" His jaw clenched, and she noticed immediately, kissing the spot just in front of his ear where all the tension lay. "I understand, Jamie. I didn't give you much room for honesty, not with how I behaved at the reunion. I think my real anger came from realizing we'd missed out, that ten years ago I could have been there for you as your friend and also something more." She pushed him again, lighter this time, and he knew any residual anger she might have felt was waning. "And then in Amarillo when I realized this could have been *our* trip from the start? It was a repeat of senior year—me falling for you and you putting that distance between us."

He kissed her, soft and light, keeping his need at bay.

"I know." His voice was hoarse. "Shit, I know."

She kissed his chest and then tilted her gaze to meet his. "It's my fault, too. I let you push me when I should have fought. And that's what I did when I got here." She groaned. "I didn't dress that way for *him*, Jamie. I bought that stupid dress in the hotel gift shop, hoping your reaction to seeing me in it would shut you up long enough to listen. I only met with Spencer to tell him about us, that I wasn't going to make it to the launch, that I was here with *you*."

He cupped her cheeks in his hands, hanging on to the last of his restraint. "You wore that for me?"

She nodded. "That was the plan—to find you, I mean. But then you found me."

"And behaved like an asshole," he said.

"And behaved like an asshole."

He slid his hands down her neck, her shoulders, her arms. When he had both of her hands in his, he brought them to his lips and kissed the tips of her fingers.

"Can we stop being assholes, now?" he asked.

"Hey, I—"

He didn't let her finish her protest, covering her mouth with his. So long, restraint. There was nothing sweet or gentle in his need, and Brynn answered him back with delicious force, tongues tangling and teeth grazing lips. He felt the skin on her arms pebbling with goose bumps and pulled her close.

"We can finish in here," he said, voice ragged. "Or I can lay you out on that really nice bed out there and do really nice things to you."

She nipped his bottom lip with her teeth.

"And maybe some not-so-nice things?" she teased.

"Jesus," he growled, and he slid open the glass door. He stepped out first and then scooped Brynn into his arms before she had time to argue. She yelped with laughter, and he carried her to the bed where he laid her down on her back.

"Just before the nice and not-so-nice things happen, I need to say one thing."

"What's that?" she asked.

"You're perfect," he started, and she took in a sharp breath. *Encouragement.*

"And you're beautiful," she said, cutting him off from his

own declaration.

He pressed a finger to her lips, and she tried to suppress her smile.

"And I'm sorry I let ten years go by without telling you how crazy in love with you I am. You're it for me, B. Always have been."

He removed his finger, allowing her to speak.

"Are you still scared?" she asked.

"Terrified."

"Good," she said. "Me, too. But here's the thing, James David Kingston."

He laughed. This must be serious if she was using his real name.

"You're it for me, too. So no matter how scary this gets, you'll always have me to help you through it."

He took her glasses off then, figuring she could do the rest by touch. She made no objection. Jamie kissed her neck and her collarbone, inching his way toward her breast. Her nipples rose in tight peaks, and he'd almost taken her in his mouth when she pushed his head up.

"Wait," she said. She raked her fingers through his hair, and he closed his eyes as he reveled in her touch, realizing he didn't care anymore how long it took her to get here, only that she was. "You had my name on the reservation." He loved the sound of joy in her voice. "I found out this morning. You *wanted* the week to end up like this."

He opened his eyes and nodded. "Am I in trouble again for not telling you?" he asked, and she shook her head. "I wanted you to be happy, and if that meant…if I stayed here alone…I would have done it for you. But yeah, I kinda hoped I'd be the reason for your happiness."

She pulled him down to her, into her, and he gasped out her name. She was so ready for him, and he sunk deep inside, enveloped in her warmth. What happened in Amarillo was beyond anything he could have hoped for, but he was too caught up in the fact that what was happening was *actually* happening—and maybe a little inebriated—that he'd missed out on the realization that they were as close as two people could get, no barriers between them.

He rocked against her, a tiny cry escaping her lips.

"Is this okay?" he asked, and she nodded.

"It's just…"

"It's different, now," he said. And Brynn nodded again.

Slowly they moved, taking their time. His hand splayed against the small of her back while she anchored her legs around him. He remembered what he'd meant to do when he first had her sprawled on the bed, and his head dipped down, his lips leaving hers so they could find the breast he'd so rudely neglected.

Brynn gasped, arching her back, and he smiled against her. It still stunned him that he could make her feel this way, that she wanted him the way he'd always wanted her. And yes, it also still terrified him to love someone this much, with every ounce of himself, and know there was always a chance he could lose her. Nothing was certain. He understood that now. But he also understood that loving his best friend was worth all the risk, because trying not to love her? Well, that wasn't an option anymore.

He could have tasted her like this for hours, but he decided not to leave the other nipple out. He was a gentleman, after all, one who enjoyed the nice and not-so-nice things he would do to this woman today.

"To think we could have been doing *this* for the past ten years," Brynn said, her breath coming in pants.

"It's pretty tragic if you think about it." His voice was low and hoarse, and he wasn't sure how much longer *this* was going to last, but they had at least another thirty minutes before they needed to head back to the tent. And then tonight. Plus all day tomorrow. Shit. He was going to need a nap at some point.

"Can we make a vow?" she asked, then paused to gasp out his name as he buried himself deep inside her and used his thumb to take care of her outside as well. "Jamie...oh my God."

He kissed her, long and slow and deep. He savored the taste of her, the feel of her, the knowledge that her heart was his just as his heart had always belonged to her.

"This vow?" he reminded her.

She grabbed his wrist, and he eased the pressure off her clit so she could speak.

"To make up for lost time," she said. "I think we might need to do this a lot more in the years to come."

He laughed, let his hand go back to work, and then nearly fell apart at the seams as she bucked against him.

"I'm sorry," he said. "But all I heard was something about coming."

With that he felt her start to throb against him, and he rocked harder, faster, and kissed her like it was the first and last time he'd get to do it, yet he knew that was far from the truth.

"Uh-huh." She strained to get the sound out, and he knew they were almost there.

"Love you," he said, their momentum building.

"Love you."

And when they climaxed together, her warmth pulsing around him, Jamie fought to keep his arms braced so he wouldn't collapse against her. It wasn't just a physical release, but an emotional one, as well, one he'd bottled up for far too long. Only now, in the safety of his best friend's love, could he finally let go. He shuddered, kissed her lips, her jaw, and the hollow of her neck where a bead of sweat trickled toward her breasts. Only then did he let his arms give out as he fell beside her, their legs still tangled and bodies connected in the most perfect fit.

Neither of them spoke for several seconds, both needing a moment to collect.

She smiled and squinted at him, so he reached for the side table where he'd put her glasses and gave her back her sight.

"It's good to see you like this," she said, and he raised a brow.

"Like what?"

"Like your heart is finally mine."

He tugged on her hair, loving the mess of curls spilling around her.

"Always was. Just took me a while to tell you."

"I should have known," she said, and he hated that tinge of regret in her voice. Enough with punishing themselves for what they missed. It was time to celebrate what was still to come.

"Now you do."

She kissed him, her lips languid and soft against his.

"You have my heart, too, you know," she said. "I lost it to you ten years ago. Just took me a while to find it again."

He nodded and kissed her back. He knew that now. And he made himself a promise not to forget it.

Chapter Thirty

L.A. was perfect. *Jamie* was perfect. Their trip back through Amarillo on the way home—yeah, there were no words for that. But now they were in Chicago, best friends like they were but also something more.

Brynn groaned.

"First-date jitters?" Holly asked, and Brynn pushed past her sister and into the bathroom for the final step in Operation Look-as-Hot-as-I-Can-in-Jeans-and-a-T-Shirt. "I'd like to remind you that this was *your* idea."

Brynn took off her glasses and unscrewed the cap on her contact solution. After the first contact was in, she spun to face her sister.

"I know. I know. And it was a good idea, right? I just can't help thinking of how this could royally backfire, you know? Like, this will either be really good for him, or it's going to bring up painful memories about his parents, which will remind him of what happened between us ten years ago, and then he'll fall out of love with me, and life as we know it will be over."

Holly burst into a fit of laughter, which did not entertain Brynn in the slightest. She closed the eye that was still contact-free so she could glare at her sister without getting dizzy.

"I'm sorry," Holly said, swiping at tears. "But I thought I was the drama queen around here."

Brynn crossed her arms but said nothing, grateful for the few moments she could let her unfounded anger hide her very real fear.

"Sweetie," Holly continued. "You know I am no romantic, but even the most cynical person could look at you and Jamie and just know that you two are the lucky ones. You found what some people spend lifetimes searching for, and tricking your boyfriend into attending a playoff game to see his favorite team is only going to make him fall harder. *If* that's even possible."

Brynn turned back to the mirror, wanting clarity before she digested Holly's words. Contact poised on her fingertip, she startled when Jamie's patented knock came at the door.

"You have *got* to be kidding me!" she yelled, and Holly cracked up again on her way to the door.

Since Galena, Kansas, Brynn had gotten into the habit of always putting her contacts in over a *closed* sink drain, but that didn't change the fact that Jamie could still throw her off-balance like this—enough to send the contact sailing from her finger. What was new were the butterflies in her belly, darting back and forth at the anticipation of his arrival.

She stood in the frame of the bathroom door and, through her good eye, watched him enter their apartment.

God, she loved this man. He startled her, infuriated her, calmed her, and right now, when she saw the broad smile spread across his still unshaven face, he warmed every part of her, all the way to the tips of her toes.

"Need some help there, Sleepy Jean?"

He wore his gray hoodie over a plain black T-shirt,

dark washed jeans, and those red Pumas. She couldn't help but smile, though, when her eye (the good one) trailed up his body to where his Sox hat rested on his head. She could tell he'd had his hair trimmed, but the facial hair remained. Yeah, she liked this look on him—different but the same. An incarnation of Jamie that was just for her.

She nodded, all anger and fear dissolving at the nearness of him. She breathed in his scent—one that she knew was nothing more than freshly showered, walked-a-few-blocks-in-the-city-breeze Jamie—and the butterflies rested for a moment while he retrieved her contact and placed it safely in her palm.

"Even cleaned it off for you," he said, but she would have known that anyway.

She turned to the mirror for a brief moment to insert the lens and then looked back to him, blinking him into focus.

"You look even better through both eyes," she said.

He cupped her cheeks in his hands and kissed her without further pretense or warning, and she sank into him, her arms curving around his waist and up his back. They hadn't seen each other in two days, which was more than normal before they started...whatever this was. People who just met were *dating*. People who'd been in committed relationships for months or years were *together*. But this thing with her and Jamie had a definition all its own, and they were still figuring out what that was. Not that it mattered. All Brynn cared about was his lips on hers after two days of *not* being on hers, and...

She let out a soft "Mmmm" against him. What was she thinking?

"I missed you," he said. Then he stepped back to take her in.

"Brynn Chandler, are you wearing a White Sox T-shirt?"

She did a slow twirl for him, his smile giving her encouragement.

"You like?"

"I love," he said. "Though I didn't expect such team spirit to go sit at the ale house to watch the game."

Brynn's smile threatened to fall, but she held it in place, reminding herself that what she was about to tell Jamie was a good thing.

"B?" he asked. "Why are you smiling like you're going to murder me?"

Okay, so maybe she wasn't quite pulling off the happy nonchalance she'd been hoping for.

Her teeth grazed her top lip.

"See, that's the thing," she started and then grabbed his hand, giving it a reassuring squeeze. Though *she* was the one who needed reassurance right now.

She slid the two playoff tickets out of her pocket and held them up for Jamie to see.

"We're not going to the ale house," she said. "We're going to the game."

. . .

He was still holding her hand. Jamie was sure of that—her skin on his, keeping him grounded. Tonight was game seven, and he was pretty sure the Sox weren't going to the Series... again. That didn't stop him from hoping, and having Brynn watch the game with him would make whatever the outcome was worth it.

But at the park?

"Okay, you've been quiet a long time," she said. "So, let me start by telling you that, yes, the tickets cost a few bucks, but Annie got them from one of the shop regulars who couldn't go at the last minute, and I just thought...it's been so long, Jamie. And you love baseball more than anything, and I hoped..."

He still hadn't said anything. He probably should before she continued her nervous verbal vomit, but it was kind of adorable.

The tension eased in his shoulders, and he felt a tentative grin spread across his face.

"You're wrong," he said and watched her expression fall. This only made his smile grow wider. "There's one thing I love more than baseball." With that he pulled her to him again, obliterating the first kiss he'd given her with one he hoped said everything he couldn't articulate with words.

"Get a room already," Holly said as she walked by. But Jamie didn't relent, only smiled against the woman he'd loved for ten long years, who stood in his arms kissing him back. *Loving* him back.

"Brynn Elise Chandler," he said, "I love *you* more than anything."

The corners of her mouth quirked up.

"More than baseball?" she asked.

"More than baseball."

"More than beer?" she added.

He scrubbed a hand across his lightly bearded jaw, but a few seconds was all she would take. Brynn backhanded him on the arm, and he chuckled.

"More than beer," he said, "but let's keep that our little secret."

She took off his hat and rested it backward on her own head, her wild curls spilling out from underneath it. She ran her hands through his hair, over his cheeks, and down to his neck.

"And it's okay…the tickets? I thought it would be good for you. For us. To do this together."

Jamie nodded and kissed her forehead. A lot had changed in the past ten years, even more so in the past two weeks.

"I don't want to be stuck where I was for a decade," he

told her. "Not anymore." She pulled him tight and rested her head on his chest, and Jamie let his chin fall to the top of her ball-cap-covered head. "There's no one I'd rather do this with—go to a place I once loved with the girl I love more than—"

"Baseball and beer," Brynn interrupted, and they both laughed.

"Baseball and beer," he confirmed.

The Sox were down by four with two outs at the top of the ninth, but that didn't stop Jamie from loving every minute he sat in the stadium. Perched above home plate, a Lagunitas in one hand and Brynn's palm in the other, it didn't matter that his team wasn't going to the Series, not without a miracle. In fact, his eyes had turned from the game after the last out, focusing on the woman beside him instead. He observed how she watched the game with sheer delight, and he knew it had nothing to do with what was happening on the field and everything to do with what made him face her now.

"What?" she asked, turning to meet his gaze. "You're staring."

"You're it for me, B."

Her eyes glassed over, and his heart squeezed with a sweet ache that he could bring her to tears with one sentence.

"Jamie…"

"I don't want to be apart from you for two days again."

Her brows furrowed. "But you had two late nights at the bar, and I'm short on days off after the trip and—"

He covered her mouth with his hand, and she quieted.

"Even when I work until two a.m., I don't want to come home to an empty bed. I want to come home to *you*. Every night."

Brynn's eyes widened, and he removed his hand. She'd need to be able to speak to answer his question.

"Move in with me, B."

He pulled her to him and whispered the request to her again before his lips fell to hers.

Whoever was at bat must have done the unthinkable and hit a homer, because the fireworks usually reserved for the end of the game shot off with a bang.

Brynn jumped in her seat, then let out a wild laugh as she watched the display up above. Then she looked at Jamie, nodding as the first tear slipped over the ledge.

"Yes." She threw her arms around his neck, kissing him between words. "Yes. I'll move in with you." She laughed through her tears, peppering Jamie with kisses—his cheeks, his mouth, his neck. And he laughed right along with her until there was a lull in the fireworks and the kissing and they had a chance to breathe—to take in the moment, the night, everything. And it was perfect.

Jamie couldn't let the perfect evening end without dragging her back to the brewery for one final celebration. He pulled her behind the bar where Jeremy greeted them both with a friendly salute.

"How was the game, Kingston?"

Jamie laughed. "You knew, too? Guess I shouldn't be surprised." He pulled Brynn in front of him and wrapped his arms around her waist. "It was perfect," he said, burying his face in her curls and kissing her neck.

Jeremy chuckled. "Dude, you do know the Sox lost, right?"

Jamie nodded, unable to contain his goofy smile. "But *I* won."

His hands still resting on Brynn's stomach, he felt her muscles contract as she took in a sharp breath. He would never get tired of all the different reactions he could pull from her.

"Look," Jamie said, positioning her in front of the tap.

It took her a moment to say something, but when she did, his heart soared.

"*Jamie.*" It was only his name, but the way she said it spoke volumes.

His name was on the door, and hers was inside on the tap. He'd see it every day, even when she wasn't around, though he hoped she and her friends would still hang out on weekends, even if it meant stealing her for a private meeting or two in his office every now and then. It wasn't just her name on the tap. It was her whole essence tattooed on his heart. He didn't know how to say these things to her, had spent so many years trying to get it right. The crack in her voice and the way her hands gripped his now told her he finally had.

Jeremy took some silent cue Jamie didn't know he'd given him and poured the two of them a pint of Chandler's.

"Thanks, man," Jamie said, and Jeremy only nodded before leaving them alone behind the bar.

Jamie raised his beer in a motion to toast, and Brynn picked up her glass as well.

"Thank you, B, for bringing me to the game tonight. To the next ten years," he said.

He watched the happy tears pool in her eyes as she smiled.

"And ten years after that," she added.

They both sipped, and as they set their glasses down, Brynn licked the foam from her upper lip.

And then, like they weren't in a crowded bar with a growing audience, Jamie took her face in his palms and kissed her before she could say anything else. At the taste of his tongue meeting hers, those fireworks erupted in his stomach as his heart slammed against his chest.

"Whoa," Brynn whispered against him.

"I think I need to see you in my office," he said with a chuckle. And he led her toward the door, finishing their toast silently in his head.

To all the years to come with the one by his side who almost got away.

Acknowledments

Thank you to my agent, Courtney Miller-Callihan, for falling in love with Jamie and Brynn's story when it was nothing more than a three-paragraph proposal. You had faith in this story from inception, and that's the best kind of encouragement. Thanks to my fabulous editor, Karen Grove, for joining me on my foray into a new category of romance and for sprinkling your magical editing fairy dust all over my words. I'm so lucky to work with you!

I have the *best* critique partners who are also the best of friends. I'm hoping that in the not too distant future we can speak via Facebook stickers only. [Insert dino sticker here.] Lia Riley, Megan Erickson, Natalie Blitt, and Jennifer Blackwood, you inspire me *and* keep me moderately sane. I love you and your words.

S and C, your snuggles and huggles are the best writing fuel. And life fuel. Mommy loves you.

And always, thank you, readers. I'm living a dream that you make possible, and I'm forever grateful.

About the Author

A.J. Pine writes stories to break readers' hearts, but don't worry—she'll mend them with a happily-ever-after. As an English teacher and a librarian, A.J. has always surrounded herself with books. All her favorites have one big commonality—romance. Naturally, her books have the same. When she's not writing, she's reading. Then there's online shopping (everything from groceries to shoes) and a tiny bit of TV, where she nourishes her undying love of vampires and superheroes. You'll also find her hanging with her family in the Chicago 'burbs.

Connect with A.J. Pine and find out more about upcoming books at AJPine.com.

Also by A.J. Pine...

IF ONLY

WHAT IF

I DO

Discover more Entangled Select Contemporary titles...

A FRIENDLY FLIRTATION
a *Friends First* novel by Christine Warner

Allison Hall is fed up with being the invisible nerdy girl. She needs confidence—and that requires a makeover and dating tips. Jared Esterly says no when his business partner and best friend Nick's little sister comes to him for advice. But when Al's attempt to make changes on her own fails spectacularly, he's there to pick up the pieces. As lessons move from the salon to the bedroom, Allison discovers change can come at a very high price.

HOW TO FALL
a novel by Rebecca Brooks

Julia Evans puts everyone else first—but all that is about to change, starting with a spontaneous trip to Brazil. Now Julia can be anyone she wants. Like someone who's willing to have a wickedly hot hook-up with the sexy Aussie at her hotel. Except, Blake Williams may not be what he seems. Julia and Blake will have to decide if they're jumping into the biggest adventure of all or playing it safe.

Just Say Yes
a novel by Alyssa Goodnight

Single mom Jade Moran isn't ready for any big changes in either her horrible '70s kitchen or her romantic life. But after meeting super-hot contractor Max Gianopoulis, she's willing to be a little open-minded. When things in the kitchen go from simmer to full-on sizzling, she'll have to decide if she believes in happily ever afters…

Temptation
by Kathryn Barrett

Laura Hayes has been acting since she was an infant, making Hollywood the only home she has ever known. But when she moves to Pennsylvania's Amish country to film her next movie, she's intrigued by the Amish simplicity. And when her neighbor turns out to be the local heartthrob, she realizes that what's missing from her life might be the love of a good man. Jacob fights the urge to question the teachings of his Amish beliefs and struggles with his longing for the sexy stranger who makes him feel truly alive for the first time. As his attraction grows, so do his doubts, until he's forced to face temptation and decide once and for all what is truly worth the fight.

CPSIA information can be obtained
at www.ICGtesting.com
Printed in the USA
LVOW10s1944191216
517962LV00001B/15/P